PROLOGUE

Ivy

The barely-there sun was peeking above the ever-expanding cornfields that laid just below the school grounds, which only intensified the nervous jitters bouncing around my stomach to a point of no return. I'd spent all morning working on my hair, making sure that the waves and bumps were long gone and burnt to a crisp by my straightener.

I'd never really cared how I looked for school, until this year. My mom fussed at me this morning while standing back against the doorway to our upstairs bathroom.

"You're growing up so fast, Ivy. Seventh grade."

She held her hand over her heart while her eyes filled up with tears. I groaned and continued to run the straightener through my hair.

"Do my hair, too! Please!"

I groaned again. My little sister, Mia, *always* wanted to be like me. It didn't matter what it was. She wanted to do *everything* I did. It was annoying most of the time, but I still found a little sliver of my big-sisterly love hanging around in the background and braided her hair before my mom loaded us up in the mini-van and ventured toward school on old, curvy back roads.

Those curvy roads did nothing to help my already queasy stomach. Why was the first day of school always so nerve-wracking to me? It wasn't like I was going to a new school. I'd still see the same ol' friends that I'd gone to elementary school with. I'd still be able to sit with them at lunch, and I'd still be able to walk to my classes with their arms interlocking with mine.

This year was *so* different, though. The usual butterflies that I got on the first day of school were flying around my stomach at triple speed. This was the first year I'd be sharing a hallway with the eighth graders.

They were intimidating.

They were bigger than me and they *ran* the school. I couldn't wait until next year. Next year, I'd be the one running the school (okay, probably not but I could pretend), and all the seventh graders would be just as nervous as I was, right now.

Or maybe not. Maybe I was just weird.

My friends didn't seem nearly as nervous as I was.

Casey and Becca were waiting for me outside the side door with their backpacks slung across their backs. They smiled brightly when I opened up the van's passenger door and hopped down, welcoming the cool morning air.

I took a huge gulp of air and turned around, smiling wearily at my mom.

"Have a great first day, sweetie. Remember to—"

I giggled, interrupting her. "*Remember to be nice.* Yes, Mom. I know. You've been telling me that every day for the last eight years of my life." I let out an exasperated sigh and waved to my little sister in the backseat.

Mia would be dropped off in a few minutes at the grade school that was only a half a mile from the middle school. She was a few years younger than I was, so it'd be a while before she was in my position.

I adjusted my jeans and brand new purple shirt right before my mom sped off. I walked up to my two best friends with a nervous smile plastered on my face.

"Ready?" Casey asked, pulling the side door to the school open.

"Yep," I muttered, nerves completely going haywire in my body.

The second we stepped foot into the gym, I scanned my eyes for an open seat. If you arrived at school before the first bell, you automatically had to wait in the gym until it rang. There would usually be a few teachers keeping watch (and by keeping watch, I mean they would be standing huddled together in the middle of the gym, talking aimlessly until the bell rang and then they'd walk to their classrooms).

As soon as I found a seat, closest to the door, a teacher raised her voice.

"Sixth graders down here, seventh in the middle, and eighth closest to the door." Then she turned around and continued talking to the other teachers.

I sighed. *So much for sitting close to the exit.*

Becca and Casey both walked ahead of me, their sneakers squeaking on the freshly waxed floor. They quickly found a few open seats on the bottom bleacher. *Thank God*, I thought. Last time I had to climb the bleachers, I tripped and busted my lip.

As soon as I sat down, I slung my backpack off my shoulders and laid it beside my feet. Casey and Becca were talking about what classes they had this year but I tuned them out. We'd already discussed this a week ago when we got our class schedules. Instead of joining in on the conversation, I looked around the gym, watching and observing.

I'd always been a little quiet and shy compared to my friends. In fact, my mom told me that I was basically a phenomenon because she and my dad were both loud and outgoing. So was my little sister. She had some serious spunk, and then there was me...quiet, ol' Ivy.

My head swiveled to my right and I noticed the tiny sixth graders biting their nails and sitting like statues along the blue bleachers. I quietly snickered because I was probably just as nervous as they were.

One girl looked over at me, with her small leg wiggling up and down, widening her eyes at the exact time they locked onto mine. Instead of turning my head, I gave her a reassuring smile and her body visibly relaxed. *Poor thing.*

I then turned my head towards the left, watching in awe as all the eighth graders sat and conversed. The girls were all huddled on the lower bleacher, just a few yards away from me, chatting away. A few of them were applying some kind of lip gloss and smacking their lips together loudly.

My shoulders fell. Maybe next year my mom would officially let me wear make-up. She told me I was too young this year, but after looking at Casey and Becca, I realized that I should have fought her a little harder. They were both sporting glittery eyeshadow and their lips definitely looked like they were shimmering under the gym's florescent lights.

As soon as I was about to turn my head back to Becca and Casey, my heart stuttered in my chest.

A few boys walked through the door and every single eighth grade girl stopped what she was doing and stared. A hush fell over the group and my heart picked up speed. It thumped hard against my ribcage as I glanced back and forth between the girls and the small group of guys. I quickly realized that these boys were the "cool" eighth grade boys.

They surely looked cool with their backpacks slung over their shoulders with only one strap, the other hanging loosely by their side. One boy had dark, cut to the scalp hair and he was super, duper tall. The one standing beside him had dirty blonde hair but it was shorter, with just a little bit of bounce on top. Then my eyes fell on the last one of the group, who had brown-shaggy hair that fell gracefully over his forehead. Right when he walked to the bottom steps of the bleachers, he shook it out vigorously. My mouth parted a little as I watched him climb the stairs with fluid steps. He glanced down at the group of girls and he must have said or done something that I couldn't see because they all giggled and huddled back together.

I watched him for a bit longer. I couldn't help it. He was fascinating. He looked like a surfer boy, only with brown hair, and I'd never seen someone quite like him before. *Maybe he was new.* He had a really nice tan, a tan that you couldn't get around here with our Northern sun. I tried to imagine where he'd come from. California, maybe? He *did* look like a surfer boy. I could totally see him with a surf-board in tow, crashing along salty waves.

Wait, why am I thinking these things? My entire body broke out into a sweat and a wave of heat flushed over my skin.

"Hello? Earth to Ivy?" I sucked in a breath and looked over at Casey. Her chestnut colored eyes were squinted in my direction.

"Wait, what? Did you say something?" I asked, trying to catch my breath.

"Yeah, why is your face so red?" she questioned,

squinting her glittery blue eyeshadowed eyes. I shrugged and then blatantly lied.

"I'm hot."

Oh my gosh. What is wrong with me? What is happening? My legs suddenly felt like two giant Jell-O globs sticking out from the rest of my body.

She laughed. "Well, then, take off your jacket."

Right before I started to strip down, trying to calm my irregular breathing, the bell sounded over the speakers with a shrill ring. I jumped instantly and noticed the teachers directing each grade to the doors in a single file line.

I stood up, keeping my eyes directed towards my friends (and not at all towards the boy with brown, surfer-boy hair) and pushed my arms through my backpack straps.

My heart was still pounding in my chest although, not as hard as before, so I was finally able to catch my breath, and thankfully, my body felt like it was resuming to its normal body temperature. 98.7 on the dot.

I glanced over at Casey, who was joking around with Billy, one of the boys in our grade who we had gone to elementary school with. Instead of laughing at their rambunctious behavior, though, my eyes wandered over to the group in front of me.

Just as Casey had a fit of loud, uncontrollable laughter, causing me to cover my ear with my lone hand, my eyes zeroed in on Surfer Boy.

My heart halted in my chest.

He was looking *right* at me.

I felt heat burn my cheeks like I'd just stepped up to a blazing bonfire, and my stomach flip-flopped. I was frozen staring into a pair of sky-blue eyes. I was locked onto him so deeply that I didn't even realize I was being a total weirdo, openly gawking at him.

I gasped, realizing that we were *still* staring at each other for what was far longer than normal, so I hurriedly snapped my head to Casey and Billy. They were still joking around with one another, and by joking, I mean flirting.

Forcing out a few laughs with them and the other friends surrounding us, I tried really hard not to let what had just happened go to my head. Even though all I did was make eye contact with Surfer Boy, I couldn't deny that I had felt a new range of emotions.

I felt alive. I felt a fire burning deep within. Like the butterflies flying around my stomach had wings made up flames.

Glancing up one more time, I noted that his back was turned towards me and he was walking out of the gym to go to class. A feeling of disappointment was rapidly approaching and I felt my shoulders slump, but then his head turned towards me, *again*.

We locked onto one another and he gave me a grin that lifted me up higher than I'd ever been before.

That was the first day I laid eyes on Dawson, and it definitely wasn't the last.

PAST

ONE

Ivy

The hum of the air conditioner and papers rustling were the only two sounds in the classroom. Everyone was working diligently to gain the perfect score on their algebra test, all except Dawson. I could see him out of the corner of my eye, leaning his tall body slightly towards my desk to get a better look at my paper.

"Stop copying," I hissed, still keeping my attention on my final equation.

He coughed and mumbled something only I could hear. "Come on, Ivy. Please."

I rolled my eyes but his pleading made me pause for a second. I moved my arm a little lower, allowing him to cheat his way through the final page.

Dawson was smart. Overly smart, but he didn't apply himself. He'd rather go to parties, flirt with girls, and hang out with his soccer buddies.

Me, on the other hand... I was bent on achieving only the best of grades. I pushed myself and I studied my ass off because I *wanted* to get into a good college. I wanted to make my parents proud and most of all, I wanted to be a good role model to my little sister. What kind of sister would I be if I goofed off in school and didn't apply myself? A bad one, that's what.

Finally, after realizing that Dawson had gotten up and turned in his test, all of which he had copied from me, I turned to do the same—but not before I checked over my answers *three* times, contentment settling in that I had, in fact, gotten every answer correct.

The second I put my test on Mrs. Goodwin's desk, the bell let out a loud screech. I ran over and grabbed my books and purse and gave Dawson a side-eye. He only smirked at me, which made my lips turn upward of their own accord.

He slung his heavy arm around my shoulders as we walked out of the classroom, but as soon as we were out of the teacher's earshot, I shrugged his arm off me.

"You need to stop cheating your way through high school, Dawson."

He leaned against the metal lockers, crossing his arms, still sporting that stupid grin.

"Oh, come on, Ivy. You're my best friend. The least you could do is let me cheat every once and in awhile."

I threw my books inside my locker and huffed. "I'm being a really crappy best friend by *letting* you copy off me! You're so much smarter than you pretend to be. Why is that?" I mimicked him and crossed my arms over my chest. He glanced down at them and then flicked his eyes back up to mine.

"It'll ruin my reputation," he smirked.

I sighed. "What reputation? You mean the one where you act like a dumb jock who doesn't know his thumb from his ass and lets girls fawn all over him?"

"That'd be the one," he answered, while following closely behind me to the cafeteria.

"Stupid. You have so much potential."

The chatter of the cafeteria grew louder as we made our way through the long hallway, passing by the clear windows of the front office. I bet if I looked at the ladies comprising most of the office staff, they'd all be craning their necks to look at Dawson. Not only did he have every high school girl drooling over his jock-like body and surfer-boy hair, he had all the grown women, too.

"You're my biggest cheerleader, you know that?"

I rolled my eyes again but then I abruptly stopped moving my feet towards the lunchroom. Dawson kept moving, making it halfway to his table, which was already full of guys wearing their blue letterman jackets, before pausing and looking back at me.

He mouthed, "What's wrong?"

My heart jumped in my chest and I instantly felt sick to my stomach. I looked from Dawson and then to another lunch table, only a few away from his.

There was my ex, Tyler Holmes, with Breanna (AKA my worst freaking enemy—like, seriously, she and her parents *hate* me) draped over his lap. She ran her hand through his straw-colored hair the second she saw me standing in the threshold and then he, not even realizing I was standing there, swooped in for a disgusting, sloppy kiss.

My face flamed. It'd been only one week since we'd broken up and there he was, already cozying up to Breanna. I was the one who'd broken up with him, but only because he basically forced me into it.

Tyler had been talking to girls behind my back (Breanna mainly, because she always wanted what I had, she just couldn't help but place her sticky fingers on my ex), so of course I had to break up with him. *What did he think I'd do? Stick around for him to cheat on me?*

*Hmmph...*by the looks of it, I was pretty certain he had cheated on me.

I was no longer hungry and even though Dawson was trying to get my attention, I slowly started to back away from the lunchroom. It looked like I was trying to mimic the moonwalk on my way out, foot sliding right after the other on the shiny, vinyl tile. I was *not* going to sit down and try to eat my packed lunch while watching Breanna stick her tongue down my ex's throat, all just to spite me.

And I especially needed to make a fast exit considering everyone was staring at me. All except Tyler and Breanna. They were making out heavily. *Where the heck are the teachers?* Wasn't that, like, breaking every single PDA rule that they had continued to ram into our brains since last August?

Ugh. Gross.

Once I was far enough away from the cafeteria, surely making Michael Jackson proud as heck of my epic moon-walk, I turned and headed straight to the doors that led to the student parking lot. Before my fingers even hit the handle, I heard a commotion. It was so loud that I instantly spun around and placed my hand on my heart.

What was that?

Then I heard the chants, "Fight, fight, fight!"

I gasped. "Oh no."

My heart dropped and I hurriedly ran back over to the lunchroom, bypassing the puzzled looks on the office staff's face.

"Dawson!" I yelled.

I panicked, quickly running over to him, foot getting caught on one of the stupid chairs. Dawson was standing over a wailing Tyler. His cries were so loud that I almost laughed. Dawson pulled his arm back one more time and slammed it onto Tyler's already bloody nose, I cringed at the sound of the thump.

Breanna was shrieking, as were all her stuck-up friends, and the guys in the lunchroom were becoming even rowdier as they egged Dawson on.

I yelled once more before he could do anymore damage. "Stop it, Dawson!"

Finally, hearing my voice, he heaved back and swiveled his head over to me. He shook his shaggy hair out of his beet-red face and pushed himself off the floor.

I glanced down at Tyler's face and my stomach lurched. His nose was gushing bright, red blood and one eye looked as if it would be bruising in a matter of seconds.

Before I could say anything, he looked from me to Dawson and then back at me.

"Contain your freaking boyfriend, Ivy," his voice was muffled as he wiped his hand under his bloody nose. "You were the one that broke up with me."

His words stung. Not only did they sting because, uh, hello, he was making it seem like I *wanted* to break up and that I wasn't at all hurt by his choices. But it also stung because Dawson wasn't my boyfriend. He had made that very clear over the last few years of our blossoming friendship. He had had so many "flings" with girls that I'd lost count, and yet, he never, ever, tried to pull a move on me.

I was friend-zoned to the max, and I went along with it. Putting him in that dreadful zone, too. Tyler always argued with me over it. He thought there was something going on between Dawson and I, but there wasn't—well, not in the open at least. I kept my true feelings hidden deep down below the surface, barely recognizing them myself.

Dawson's eyes scanned my face and I knew he could tell I was hurt by what Tyler had just said. Dawson knew me too well. We had our own way of speaking. I knew what he was feeling before he'd even tell me and the same went for him. He just *knew*.

Dawson turned his attention back to my pitiful ex-boyfriend, who was still lying on the dirty cafeteria floor, and seethed, "If you ever, and I mean *ever,* fucking look in her direction again...I will put you in the hospital."

Tyler stared up at Dawson and then slowly slid his body away from him. Dawson didn't get into fights often. He was the guy who was *always* happy and joking with people. He didn't have any enemies, unless of course, you count the girls that he used for "fun" and then so casually ignored afterward (yet they still fell for it every time—stupid, stupid girls). But honestly, he didn't have beef with anyone.

Unless they messed with me.

It made half the guys afraid to even look in my direction, which was just *grand.* That was probably another reason why the break-up with Tyler hurt me a little more than I'd like to admit. He was my first *real* boyfriend.

Sigh.

"Let's go, Mr. Lanning."

I didn't even realize that Mr. Williams, the P.E. teacher, was standing only a few feet away from us with his arms crossed over his stark white t-shirt, his whistle resting over his pot-belly. Dawson let out a loud breath and swiftly walked away from a bleeding Tyler and the rest of the gawking stares of our classmates.

Right when he was about to stride past me, he stopped. Mr. Williams let out a frustrated sigh but didn't say anything.

Dawson's crystal-blue eyes softened. "You okay?"

My eyes almost fell out of my head. Am I okay? *That would be a big, fat no.*

"Why did you do that, Dawson?" I whispered, still aware that everyone's eyes were still on us.

He smiled widely as he tucked a loose hair behind my ear. "Because *no one* messes with you. Not on my watch."

My eyes instantly welled up and I realized that even though we were only friends, best friends at that, it didn't mean I couldn't love him. Because I did and I probably always would.

I smiled up at him, trying to keep my emotions under control. He smiled back and then sauntered off, walking lazily behind Mr. Williams.

I felt Becca slide up beside me as I watched everyone turn their attention back to the strange-smelling cafeteria food.

"That damn Dawson. He's got you all tied up, doesn't he?" Her greens eyes twinkled as I slid my gaze over to them.

I shook my head no, but we both knew I was lying.

TWO

Dawson

"You're not grounded for getting in-school suspension for the last two days?" Max asked, following me out to my baby.

My baby = my cherry-red Camaro.

"Nah," I answered, pulling out my keys and searching the parking lot for Ivy. *Where is she?*

Max whistled. "You are one lucky dude. My dad would probably beat my ass for fighting in school."

I shrugged. Max's parents were the type that cared about stuff like that. My parents were too wrapped up in keeping my brother out of trouble and burying themselves in endless amounts of work. They probably weren't even aware that I'd gotten into a fight. Which, it wasn't even a fight. In order for it to be considered a fight, Tyler would have had to fight back and he didn't. *Pussy.*

"Hey, you goin' to Shane's tonight?"

I pulled my door open and rested my arms on top of my Camaro. He did the same on the other side.

"Yeah, I'm taking Jessica." I grinned.

He laughed. "Dude, you are so fucking lucky."

I wiggled my eyebrows. I was lucky. Jessica was smokin' hot and I knew when I'd ask her to go the party with me earlier in the week (before I got in-school suspension and had to stay inside one stupid room, all day long) that she'd be more than willing.

Jessica was more than willing to do *anything* with me.

"I know, she's pretty hot."

He laughed, shrugging off his letterman jacket. It was nearing spring in Ohio, which meant that it wasn't quite warm enough to go without a jacket in the morning, but now that it was three o'clock in the afternoon, with the sun directly over our heads, it was becoming stifling.

"Yeah, she is, but I was saying you were lucky for an entirely different reason."

I wrinkled my forehead, scanning the parking lot, once again, for the sight of a chestnut-haired girl.

"Why?" I asked, still searching. I saw Becca and Casey standing by their cars. They were talking closely to one another, but their gazes were also grazing the parking lot every few seconds. Probably looking for Ivy, too.

"Dude, because you have all these girls basically jumping your bones every chance they get *and* you also have, like, one of the hottest girls at this school right at your beck and call."

I inclined my head towards him, still leaning forward with his arms over my Camaro.

"What do you mean?"

He rolled his eyes dramatically. "Dude... you're fucking blind."

I still wasn't catching his drift so I only lifted my eyebrows.

His eyes widened. "*Ivy*, bro. I'm talking about Ivy."

Just the sound of her name on someone else's lips made my blood boil. I was extremely protective of her. Almost borderline psycho. I'd always been that way with her. Ivy was just... different. The first time I saw her, during the first day of the school that I'd started attending in eighth grade, I knew she was the type of girl that you treated with respect. Her smile lit up the entire gymnasium. It did it then and it does it now.

I still remember the first time I'd ever stuck up for her, too. It was only a few weeks into my eighth grade year. The seventh and eighth graders shared a hallway, which was unlike my last school but I thought it was kind of cool, nonetheless.

Anyway, I had walked over to the lockers with a few of my "new" friends and two eighth grade girls were bullying *my* Ivy. Well, she wasn't really "mine," per se, but the moment I told those eighth grade chicks to take the tissues out of their training bras and to fucking stop bothering the prettiest girl in school, I'd claimed her.

That was the start of my feelings for Ivy and they'd only intensified over the years.

Intensified into what? I wasn't sure. All I knew was that I cared about her more than I'd cared about anyone or anything in my entire life. She was just... *Ivy*.

"Bro, don't get pissed." Max's voice brought me out of the memory, quickly dissolving the image of the sweet, little, seventh grade Ivy with wide, doe-like, green eyes from my brain.

"I'm not pissed," I huffed, still slightly annoyed that he even brought her up. "Ivy isn't like that. We aren't like that."

He gave me a knowing look, and I responded by my narrowing my eyes at him.

"So you're saying that if I wanted to ask her out on a date, you'd be cool with that?"

I growled and slammed my hands down on the top of my Camaro.

"Fuck no. She deserves better than you."

He fucking fell over from laughter which only pissed me off more. Once he straightened up and got his shit together, he plastered a shit-eating grin onto his olive-skinned face.

"You are full of it, Lanning."

"Full of what?" I prodded. The sound of car doors being slammed and people whipping out of the school parking lot momentarily ceased the pounding of my heart in my eardrums.

"You are so into her and she's so into you but for some reason, you both deny it."

I scoffed. "What the fuck ever, dude. She's just my best friend, so leave it at that."

He snickered, pulling open the passenger door a little further. "So why do you become livid whenever a guy takes an interest in her? I mean, you pummeled Tyler pretty fucking hard a couple days ago..."

My chest tightened. "Because she's my best friend and those guys aren't good enough for her and Tyler deserved to get his ass beat for fucking around on her."

Max's face twitched and then he chuckled, sliding his body into the passenger seat and out of my sight.

I leaned my head down into the car. "And don't even fucking think about asking her out."

Max pulled his hands up like a surrender but not before he grinned.

Once I stood up again, still looking around the parking

lot for Ivy, I replayed the mantra over and over again in my head: *"She's just my best friend, so leave it at that."*

Yeah, fucking right.

THREE

Ivy

Holy moly, holy moly, holy moly!

My breathing had never been so crazy from a single conversation until now. But after all, what did I expect after hearing Andy call my name? My heart halted in my chest when I turned around and realized that he was, in fact, talking to me.

Little ol' me.

Andy was probably the hottest guy at our school, besides Dawson, of course. But Andy...he was a senior and he was the star baseball player for our school; the mighty Wildcats baseball team was led solely by him hitting multiple homeruns every game. And to top it off, he had already signed with one of the D1 colleges next year to play for their team. Andy was the epitome of *cool*.

He was dreamy and totally swoon-worthy and I knew for a fact that every single girl would unashamedly agree. I took in the shine of his kelly-green eyes as he sauntered up to me (standing awkwardly, no doubt) adjusting the straps on his backpack. He had on a sly grin, one that made butter-flies awaken in my lower belly.

"Hey," he intoned and I swear I almost fainted right then.

"Uh, hi," I replied. My voice came out shaky and inse-cure but I gave myself a three second mental pep-talk and was able to calm down (a little).

"So I saw what happened a few days ago...during lunch."

My face instantly felt hot. Of course he did. The entire school was talking about Tyler being an asshole and then Dawson losing his shit. *Still,* even three days later *and* after Mrs. Smith had fallen off the stage during an assembly and flashed everyone her hot pink, unicorn underwear. No one cared about that...

"Yeah," I said, not really sure what to say. I was embar-rassed. I knew that much.

"I just wanted to let you know," Andy said as he leaned against the wall closest to the exit. He crossed his tanned forearms over his tightly-fitting t-shirt and smiled genuinely at me.

"Yeah?" I asked, because he didn't finish his sentence.

He took a deep breath. I watched his strong chest rise and then fall deeply. "I just wanted to let you know that I think Tyler is an idiot for letting you get away."

Whoa. Whoa. Whoa. Whoa...

Just woah.

Those butterflies that were awakened earlier? Yeah, they'd completely filled my stomach to the point that I was forced to swallow back puke.

"And," he started again, his eyes took in every bit of my face and I couldn't help but feel like he'd just captured me up in a single whoosh. "I think that Dawson is absolutely nuts for not making you *his.*" My face flamed, again, as I sucked in a shallow breath.

I whispered, "Dawson and I are... just friends."

I'd said the same sentence for the last few years, over and over again, and finally... it actually sounded believable.

"Good," he smirked. "Then he won't mind if I take you to Shane's tonight."

I felt my jaw fall and then he chuckled, looking down at the floor. A timid smile broke out on my face when he looked back up at me.

"Why would you want to take me?"

His eyebrows folded. "Why wouldn't I?"

I just stared at him, which made him smile, causing the one dimple on his cheek to grow deeper.

"I'll pick you up at 8. Okay?"

He didn't wait for me to confirm. Instead, he reached for the door and opened it, throwing back a wink and walked out, leaving me standing there like a mystified idiot.

In haste, I called out after him, running through the threshold of the doors. "I'll be at Becca's."

He turned around and gave me a nod. "See you then, beautiful."

Warmth slowly replaced the jittering feeling in my body. I almost squealed right then and there outside the doors to the school. I was cheesing. My smile stretching from ear to ear.

When I started to make my way over to Becca and Casey, they were both eyeing me suspiciously. I basically flew over to them, wings coming out of nowhere, and filled them in. We all three jumped up and down in the middle of the parking lot, with cars whipping by.

"This is insane!!" Casey piped. I locked on to her face

and then she squealed so loud that a few other students looked over at us.

"I know, I almost can't believe it!" I felt exhilarated. Then the confusion started to set in.

Really, though. Why me? Why would he ask me to go to the party with him? I was a sophomore, and definitely not like the other girls in my grade. I think I was one of the last virgins there was. Even Casey and Becca had had sex.

Not me.

Which was a major disappointment to Tyler. Just ask him; that's why he basically forced me to break up with him.

"Hey, Ivy. Come here." My head snapped up to Dawson and Max in Dawson's bright red Camaro, idling a few yards away.

"Hold on," I said to Becca and Casey. They nodded and hopped inside Becca's Honda, still yammering on about what I should wear tonight.

I skipped over to the rumbling of the Camaro's engine and bent my head down to Dawson. I rested my arms on the black paneling inside the door.

"What was that?" Dawson asked, his jaw clenching every few seconds.

"What?" I played stupid, trying to force the grin off my face.

I peeked around his body and looked at Max. He was sitting mindlessly in the passenger seat, looking down at his phone, not making any eye contact, whatsoever.

"Why was Andy talking to you?"

"So what if he was?" I snapped.

Dawson's head twitched a little and then his face scrunched.

"Whoa, killer. I was just asking."

I let out an even breath.

"Sorry, I'm just as confused as you are. He wants to take me to the party tonight."

Max coughed uncomfortably in his seat and I looked over at him once again, but he still wouldn't meet my eye.

"Oh..." I brought my attention back to Dawson. "So what did you tell him?"

"I told him yes. Duh."

He nodded his head up and down harshly and I could have sworn I saw a reddish tint on his cheeks. But all he said was, "Great."

Now I was even more confused but before I could say anything he asked, "Do you want to go to Ronnie's?"

I licked my lips. *Mmm.* Chili fries sounded damn good right about now and chances were, I wouldn't be able to eat much before the party due to the already-there nerves that would surely amplify in a few hours.

"Sure, right now?"

"Yeah, get in."

"K," I answered. "Let me go tell Becca. You'll drop me off at her house after, right?"

"Yep," he said, looking straight ahead.

Dawson was being totally weird but there was no way that his weirdness was going to ruin my high right now. One of the hottest boys in school just asked me out (insert high-pitched girly squeal here), and I totally agreed! I was going to a party with a senior. A really, really cool senior.

"HERE YA, GO." Dawson said, handing me the steaming, cheesy chili fries through the passenger window.

After we'd dropped off Max at his house, I jumped up

front and Dawson sped to Ronnie's—the *best* eating establishment in all of Ohio. Mr. Ronnie made the most INCREDIBLE chili fries, and they went perfectly with his famous shakes.

I slurped on my chocolatey drink before devouring the chili fries sitting on my lap. I turned down Dawson's blaring radio, which was playing "Ohio is For Lovers" (our favorite song) and looked over at him.

"What's wrong, Dawson? You've been acting weird since after school."

He shrugged, taking a huge bite of his Coney dog. He chewed vigorously, jaw chomping up and down, and then he wiped his mouth with his forearm.

He looked over at me and realized that I wasn't giving up. I noted how his blue eyes looked a little duller than normal and my heart ached.

"Dawson, tell me," I pleaded, still staring at him intently.

"I just..." he started. He turned his head and looked out the windshield. I did the same, noticing the pretty, blooming flowers just outside of the building. "I just don't think it's a good idea for you to go out with Andy."

My heart tumbled in my chest.

"Why?"

He shrugged again.

"Dawson, why? Did he say something?" Suddenly, I thought back to every movie I'd ever watched regarding a really popular guy and a less than popular girl. *What if this was a trick? What if Tyler put him up to this? Better yet, what if Breanna put him up to this?!*

He shook his head no, causing my wild thoughts to simmer, and then glanced back at me. His eyes searched my face and then I watched them soften. "Never mind, Ivy."

I scoffed and paired it with an eye-roll. "You can't just say something like that and then tell me never mind."

He cleared his throat, placing the hot dog on the center console, mere centimeters from my arm.

"I just don't want you to get hurt."

My body relaxed and I smiled. I reached my hand over and placed it on his face. His barely-there facial hair scratched the palm of my hand and I couldn't help but notice that his cheek fell inwardly toward it. "I'll be fine, Dawson. I'm a big girl... but," I took a deep breath, stopping myself.

"But what?" he asked, grabbing my wrist with his hand.

I clenched my teeth before answering. I'd never really been that nervous around Dawson, not since we became best friends, that is, but right now... I was feeling a little panicky to be admitting something so personal out loud.

"Ivy?"

I blew out air and then removed my hand from his face, flinging my attention to the windshield. "Why me?"

"What?" he questioned.

"Why me? Why would he want to take *me?*"

Sure, Andy had called me beautiful but still. Why me? I wasn't special. I wasn't like the other girls. I didn't spend hours in front of the mirror every morning applying endless amounts of make-up to my face. I didn't dress like a slut. I was just... normal. Ordinary.

Dawson rushed through his words. "Why would you ask that? Why wouldn't he ask you? I'm surprised it took him this long."

I was quick to respond. "Do you think I'm pretty?"

He stuttered. "Wh—what? You know I think you're pretty, Ivy."

I shook my head so hard the Camaro actually bounced a

little. "No, no. I mean, like, try to imagine I'm not your best friend who you met in middle school. Try to forget about the fact that I used to wear high-water jeans and dingy ol' Converse. Think of me like a normal girl, someone you just saw on the street somewhere. Would you actually stop and stare for a second?"

I turned to face him, grabbing a few chili fries on the way. The chili and cheese mixture hit my tongue and I let out a moan. So, *so* good.

I stopped chewing when Dawson started to choke on his milkshake, laughing before asking if he was okay and giving him a slap on the back.

"I'm fine," he grunted. Then he turned towards me, eyes blazing with something I'd never seen before. It had me pausing with my fingers inches from my face, a few chili fries dripping their melty cheese back onto the plate.

"Ivy," he whispered. "I think you are the most beautiful girl that I've ever seen."

I stared at him for a few long seconds, his blue eyes pulling me in like the ocean drawing in the tide. Then I busted up laughing. His face contorted quickly as confusion washed over him.

"You're not," I laughed harder, smacking his bicep. "You're not being serious."

He gulped, still staring at me. He didn't even so much as crack a smile, which had my laughter fading. A strange silence filled the Camaro, and even though the windows were open, I could have sworn that even the wind stopped moving.

"I am. I think you are so beautiful, Ivy. Inside and out."

Suddenly, I felt like I knew how Alice felt when she fell into the rabbit hole. Confusion filled my body but at the same time, so did anticipation and excitement.

Dawson thinks I'm beautiful? Why does that mean so much to me?

"Really?" My voice was near a whisper and he nodded, causing my heart to skip a beat.

"But, I look nothing like the girls you always pursue. How can you think I'm beautiful but then cozy up with Angela or Jessica?"

I immediately thought about how different I was from the girls he surrounded himself with. Angela had bright red hair and her boobs were what wet dreams were made of. Then you had Jessica. She had strawberry blonde hair, and the clothes she wore... made her *seem* like she had the same type of boobs as Angela. Except, I knew she didn't. I'd seen her without a shirt on in the locker room.

Then there was me: brown hair, usually wavy because I had a crappy straightener. By the end of a school day, it was always piled high on my head or in a braid that fell over my shoulder. I had forest green eyes which I always thought were dull looking. I wore jeans that weren't meant to be super tight and usually some type of Hollister shirt that didn't show any of the cleavage that I *didn't* have.

All the girls Dawson had had his feel of were the same: slutty but pretty, and they gave guys their *everything*. That wasn't me. I was totally different from every single girl he'd ever been with. Yes, there had been times that he'd snuck some touches in, and there had been times that I'd caught him staring at me, but I figured that was probably because I had something on my face. The butterflies that erupted in my stomach every time he did do something like that just taunted me. They reminded me that Dawson only saw me as a friend and that I should do the same. *Besties for life.*

"I never tell *them* they're beautiful," he quipped, taking back his hot dog and shoving the rest of it into his mouth.

I let out a shaky breath, ignoring our weird and out of character moment.

"But you're still attracted to them..."

"I guess," he answered, his mouth full of food.

A few minutes passed and he finally spoke again.

"Ivy..."

I moved my head towards him, taking a huge gulp of the creamy, chocolatey milkshake.

"Just don't let him use you."

"I won't."

He smiled weakly at me and reached his hand up to my face. His hand wavered for a second before he brought his eyes back to mine. I couldn't ignore the way my heart suddenly felt fuller in my chest and how all the oxygen from my body seemed to have disappeared.

His finger reached up and swiped my lip (which probably had leftover milkshake on it), but it lingered there for a moment too long. My eyes snapped to his and we stared at one another, saying nothing.

The air had shifted around us and I felt myself inching towards him. His eyes widened at the same time my breath hit his face, and then we both paused. My body felt hot, my mind was backtracking in my head, but my heart was chanting, "Do it! Do it! Do it!"

Do what? I asked it back, and then I hastily jolted myself backwards, slamming myself onto the back of the seat when it answered, "Kiss him!"

Then I let out a yowl.

"Jesus, Ivy," Dawson groaned, reaching in the center console for the napkins.

The chili fries were everywhere. My capris were going to be stained from the rust-colored sauce and yellow cheese, and I would likely have burn marks from their simmering heat.

"You are a walking disaster," he muttered while chuckling and handing me napkins.

I chuckled, too, ignoring the fact that I literally had just tried to *kiss* my best friend.

"And to think, I wasn't even walking..." I said, although I was truly screaming on the inside. I was dying. *DID I SERIOUSLY JUST TRY TO KISS HIM?*

Dawson started to laugh at my little joke and then I nervously joined in. We laughed together for a few seconds and then began stuffing our faces with our food and shakes. It was completely obvious that we were both trying so desperately to cover up what had just *almost* happened.

...But maybe he didn't notice?

FOUR

Dawson

Chipped red fingernails trailed over my thigh, scratching along the fibers of my jeans, inching closer and closer to my dick. Jessica's cleavage was in full action, spilling out of her tight V-neck shirt. I stifled a groan, and not the kind that meant I wanted her hand to creep higher. Her hand on my leg was doing absolutely nothing for me right now.

This morning when I squeezed her ass as she breezed by me in the school parking lot, I was more than excited to know that we were going to Shane's together. She gave me a flirty smile, smacking my hand away but I could see in her eyes that she was egging me on. I knew we would probably end up in my Camaro or somewhere deep within the woods, the smell of a bonfire laced within her blonde strands and her tongue tasting of some cheap beer, coaxing the life right out of me.

So why was I no longer eager?

I knew why, but I would never admit it out loud.

The bonfire was lit so high that I could see the flames

before I even rounded the bend of the road. Shane lived with his mom and stepfather, who were currently out of town for his little brother's baseball tournament. He threw parties every single time they left town, and since they lived out in the middle of Bumfuck Egypt, there were no neighbors to call and rat him out.

Plus, I was pretty sure they knew that he threw parties all the time. They just didn't care.

The drive to his house was long. It was well beyond the city limits, surrounded by tall oak trees and open fields. Cows mooing in the distance, coyotes howling with the wind. Even through the thirty minute drive and through Jessica's nonstop blabbering, the only thing I could focus on was Ivy and how she would be here with Andy.

Oh, and let's not fucking forget that I almost kissed her a few hours ago.

My God, if she hadn't pulled herself away, I would have kissed the life out of her. I swear it. I could almost taste the chocolate on her mouth. I could almost feel the touch of her soft, heart-shaped lips on mine.

But it was a good thing she pulled away. If she hadn't and I really did kiss her, everything would have changed.

I know that whenever I did kiss Ivy, there would be no going back. There will be no going back to being *just* best friends. It'll be something entirely different and let's face it: I'm not ready to tackle that obstacle yet; I need to get my shit together first. I just wasn't good enough for her.

No one was, but especially not me, the dumb jock with parents who were too busy worrying about their other fucked-up son...that is, when they weren't arguing over money or having a pissing contest over which one could bring home the larger paycheck.

At this point in my life, I had no ambitions. I had no

goals. I was pretty much coasting through high school, messing around any girl who gave me a second glance. Which was more often than not.

Sure, I was popular, but that's not what Ivy deserved. She deserved someone with dreams like hers, someone who would apply himself in the future and take care of her. Someone who hadn't slept with most of the school because he was simply bored.

I couldn't have Ivy that way, no matter how badly I wanted her. Instead, I would stay her best friend and fuck up any guy who hurt her.

That's what I was to Ivy. Her best friend, her protector. I loved her, I did. More than anything, but because I loved her, that also made me realize that I couldn't have her. I just... wasn't ready to cross that bridge. Maybe in the future. Maybe if I ever got myself together and actually tried to be the guy she deserved, but right now... no.

I don't think I'm ready.

Shit, maybe I am.

Max's words echoed in my head from earlier in the background of replaying the almost-kiss with Ivy. It was like an old VCR that just kept rewinding and then playing over and over again. Was I ready to tell her? Was I ready to risk it all? The near-kiss was like a hand squeezing my throat; I couldn't get away from it. It was consuming me.

Jessica's hand crept up higher along my jeans, causing me to cease fire on the argument over Ivy. "If you want, we can just go to back to my house. My parents aren't due back home for a few hours." Her voice sounded more like a purr. A sexy purr, but it just wasn't workin' tonight.

"Nah," I said, sliding her hand off my leg. "Let's just go in. People are expecting me."

People = Ivy.

She popped out her bottom lip and I almost laughed. She resembled a five-year-old, which wasn't the least bit attractive.

You know who was attractive when she stuck out her bottom lip? *Ivy*.

I quickly pushed open the driver's side door and jumped out, slamming it hard. It slammed so hard that Jessica actually yelped.

"Jeez, Dawson."

"Sorry," I mumbled, still irritated with myself.

As soon as we made it around the curve of the concrete driveway, I spotted the giant, blazing bonfire in the middle of the yard. Most of the guys were standing around it, wearing their letterman jackets with red cups in hand.

Jessica spotted some of her friends and whispered that she'd be right back. I nodded but I wasn't really paying attention. I was looking for someone else.

Someone who I'd give my full attention to.

I found her within half a second. Her brown curls landing halfway down her back. She looked so different than any other girl at the party, with her Hollister jeans and dark purple hoodie. That was one of the things I loved about Ivy. She never dressed to impress. She just dressed normal, and it worked for her.

She was effortlessly beautiful.

Which was absolutely alluring. I was almost tempted to just grab her arm and pull her back into my Camaro and tell her that if she gave me a couple years, I could change and be the guy that she deserved, that I just needed to figure my shit out...but then my eyes locked onto Andy, standing only a few feet away from her. His head was inclined to the left, peering down at her with a smile on his face. My blood ran cold.

I wanted to knock the stupid fucking smile right off his face because it was damn near torture for me to see him looking at her like that. As if she walked on water. *I* was the only one who could look at her like that, just me. No one else.

I let out a huge sigh and walked over the freshly-cut grass to Max and Clay.

"What up, bro. Where's Jessica?"

I shrugged, not answering and not really giving a shit.

I was already in a piss-poor mood after dropping off Ivy at Becca's. We'd completely acted as if the two of us almost kissing wasn't the least bit significant. As if it was this huge secret, which kind of stung. Did she realize that she didn't want to kiss me? Or was she concerned with the same thing I was – *best friends don't kiss* - and if we did, we could say good-fucking-bye to our comfort zone.

My piss-poor mood cranked up another notch when I got home. I walked in on my older brother punching a hole through the living room wall. Small pieces of dry-wall clattered to the floor, dust flying around the room. My mom was screaming with her high-pitched voice at him to "get his shit together," and then he stormed off to his room, slamming the door shut so hard the frames on the walls rattled.

My brother, Emmett, was only a year older than me, meaning he was a senior and should be at the same school as me, except he attends a military school. It was all very hush-hush in our family, telling neighbors and friends that he went to military school because he got accepted on some scholarship and wanted to join the military right out of high school. That wasn't true. My mom, dad, and I... we knew that Emmett was really in the military school because he was a rebel. He *enjoyed* breaking the rules. Even more so than me.

He'd been arrested, he'd been on probation, and he'd been in more fights than I could even count. Emmett was the epitome of a hothead and now that he was on spring break, back in town for a few days, things were right back to how they were before he left. Bad.

I was almost certain that it was because at military school, they didn't allow the students even an ounce of freedom. He was caged up like a fucking lion at the local zoo. I felt bad for him, but not bad enough to check on him before I picked up Jess.

I'd tried that before and he almost ripped off my head. *No, thanks.*

I pulled out my phone, sitting my ass on one of the foldout chairs surrounding the bonfire, ignoring everyone and their relaxed conversations and laughter. Usually I was the life of the party, joking around with everyone with a girl on my lap, gaze staying close to Ivy, who would be hanging with Becca or Casey somewhere in the distance.

But that wasn't the case tonight. She was with Andy and I was *not* joking with anyone. I was pissed off and uncomfortable. Like there was a pit in my lower stomach, growing larger and larger with each crackle of the fire.

My head twitched when I heard a soft, familiar laugh a few feet away, but instead of looking in her direction, I stared down at the tweets lining my phone screen.

The very first one made me cringe.

Emmett @emmett09 – 6 h

Don't drink and drive. But if u do, make sure you live in a small town with hella chill cops. #smalltownperks

Then the next one.

Emmett @emmett09 – 4 h

I can't believe I'm saying this but I can't fucking wait to get out of this hellhole town. #fuckingparents

I blew out a long breath, feeling tension crawl over my shoulders. *Why the fuck was my brother doing this shit?* Sure, my parents were kind of neglectful, but Jesus. He was turning out to be a fuckup and I hated that because I used to look up to him. He used to be my hero.

I pressed my hand against my chest, feeling a pain wedge itself deep within. I was a junior in high school and here I was fucking worried about my brother getting into even *more* trouble and my parents investing so much time into their insane competitiveness to make more money than the other that they didn't even realize how messed up he really was.

And, the only person who could make me feel better was sitting five feet away with a dumbass baseball player. Ivy was like my cushion. She was my comfort, she was the one who could smile in my direction and make my worry fall away. I didn't want to ruin that.

I couldn't ruin that.

I couldn't afford to ruin that.

I'd rather have her as my best friend then fuck everything up by trying to be her boyfriend. I would mess shit up, because let's get real – I had no fucking clue how to be a boyfriend, and then our friendship would fade faster than the fucking sunset.

Jess's soft voice wafted around me at the same time her arms wrapped around my neck. "Hey, wanna go inside?"

I cringed.

I openly cringed. *Shit.*

Her voice made my skin crawl. Her skin on mine irked me so badly I wanted to throw her arms off my shoulders.

I couldn't get Ivy's green eyes out of my head, or the way her breath felt against my mouth. If I'd just leaned in a fraction and kissed her... what would have happened? I mean, there had been times that she'd wandered into my deepest dreams, taking a hold of my heart, but I'd eventually wake up and shake it off. And there had been times that I physically couldn't help but touch her but I just chalked it up to... being extra friendly. *Friends flirt, right?* I was realizing pretty fucking fast that I'd been lying to myself over and over again. Like the near-kiss from earlier was untying those knots I'd so carefully tied around my deepest wants. And top that off with seeing her with Andy... it drove me fucking nuts. There was no tying up loose seams. There was no denying my inner feelings.

I think it was particularly driving me mad right now because she actually looked as if she was truly into him. She wasn't like this with Tyler. If anything, he annoyed her. She told me about all the things that irritated her when they were dating, as if she wasn't that into him but watching her eyes light up as she stared at Andy's angular face...holy fuck.

"No," I said harshly. Jess's arms unwrapped themselves from around my body quickly and I heard her gasp.

Max snapped his head over to me because he knew me almost as well as Ivy did. He knew something was up if I was denying a girl.

I briskly stood up, my chair falling backwards, landing with a soft thud on the grassy ground. My head turned slightly to the right and I saw Ivy staring at me with confusion and worry written all over her face.

The red and orange tint of the bonfire danced along her high cheekbones and she appeared even more alluring than before. Her eyes scrunched and her mouth puckered, high-lighting those kissable lips.

I was so close to walking over to her and dragging her off with me, but then my eyes flickered to Andy standing behind her, who was eyeing me with severe suspicion. For just a second, I pictured myself leaping over the remaining chairs in between us, like a real-life Superman and plummeting my fist onto his face, but I quickly brushed it off.

Turning away from Ivy and her pounding stare, I stomped past Jess's stricken expression and snatched Max's cup out of his hand, heading off towards the woods.

I just needed to be alone.

FIVE

Ivy

The only thing I could think, even with one of the hottest boys in school wrapping his hand around my waist was, *Something's wrong with Dawson.* Then that thought was quickly replaced with a surge of panic because I realized that I was more concerned about Dawson than the lack of butterflies in my stomach from another boy touching me.

After Dawson had dropped me off at Becca's, I watched his Camaro take off down the road, spinning wheels and all. My entire body was in a frenzy and if I thought that Andy talking to me earlier had made me nervous, that almost-kiss from Dawson was from a different freaking universe.

I didn't admit this out loud to Becca or Casey, even after they rambled on and on about how hot Andy was and how lucky I was to be going to the party with him. I acted as if I was excited when he pulled up in front of Becca's house, but I wasn't.

I could only focus on Dawson and how his eyes almost looked uncontrollable when I leaned over his center console, near centimeters from his mouth. He looked like he *wanted* me to kiss him. Then, my mind started wandering in every flipping direction... all leading back to two words:

What if?

What if I kissed him? What if he wanted to be with me like that? Does he like me more than a best friend? I mean, I knew he and I had a really strange, deep bond that people found peculiar. Dawson and I just... worked. I didn't know why, but we did. We were so in tune with one another, so much so that I knew when something was bothering him just by way his body felt near mine. The way his shoulders were stiffer than normal, the way the smile on his face didn't quite reach his eyes.

I knew him better than anyone, but why couldn't I figure out what he wanted with me? Was I imagining it? Was the inner hopefulness of my 15-year-old teenage heart making stuff up? Was something holding him back? Or was something holding *me* back?

Our friendship. That's what's holding us back.

Everything will change.

Everything will change if he and I kiss or date, or worse... have sex.

A surge of jittering nerves hovered above my skin. The thought of Dawson taking my virginity wasn't just appealing but it was completely consuming. I wondered what it would be like...

Perfect.

The second I let my mind dig into those feelings I'd shied away from since I was a dweeby seventh grader, I internally gasped.

Oh, my God!

I'm totally in love with my best friend! He's hot and

funny and sweet, and he cares about me, and oh my GOD, get it together, Ivy!

Letting out a deep breath, I looked over at Andy's sturdy jaw and twinkling eyes, feeling a small amount of guilt in my gut. "I'll be back."

I felt totally guilt-ridden coming here with him but running off to be with Dawson.

But... Dawson needed me.

I didn't give Andy time to respond; I spun on my heel and wandered in the direction that Dawson did.

The dormant butterflies in my belly, the ones who'd been asleep just now while with Andy, were slowly starting to stir. They were swirling and whooshing around faster and faster as I took each step, hearing sticks and branches break beneath my white Converse.

Why is it that I was totally into Andy earlier when he'd asked me to come here with him and now I can't get away fast enough? I rolled my eyes at the thought... I knew exactly why.

"Dawson?" I yelled out, my ears perking to attention.

"Ivy?" he answered back. My heart leapt in my chest but I ignored it, swallowing every ounce of excitement and focusing only on the relief that also filled my body. "What are you doing?"

"What's wrong?"

I finally found him sitting on top of a large log lying horizontally on the wooded floor. The sharp smell of the forest filled my nose with its refreshing pine scent, and it was honestly nice to be away from the smoke of the fire.

"You should go back to the party, Ivy."

I huffed, sitting down beside him, rubbing my hands along the bumpy bark of the log. His body was tense beside mine and I almost reached my arms around his expansive torso. "What's going on? You're definitely not acting like yourself, especially since after school..."

Silence stretched around us to the point that it became awkward and that didn't sit well with me, because things with Dawson – they were never awkward.

"I just...I don't like you with him." His voice was so low that I could barely hear him, but I did. I heard exactly what he said.

"Why? He's not going to hurt me, I don't even like him that much." I laughed and he whipped his body towards me.

"You don't?"

Shadows from the night sky imprinted themselves along his chiseled face, the same face that I'd always turn to when I was upset about something. The same face that made me laugh and gave me comfort, and maybe a little something else, too.

"Not really. I thought I did, but I realized that he doesn't really give me all those swoony butterflies that girls always feel when they're around a boy they truly like." *You know, like I feel when I'm with you sometimes.* I laughed again, turning my attention to the ever-expanding trees in front of us. "Like, every girl who's ever around you probably has those butterflies."

"Do you?"

I paused. My entire body stilled. Even my breathing. *Can he read minds?!*

"Why are you asking me that?" I whispered, heart rate accelerating to an alarming rate. *What the heck is going on!*

He let out a raspy chuckle. "I don't know, never mind."

And...just like that, my heartrate decreased dramatically.

"So what's really wrong?"

He answered, "Nothin'."

I rolled my eyes. "I know you way better than that, idiot. What's wrong, Peanut?" He chuckled at my nickname for him.

One time, my dad had called us Peanut Butter and Jelly because we were literally stuck together all summer, the summer after my eighth grade year. We'd spend most of our days in my back yard, fixing up the old treehouse that my dad had built Mia and I when we were in grade school. It was the summer that all of our friends had told us we were weird for being so close – no one ever quite understood our friendship. Sometimes even I didn't. It's not often that girls and guys can be best friends like us, so yeah, we were like one in a million.

After I giggled, taunting him with the name Peanut again, I paused and pulled my phone out of my hoodie pocket. I scrolled down to the last tweet I'd seen before coming to the party, knowing that it was more than likely what was troubling him. "Is it because of this?"

I shoved my phone up to his face, illuminating his blue eyes.

They scanned it for only a second before he turned his head away.

"Yeah."

I whispered, taking my phone back. "Things bad?"

I knew that his brother was into some rough stuff and that his parents weren't really... the caring type. They were the polar opposite of my parents, that's for sure. We didn't talk about his family much, especially since Emmett had to go away to military school, but I knew it bothered him. He was pretty upset about it when Emmett had left; in fact, in an attempt to make him feel better, I had gone to the video store and rented all 10 seasons of *BattleBots* (the bane of my existence- I can only watch robot-like things obliterating one another for so long until I want one to actually come through the TV to obliterate me). We watched them all day long, in the privacy of my finished basement...that is before my dad came down and joined in on the fun. I was basically nonexistent at that point.

Dawson's voice tore me from silently cursing *BattleBots*. "No worse than usual, but he's just being such a dipshit and it's pissing me off. He's just... being stupid."

I jutted out my lip and nodded. Then he started talking again.

"I don't feel like being here tonight. I feel off."

I pursed my mouth, letting out a held breath and ignoring the replay of the near-kiss from earlier scratching the inner walls of my brain. "Then let's get out of here."

He pulled back, his shaggy hair falling into his eyes. "What about Andy? You can't leave your date."

I giggled. "Says who? My best friend needs me tonight, he can eff off."

That had him laughing out loud, then he abruptly stopped when I asked the same about Jess.

"*I* need my best friend so she can eff off'."

Then we both laughed together. He shot up onto his feet, the ground loudly crunching beneath his football play-er's build. He extended his hand down to mine and I eagerly placed my hand in his, letting him pull me upward.

We didn't go back to the party.

We didn't even say goodbye to our "dates." We walked hand in hand to his Camaro and drove off, together.

Right where we belonged.

AS SOON AS we grabbed some McFlurries from Mcdonald's, we drove straight to Dawson's house. It was only a block away from mine—talk about convenient. I shot Becca a text and told her to let me know when she was going home so Dawson could take me over to her house, since I was staying there tonight after the party.

My parents knew I was at the party and they didn't mind. My mom and dad were probably the most laidback parents in the entire world, but I think that's because they knew I had a good head on my shoulders (that's what they told me, anyway). I wasn't a rule breaker by any means. I'd never been like that. I hated disappointing people and I hated when people were upset, so I'd always done my best to do what I thought they wanted of me.

"I see my parents are gone, go figure," Dawson gruffed from the driver's side seat of his Camaro. I glanced up at his two-story home and saw that there were absolutely no lights on inside. Despair fell over me for a tiny second. How strange would it be for my parents to never be home like Dawson's? How strange would it be to feel like you were living with complete strangers?

Lonely.

I bet it was really lonely.

"Is your brother gone, too?"

Dawson slurped up his McFlurry and I watched in awe as the corded muscles in his neck tensed with every gulp. I gulped too, but only because I realized that I was staring at my best friend's muscles with a weird feeling in my lower stomach.

He chuckled. "He's probably at a party. I'm surprised he didn't show up at Shane's."

I bit my lip. I was so lucky that my sister was an angel and that she was younger than me. I could set a good example for her, unlike Dawson's older brother, Emmett.

"Well, do you wanna go chill before Becca texts me?"

He thought for a second, staring up at his house with a desolate look in his eye. Then he nodded and started to climb out of his car, welcoming the cool, spring air.

Once we were inside, Dawson didn't even bother turning the lights on in his house. We both stormed up the carpeted stairs, me tripping a couple times and Dawson laughing, and made a bee-line for the only room he truly felt comfortable in: his bedroom.

I'd been in Dawson's bedroom so many times, but I was never as nervous as I was right now. Even in middle school, I'd come over and hang out with him after school for a few hours before heading to my own house. Usually, we'd just lay on the floor and do our homework together while MTV played in the background but over the last year or so, we'd either go to my house (where my parents constantly interrupted our homework doing by continuously talking to Dawson—they loved him) or we'd just drive around the backroads of our town, blaring music.

He'd never come out and tell me he didn't like to be here, at home, but I knew him so well that he didn't have to say anything.

He wore his emotions on his sleeve—at least with me, he did. I could read him like a Jane Austen novel, over and over again, feeling the depth of his feelings so deeply that they felt like they were mine. Unless, of course, it came down to deciphering his feelings for me. I was still contemplating the notion that I may have just made up the almost-kiss from earlier. Actually, no, I was certain that I was making stuff up from earlier.

Absolutely certain.

As soon as we walked into Dawson's bedroom, he flipped the lamp on and I jumped onto his bed, sliding my

Converse off. My white-socked feet wiggled at being freed from my shoes and I finished off my McFlurry before looking up at him

He was being totally weird.

"Why are you being weird, still? Do you wanna go to my house instead? My parents won't care, you know they love you." I laughed and he grinned.

"Can you blame them?"

I smiled, watching him cross the room to get on the other side of the bed.

He let out a huff and pulled his body up to rest against the headboard. He checked his phone for a few seconds and rolled his eyes. Before I could ask what he was rolling his eyes about, he turned his phone to me.

I scanned it quickly and had the same reaction.

Sure enough, there was a picture on Facebook of Andy and Jess, who were sitting together on the hammock at Shane's, hands intertwined. It probably *should* have bothered me.

But it didn't.

"They're perfect for each other," I mumbled, reaching over Dawson's body to grab the remote.

His entire body stilled. My body was hovering slightly over his, one arm leaning on the bed beside his hip, the other reaching for the remote on the side table.

I noted the way he tensed so I craned my head over to his. Our faces were so close that I could feel his breath on my face. I wanted to ask why he was being so strange, but the words got jumbled up in my throat. My heart was pounding ferociously in my chest and I instantly felt a dazing wave of heat flow through my body.

It freaked me out.

I had felt this exact way earlier in his car, when I'd inched my face closer.

He cleared his throat and I hurriedly grabbed the remote and shot my body back, crawling up to rest against the headboard, just like he was. Except I made sure that our bodies weren't touching, not even our legs.

My eyes stayed glued on the TV placed on the dresser in front of us as I tried to clear the tense air surrounding us.

What in the actual hell is happening? It's like a switch had been flipped earlier in the day. My heart was acting in a way that I'd never felt before and I kept getting hot flashes.

Maybe I was having a stroke.

Dawson mumbled from beside me, "Don't even think about it, Ivy."

I let out a giggle and pressed my finger down on the small, rubber button.

He groaned and threw his head back against the bed, looking up at the ceiling.

"What's wrong with this?" I prodded, my voice full of mirth.

He turned to look at me. He was *trying* to act annoyed but he was failing miserably. His grin was slowly stretching across his face, which caused me to smile.

Then he laughed and shook his head. "We've watched this, like, 500 times. Pick something else."

I gasped. "But it's my favorite!"

"Last time we watched this, you tried to act like you were an actual Charlie's Angel and you literally almost broke your parents' coffee table."

I jumped up to my knees, throwing the remote over to him. He grunted but caught it at the last second. His eyes were wide and his mouth was opened half-way.

"What're you doing?" he asked, acting mildly frustrated.

I smiled wickedly at him. "I've been practicing." Then I wiggled my eyebrows at him.

He barked out a laugh and I swear, I felt it all the way to my soul. I loved making him laugh.

"Come 'ere," I whined. "I need a dummy."

His expression was wary. "No. I'll let you watch this movie, only because the chicks are seriously hot in that get-up," he swirled his finger toward the screen, "but, I am not letting you perform some half-ass karate kick on me."

I stuck out my bottom lip. "Pleeeeeease. Let me show you my self-defense moves."

He quipped an eyebrow and then jolted his eyes down to my bottom lip. Several seconds passed as he stared at my mouth and once again, my body started to feel hot. Like I needed to fan myself.

Is this PMS? Why am I so hot all of a sudden? I felt out of breath.

"Fine," he huffed, swinging his long, jean-clad legs over the bed. His red t-shirt clung to his upper body, even after he shook his arms out like he was getting ready for a brawl.

I giggled again and he came and stood out in front of me. He laughed, his shoulders shaking a bit.

"I have so much fun with you," I said.

Dawson's laughter faded. His chest heaved up and down heavily and I watched as he swallowed harshly, the muscles in his neck straining.

Then he popped his neck, his caramel-colored, shaggy hair falling over his forehead. "Alright, come on. Show me whatcha got."

Instantly, I felt giddy. I took a few steps back from him, angling my body towards his. His eyes were dancing with excitement and anticipation, and then I spun around, whipping my back leg up and towards his torso.

His hand caught it at the last second as he let out a grunt and then we both tumbled to the floor.

I was rolling with laughter when I looked up at his face. His mouth was opened wide but there was still a smile on it. He didn't think I'd actually use that much force to kick him, but I was serious when I'd told him I'd been practicing.

I'd been going to kick-boxing with my mom for the past few weeks. I was channeling my true, inner Charlie's Angel.

As soon as I stopped laughing and my body relaxed, my eyes slowly trailed down to his hand. He was sitting upright on his butt, but his palm was still splayed, wide-open on my upper thigh.

I stared down at it, feeling the air shift around us. It was like a nice, warm blanket encasing us, for just a second. No scary overthinking clouded the moment. Just his hand on my thigh, causing butterflies to erupt from deep within. I felt a strange pull in my belly and goosebumps spread along my arms.

The TV was still playing in the background but the only noise I could focus on was his breathing. I wasn't sure how long we stayed like that, but what I was sure of, was how *alive* I felt with his hand on my leg.

I wanted him to leave it there.

I wanted the thrill of his hands on my body.

I wanted him.

I wanted my best friend.

SIX

Dawson

My hand is on her thigh. My hand is on her thigh and the only thing I can think about is how I want to inch it upward, towards her sweetest part.

What am I doing?

I'm ruining everything.

But I didn't care.

My hand twitched upward, just a fraction of a centimeter. I waited to see her reaction. I waited to see if she would pull her leg back and scramble to her feet, but she didn't. She took a sharp inhale of breath and I flicked my eyes up to hers.

The gold specks within her emerald eyes were sparkling, like they were egging me on. And did they ever.

I moved my hand upward, just an inch, feeling excitement run along my veins. She was so perfect, and beautiful. So breathtaking. My breaths were uneven. They were coming in spurts. I wanted to pounce on her. I wanted to lay her on her back and claim her mouth with mine. I'd imagined the way her tongue would feel along mine all fucking night.

Things were moving at a wicked fast pace. This morning, I looked at her like she was my best friend, but now I was looking at her like she was my lifeline.

Like I'd literally die if I didn't feel her lips on mine in the next three seconds.

Slowly, I pulled my upper body upright, so I was caging her body within mine. There was nowhere for her to go. She could either sit here and push me away or lay back and allow me to claim her like my entire body was telling me to do.

She didn't move, at all. Only her mouth. My eyes left hers and I stared down at her pale pink, heart-shaped mouth. It opened, just slightly, and I could smell the sweet, vanilla ice cream on her breath. I licked my lips, mere seconds away from kissing her, and then she jumped, letting out a small scream.

I shot my head up and looked in the direction of my door.

"Whoa, my bad. I thought you were alone."

I clenched my eyes shut tightly and then opened them to stare at my older brother. I was about to tell him to get the fuck out and shut the door but my mouth halted when I realized he had an awful-looking, swollen black-eye.

My shoulders slumped as I took in his appearance. He'd been in a fight. That part was obvious. Dark green grass stains covered the knees of his jeans, and his t-shirt looked loose around the neck, like someone had pulled on it. His dark hair was sticking up in several different directions and in addition to his blackening eye, his nose had a little dried blood just below his right nostril.

"What happened?" I asked, not taking my hand off Ivy's

leg. She was sitting with her back bone-straight to my brother. Her lips were smooshed together and she was staring directly at my face.

I glanced back up to my brother and his forehead furrowed before he asked, "Ivy?"

Her shoulders slumped and then she slowly swiveled her body towards the door.

"Hi, Emmett." I couldn't help but notice the pink blush that crept across her cheeks. It made me grin and when she looked back at me, she was acting totally opposite of the Ivy I knew; she was being shy. Ivy wasn't normally shy around me, even with other people around. But looking at her right now, she looked ready to bolt out of my room in less than five seconds.

"I'm sorry, I didn't know you two...were...um." My brother stuttered over his words and it made a sharp laugh fall out of my mouth. He started to ramble even after I laughed. "I saw the light on and I figured if you were in here with a girl, it would be Ivy and you two would be goofing off, but..."

Ivy coughed out an uncomfortable noise and I smirked.

"I'll just leave you two to it then," he hastily murmured and then backed away from the door and all but ran down the hall.

I had no idea why he was being so weird about this. I mean, sure, it was Ivy. My best friend. Emmett had been around her before, and when he went to school with us last year, he protected her like she was his little sister...but, I guess he hadn't realized that I felt this way about her.

I hadn't fully realized it either, until about five hours ago.

I mean, yes, I'd always loved her and cared for her and I'd definitely dance around the line of flirting versus being friendly many times, but it'd never been like this. I'd never touched her with the real intention of actually kissing her. I'd touched her because it just felt right.

It felt even more *right* after what had just happened.

"Uh, I need to go talk to him, I think." I said, finally taking my hand off her leg.

She looked down, her brown hair falling wistfully in her face, shielding it completely from me. I didn't like that. I needed to see what she was thinking.

Her voice fell over me in the softest way, like a leaf falling gracefully from a tree in the middle of fall. "Yeah, definitely. He looked... bad."

I sat there for a second, feeling my heart thump wildly in my chest. I wasn't going to pretend like what just happened, didn't.

I was not shoving this under the rug like earlier.

"Look at me," I pleaded. Ivy's head popped up so quickly that her chestnut hair flew back out of her face. Her green eyes were vividly scared and confused which was a lot like being punched in the gut.

"We're going to talk about what just happened when I come back in here, okay?"

Ivy sucked in her lower lip, biting on it gently with her teeth...which was not helping matters, whatsoever. She swallowed, allowing her mouth to close once again. Then she slowly nodded her head and I just couldn't help but let the next words tumble out.

"I don't regret it."

She sucked in a breath, widening her eyes.

Her voice almost quivered. "You don't?"

I smiled. "Never."

Ivy let herself smile, just a small one, which was probably forced. Even through her weak smile, I could see the weary expression on her face. That's when I took my hand and placed it underneath her chin. My heart was hammering in my chest and I can honestly say that I'd never felt so compelled to make someone calm in my entire life. "Just relax, Ivy. It's still me you're talking to."

She let out a sigh and nodded, a small smile still lingering. I knew exactly what she was thinking in that moment, though. I knew her so well that it was obvious. It was also very clear to me that I was thinking something similar: *This is gonna change everything.*

WHEN I WALKED out my bedroom door, I turned the corner and rested my back against the wall. I angled my head up and looked at darkened ceiling, letting out a huge breath and trying to reassure myself that it wasn't a dream and that I had, in fact, just tried to pounce on my best friend of the last four years.

All those taunts and remarks from my friends reverberated in the back of my mind. I think everyone had known that there was always something different with Ivy and I. Memories slammed into me and I truly couldn't comprehend how it had taken me this long to recognize the way my heart beat a little faster in my chest when she walked out her front door in the morning to climb into my Camaro. Or the way I felt blinded with anger when I'd hear some guy talking about how attractive she was; much like I felt a couple days ago when I saw the hurt flash on her face from Tyler. Whenever things were going wrong in my life, I turned to her. She was the only person I knew that could make me feel better, that could make me feel a little lighter.

I was pretty sure I was in love with my best friend, and I wasn't the type of guy who fell in love. I wasn't the type of guy who was sweet and tried to wow a girl, just to make her smile. I wasn't the type of guy who could grow a weird fluttery feeling in his lower stomach just from the mere touch of someone's skin.

I mumbled under my breath, "Jesus," and then pushed off the wall and walked towards my brother's room, opening his door quickly and marching inside.

He spun around, a huge smirk covering his bruised face.

"Dammmmmn, took ya long enough, bro."

I rolled my eyes. "What?"

He barked out a laugh and landed with a thud on his messy bed. "Dude, I knew that you'd fall for her eventually. I honestly didn't think it'd be this soon, but I knew it'd happen."

I wanted to deny it. I wanted to tell him to shut the fuck up and that she was only my best friend. But the words literally evaporated on my tongue when I opened my mouth.

Walking a little further into the room, I leaned my back against his closet door and sighed. I rubbed my hand through my hair and finally met his eyes.

"I don't wanna fuck it up."

Emmett only stared at me, taking in what I'd said.

My brother and I, we hadn't had a decent conversation in so long. He'd been away at his hell school for the last year and when he'd come home for a visit, he'd stay holed up in his room or be out behaving raucously with friends.

Just like tonight. Except tonight, whatever friends he had been with weren't the best, apparently.

I would never admit it aloud, but I missed him. I missed my older brother and I hated that he was so closed off and angry at the world. I didn't understand it. Not entirely, anyway. He was just unhappy, all the time.

"You won't fuck it up, Dawson. You care about her too much to fuck it up."

My heart was heavy and I felt like I was being smashed by a tidal wave of uncertainty.

"So, what's going on?" I asked, changing the subject.

He blew out a sigh and popped himself back up on the bed.

"I was just coming to tell you that I was leaving."

My brows folded. "What do you mean you're leaving? I thought break was for another week."

Emmett stared at me for a few uncomfortable seconds and then let it all pour out.

"I'm tired of being here. I hate it here. I hate this house. I hate how Mom and Dad are always breathing down my neck and telling me to 'get it together.' I fucking hate how they don't know me at all. They don't know you, either. They don't know anything but how to bury themselves in work; they think that if they make enough money, all will be right in the world. I'm sick of it. I'm angry here and I become angrier with each passing second that I'm in this town and this house."

Silence crossed between us. I heard everything he was saying and I understood every single bit of it.

He was right. He and I – we were basically on our own. We'd been on our own for so long. I honestly can't remember the last time we all ate as a family. I think back, and it must have been when we were still in grade school, and even then, our parents probably talked nonstop about their jobs, or bickered. It was kind of depressing, now that I truly thought about it.

Our parents weren't terrible. It wasn't like we didn't get fed or had to fend for ourselves. We weren't forced to get jobs to pay our car payments and insurance. They've always showered us with materialistic things and we've always received a load sum of money each month into our accounts, but that was it. No lengthy but helpful conversations about school, or college. No talk of an upcoming family vacation. We didn't really talk at all.

And the only time I heard my parents converse was if they were discussing work or if they were arguing.

It made my chest ache to think about it. I felt suffocated by tension in my house. Like the walls were closing in on us.

"Where are you going to go?" I asked.

He looked around the room for a brief second before answering. "I'm staying with a friend. I'll finish the next couple of months at the school and then I'll get a job and figure out what I want to do for the rest of my life. I'm just... I'm done, Dawson."

I nodded, my back still pressed along the wall. I briefly thought about how freeing it would feel to just *leave.* My future was kind of blurry when I looked into it. I figured I would just work with my dad after high school, or maybe go to college and then work with him. He'd have to retire eventually from his contractor's job; he owned the business and he used to tell Emmett he wanted him to take over.

Maybe I would take over one day. Did I want to? I wasn't sure. I hadn't really put much thought into it. All I knew was that I liked to play soccer, hang out with my friends, and be with Ivy. Those were the only things I cared about.

It wasn't like that with Emmett, though. He was very adamant and made it clear to my parents that he didn't want to work with my father. He didn't want to take over the business—if I remember correctly, he liked to draw.

He was always drawing and creating stuff when we were younger. My mom used to encourage it when we would sit on the living room floor and play as kids, but as he got older and more interested in art, she stopped noticing or caring. One or the other.

My father used to encourage him to focus on school. To focus on woodshop or math (two things that would pertain to his line of work). Emmett wanted none of it, which was more than likely the culprit to him acting out so much.

"I'll help you pack," I finally said. Emmett looked surprised, like he'd thought I was going to tell him not to go. Like I wouldn't understand what he was feeling or where he was coming from. But even if I hadn't understood, it didn't matter. The only thing I wanted was for him to be happy.

"What are you going to tell Mom and Dad?" he asked, pulling out a duffel bag and shoving some of his clothes inside.

I grabbed another, pulling things out of his dresser.

"I'll tell them that they probably should have acted like they cared a little more."

He chuckled but then his expression turned stormy. His blue eyes darkened to the point that the color blended in with his swollen black eye.

"Are you gonna be okay?" he questioned, pausing his packing.

I grinned. "I have Ivy. I'll be fine."

He nodded as a smile worked its way on his face.

"Don't fuck it up."

I gulped, turning my attention back to filling up the other bag.

I won't fuck it up.

I couldn't.

SEVEN

Ivy

Something jolted me awake, but I wasn't sure what it was. The dim light of the small lamp beside me caused my eyes to adjust quickly. My heart pounded in my chest when I realized that I wasn't where I was supposed to be.

I was in Dawson's room. I wasn't alarmed that I was in his room; it's not like I hadn't been in there before, but I suddenly remembered what had happened before I accidentally fell asleep.

Us almost kissing *again*, the proximity of his body near mine, the way my body burned with his hand on my leg. Then, his promise to discuss it when he got back from talking with his brother.

As soon as Dawson's hand left my thigh and he exited the room, I jumped to my feet and had to cover my mouth before a girly squeal fell out of it. I was prepared to pretend like it hadn't happened, just like we'd done earlier in the day, but he told me *didn't* regret it.

That meant he wanted to kiss me, right?

That meant he wanted things to change, right?

Doom washed over me like I'd just walked through an open waterfall. Things *would* change. Feelings that I'd buried deep within would surface and I would get even more attached to him. Dawson and I were the best of friends; we'd been that way since I was in seventh grade. I had enough memories of us to last a lifetime and the thought of adding in intimate memories, things like knowing what his mouth would feel like on mine...those would haunt me until the end of time if things didn't work out between us.

I'd watched enough movies and read enough books where two best friends fall in love and then things go wrong and then never return to how they once were. Sure, in the movies and books, the two characters always end up back together in the end, blissfully in love and happily married.

But those were fictional. I might be young and naïve but I knew, for a fact, that reality didn't play out like that. The guy doesn't always get the girl in the end, and the girl doesn't always end up with her happily-ever-after.

Dawson and I could fall madly in love, he could take my virginity and I'd hang off his arm like I'd seen so many girls do at my school, but what would happen if things went in a different direction? What would happen if he got sick of me and wanted to be with another girl?

I was totally out of my league compared to all the other girls Dawson has been with. I was a big, fat virgin! I had no idea how to have sex. I mean, okay, I had a little bit of an idea from what Becca and Casey had told me but I was more of a hands-on learner.

Awkward.

I honestly would be destroyed if something happened between us, causing our friendship to go up in flames. And, even if we did salvage our friendship, I would never be able to deal with him being with someone else, knowing that I hadn't been good enough or that I hadn't made him happy. Our friendship would be based on a lie. And then it would cease to be.

Dawson and I would cease to be.

Things were going to get complicated and messy and I could openly admit that I was scared to death for things to change. That was the last thing I remembered thinking about before I fell asleep with *Charlie's Angels* playing in the background, curled up on Dawson's bed.

Now, the TV was on low and an infomercial was playing, advertising some super-amazing pan to cook eggs in. My legs were intertwined with Dawson's and his muscled arm was laying heavily across my stomach.

I'd taken my hoodie off after he'd left the room earlier because I was completely burning up (probably something to do with the way he'd looked at me and the way his hand had felt on my thigh), and my grey t-shirt had risen up a few inches...meaning that Dawson's bare forearm was lying on my bare stomach.

The wild fluttering that occurred in my lower stomach was almost embarrassing.

Turning my head to the side, I took in his peaceful, sleeping face. He was so incredibly attractive in the simplest way.

His tousled, shaggy cinnamon-colored hair was hanging off his forehead, covering his eyebrows. I giggled because he needed a haircut in the worst way, yet he still looked perfect. His long eyelashes, that most girls were probably jealous of, fluttered along his smooth cheeks. His straight nose led down to his unmoving, blush-colored lips. My eyes naturally zeroed in on them and I could feel my lower body start to feel funny in the way that I really, really wanted to kiss him.

I felt my face getting warmer with each passing second that I studied his face like he was some fancy statue in the middle of a museum. I slowly turned my head away and took a deep breath. I let it out slowly, careful not to wake him up.

I reached my other arm over and grabbed my phone from beside me.

My eyes sprang wide open when I took in the time. *How was is almost two in the morning?! How long were we sleeping and why didn't he wake me up when he came back in here?*

Thankfully, my parents thought I was staying with Becca so I wasn't missing curfew or anything. Heck, they probably wouldn't even be mad if I told them I fell asleep with Dawson. They truly did love him. I wonder what they'd think if I told them that Dawson and I were becoming a *thing*. Were we? Maybe that's why he didn't wake me up. Maybe he changed his mind and *did* regret almost kissing me...again.

Embarrassment surged through my body but I pushed it away, quickly texting Becca back.

Sorry, I fell asleep at Dawson's. Can I still come now?

I giggled when I read her messages from earlier in the night.

At 11:07 she texted: **I'm on my way home now so u can tell Dawson to drop u off**

Then at 11:50: **Where are u**

Then at 12:01: **I would bet my left arm that u**

and Dawson are either out cow tippin or u fell asleep

Three minutes later: **K Case and I have a bet we think u two fell asleep and she thinks u two are seriously out cow tippin**

Then an hour ago: **I win cuz you can't still be cow tippin Casey is mad that she lost but I'm going to bed so call if u end up waking up and still need to come here**

I didn't realize I was laughing until Dawson started to stir beside me. His arm twitched on my stomach and I froze. I kept my face turned down toward my phone, afraid to look over at him. My smiled had disappeared, as had my laughter.

Dawson's voice was in full-on sleep mode with the roughness of a deep rasp. "You go cow tippin' one freaking time and no one will let you forget it."

I cracked up, shoulders shaking so hard that it caused him to laugh, too.

I looked over at his droopy eyes and sleepy smile. "That was such a fun night."

My cheeks lifted when I thought back to last fall when Dawson and I had skipped out early of the bonfire after a rival football game because Max had dared us to see if cow tippin' was a real thing. He didn't believe that cows really slept standing upright.

Turns out cows do...but they really don't like it when you tip them over.

One cow came charging at Dawson, and I, being the person I am, of course got the entire thing on camera. He had to leap over the barbed-wire fence that surrounded the pasture and cut his leg in the process.

The grassy meadow was right behind our high school, up on a bank that overlooked the town. We weren't allowed to go up there, according to the principal. He had made a huge announcement one day because apparently some kids had been going up there and making out during school hours.

But Dawson and I didn't really care. There weren't any school faculty members at the rival bonfire; only the football and cheerleading coaches and they were too busy flirting with one another to worry about two high schoolers sneaking away to see if cows really did sleep on their feet.

Dawson's laughter broke me out of the memory. "Remember Betsy?"

I giggled. "Betsy was really freaking fast for a cow."

"I almost died."

I laughed again, pushing his shoulder. "You're so dramatic, Dawson."

He pulled back, the bed moving under the weight of his body. "Are you kidding? Do I need to pull up the video? I'm almost positive that her eyes were red like she was some demonic cow; she was ticked!"

I threw my head back and cackled, closing my eyes. I put my hand up on my cheek and then peered up and over at him once again.

Our laughter quickly died down and then a feeling of dread came over me. The giant elephant in the room was trampling toward us and I wish I could lie and say that I felt totally cool, calm, and collected, but right now, I felt anything but.

Dawson's oceanic eyes became darker, his pupils dilating as he stared at my face. He ran a steady hand through his hair and rolled his lower lip between his teeth. My eyes took in every bit of his lips, the way they slightly curved inward at the top and the way the lower one was slightly plumper than the top.

He had to be a good kisser; he had kissed tons of girls and they just kept on coming back, even after he'd all but thrown them away, spewing that he didn't want a relationship.

I had to believe he wouldn't treat me that way, though, or else I was going to be in big, big trouble. What if he *didn't* want me as a girlfriend? Maybe he just wanted to kiss me. Or maybe not.

The low wail of sirens from outside sounded around us, and it was a welcome noise from the silence that had entrenched the room.

"So, about earlier," he started, cutting right through the awkwardness.

My heart pounded viciously in my chest and I couldn't help but start to feel like my world was about to come crashing down.

I blurted, "It's okay, Dawson. You don't have to pretend like it meant anything. We just—"

All the words dissipated on my lips when his rough palm rested on my cheek. I sucked in a sharp breath as my body jolted backwards from his touch, but at the same time, he lurched forward. We were like magnets; as soon as I'd pull away, he'd come closer, like there was no other way for us to be.

"Dawson," I whispered. "You're," I gulped, ignoring how amazing his hand felt on my face. "You're my best friend..."

He nodded his head slightly and I continued, still whispering. "This will change everything..."

"I don't care," his tone was guttural and it caused something to explode inside me. Instantly, I didn't care either. All the well-thought out arguments I had made earlier were diminished. Not a single one left in the background to keep me from making things messy or risky. I think, after hearing what he was trying to imply, after feeling his warm breath on my cheek, after waking up and feeling his bare skin on mine...that kissing Dawson was worth the risk.

He was worth the risk.

Things were shifting dangerously, but nothing could stop the way my body felt. Nothing could stop the thumping in my chest and the ringing in my ears. Nothing could penetrate what was happening in this moment. Not even the increasingly loud sirens outside his window.

He leaned in a little closer, dipping his body down to mine, eyeing me, watching to see if I'd pull away—but I didn't. In fact, I moved closer.

Our lips were only millimeters apart; I could almost feel the softness of his on mine.

My heart strummed and my entire body felt electrified, and then his mouth fell onto mine in one swift, perfect moment.

And everything went calm.

Dawson's kiss was dangerous; it shut the entire world out. It was the type of kiss that made you close your eyes even when you begged them to stay open.

I innocently fell into his body, moving my lips along his like they were meant to do that exact movement for the rest of my life. His tongue moved languidly across mine and if there had been real butterflies in my stomach, they'd be flying so fast that my whole body would probably take flight.

I let out a sound, one that I'd never even made before, and it quickly brought me back to reality. I was kissing

Dawson so thoroughly that I didn't even realize my phone was vibrating in my lap.

As soon as he felt the shift in my body, he pulled back, taking his lips off mine. Both of our chests were heaving up and down with such intensity that you'd think we'd just completed a triathlon.

I etched every inch of his face, wondering if he felt the same way that I did. If he had felt how *right* and life-altering that kiss just was. As if every single wrong in the world had suddenly been righted.

By the looks of his face, he had. He had felt it too. His mouth was opened a little and his eyes were widened beyond their normal size. The sharp angles of his cheeks were pinker than before and then he let out a sigh.

"Wow."

The kiss was so powerful that my eyes had glossed over, suddenly blurring the edges around Dawson's face.

I was at a loss for words, completely stricken to the point that I didn't even know where I was. All I knew was that I'd just kissed Dawson and that it was the best kiss I'd ever had.

I wanted to spend the rest of my life feeling the way I just had with him.

My forehead scrunched when he tipped his head to my still vibrating phone, and then his attention went to the window.

The sirens I'd heard earlier seemed close, and they weren't fading away. They should have moved on by now. They wouldn't still be *that* loud.

Dawson's brow furrowed because the same thing must have occurred to him.

I finally glanced down at my phone and picked it up without even seeing who was calling.

"Hello?"

Annie, one of the girls I'd run track with, who also lived a block away from me, shouted into the phone. "Finally!! Where the heck are you, Ivy?!"

"What? Why? I'm at Dawson's."

Her voice was muffled, like she was crying. "Oh my gosh! Thank God! Ivy, you need to get home."

A deep chill went down my spine as Dawson's tall frame pulled away from the bed. He went over to the window and looked through the crystal-clear glass. He turned around, watching for my reaction to the phone call.

Annie's voice was troubled with distress. "Your house is on fire. I can see the flames from my bedroom. It looks really bad."

And just like that, I bounced to my feet, phone falling to the side. I took off through the bedroom door without even putting my shoes on. He was right behind me, asking what was wrong.

I didn't have time to answer. I jumped the stairs, landing with a loud thud, the bottoms of my feet stinging so badly it caused me to pause for a half second.

I had no idea if his parents were home but if they were, I didn't care. I didn't care if they thought I was a crazy person running through their house like it was on fire... because *mine* was.

I swung open the front door and ran down the street, tiny bits of asphalt and gravel cutting through my socks. They didn't stop me from running. I could see the orange and red flames from the stop sign at the end of Dawson's street.

My feet pulled me through the cool grass of neighboring houses, cool dew grass soaking my socks. I saw a fence coming up and thankfully, I'd run hurdles in track so I was well-equipped for leaping over stuff.

As soon as I came to the chain-link fence, I used my hands to help push off the top rail, and catapulted my legs over it. I ran straight through our neighbor's yard, my foot getting caught in a hole her dog had dug. I hit the ground for a second but Dawson was right beside me, helping me up.

He kept shouting at me to slow down but I couldn't. I just kept running.

Once I was through that yard, I could actually *feel* the heat of the fire.

My stomach convulsed as I rounded the last house blocking my view. I moved around the looming firetruck and I was instantly met with thriving, raging flames. They were coming from every single angle of my house.

Where are my parents?!

My eyes desperately scanned the surrounding people. I noted the firemen in all their glory, dressed head to toe in suffocating uniforms and as they sprayed my house with giant hoses hooked to their trucks. I searched for an ambulance but I didn't see one...yet.

My eyes found my next door neighbors: Judy and Bob St. Clair. I ran over to them, not hearing a thing except my heartbeat pulsing in my ears.

"Oh, honey," Judy pleaded. Tears were running down her face with her husband's arm around her sloped shoulders. "Thank God you're okay."

"Where's my mom?" I asked, as she enveloped me in a bone-crushing hug. "My dad? Where are they?" I pulled back and her face contorted and my heart fell out from beneath my stomach.

"Where are they?!" I screamed frantically, as if my life depended on it.

Dawson's strong arm wrapped around my torso, pulling me backwards. I knew I was crying by the way my face was wet, but I couldn't concentrate on that. The only thing I could focus on was the hellish orange hue gleaming around everyone and everything in front of me.

Oh my, God. It felt like my heart had died in my chest.

"Mia!!" I shouted. Dawson was caught off guard at the way my body sharply pushed off his. His arms fell down my torso just enough for me to slip away and run to my house, right toward the blazing fire.

"Mia!!" I yelled again, my voice so hoarse and jagged that no one would be able to make out what I was saying, even if there hadn't been a roaring fire surrounding us.

Someone pulled me back before I even got to my front lawn.

"Miss, stop! PLEASE, stop!"

The scratchy material of a fireman's uniform rubbed my bare arms raw. I clawed and kicked at him only to realize that he wasn't going to let go and that he was much stronger than me. I didn't care, though; I continued to fight as raw sobs tore out of my mouth, unable to form any other word but Mia's name.

"You need to calm down because I can't understand you."

I shook my head harshly, crying uncontrollably, hair sticking to my wet face.

"Her sister. She's asking about her sister." Dawson came out of nowhere, his voice stern and demanding.

I snapped my head over to Dawson and the second I met his eyes, I felt myself break in half.

Oh my God, oh my God, oh my God. My sister. Where is my sister? Mia. No, God, please don't take her.

"We only found two bodies in the house. No one else."

I repeated the sentence in my head, *We only found two bodies in the house. Only two bodies.*

Two bodies.

My parents.

My body went limp and I stopped struggling. I was still enclosed in the stranger's grip, his strong arms wrapped around my body so tightly that it was hard to breathe. The flames were dying down a little but it didn't matter; my entire house was burnt to a crisp. There would be no salvaging anything.

"Ivy!!" My head whipped over to a barely audible voice but I knew instantly that it was my sister.

My entire body sagged with relief. *Thank you, God.*

I cried harder and the man finally let me go after Dawson looked as if he was going to kill him. I ran past Dawson and opened my arms for my younger sister to burst into them.

She was wearing her cotton, lilac-colored, star PJs, her best friend's parents following closely behind her. As soon as she was in my arms, we both collapsed onto the rough ground, hot from the fire. The volume of her cries eclipsed mine by a landslide. She pulled back just slightly and looked up into my eyes. "Are Mom... and Dad... okay?"

She could barely get the words out and I was hoping with everything I had that she wouldn't make me answer. I couldn't. I couldn't form the words.

My silence was enough. She buried her head into the crook of my neck, sobbing even harder than I thought possible. Her tiny frame convulsed in my arms as the tears kept falling from my eyes, even though I was trying my hardest to get them to stop. They were silent tears. I wasn't sobbing anymore. My body wasn't hijacking its frame with uncontrollable shakes, like my sister; there were just rivers streaming down my face in silent pleas to make this all go away.

I turned my head to the left, staring at the dying flames and the firefighters working so diligently to get them under control.

My entire house just went up into hot, simmering flames, leaving *nothing* in its wake.

Nothing at all.

Dawson

Her cries would stay with me for the rest of my life. I had never known true pain until the moment I saw Ivy collapse in front of her burning house with her sister in her arms. I literally wanted to pick her up and just carry every single bit of hurt that was suffocating her. The second her eyes met mine, when she realized that her life had just gotten turned completely upside down, was the moment I realized that I loved her so fiercely that I would do anything to put the light back in her eyes. I would do *anything* to put a smile back on her face.

I promised myself right then, that I would spend the rest of my life making her happy again. I promised myself that I would spend every waking moment, surrounding her with love, making up for the fact that her parents had just been stolen from her.

I just wish I could have known that seeing her curled up with her sister in front of the smoking embers of her house was the last time I'd see her for a long, long time. Then maybe I wouldn't have made promises I would be forced to let go of.

EIGHT

Ivy

It'd been three weeks since the fire.

These three weeks had been such a blur that I couldn't even conjure up images of anything other than the four paneled walls that surround my sister and me every night. We shared a room, which was fine; I wouldn't want her to be away from me, anyway.

As soon as things calmed down on the night of the fire, the police had contacted the only person who I knew would take us in.

Uncle Timothy.

He was my father's brother who lived four hours away, up north. My grandma, really the only family member my parents had forced us around when we were younger, had been put into a nursing home a couple years ago with Alzheimer's. My sister and I had one more aunt, but she lived in a different country due to work, and that was about all the family members we had.

Uncle Timothy was it.

He was also a recovering alcoholic who had a serious gambling problem – hence the reason that all the money my parents had to their name was already gone. He paid off his debts in order to stay out of jail...in other words, in order to be considered a "fit" guardian.

I should feel thankful that he'd taken us in. If it weren't for him, my sister and I would have been thrown into foster care, at least according to CPS, who had taken us in for the couple days that it took to get things settled with my uncle. They had to come up with a plan, figure out the money issue, and so on.

I no longer had my cell phone, I no longer had the clothes that I'd obtained over the years from shopping with my mom...I had absolutely nothing, except for my sister and the clothes on my back.

We didn't even get to have a funeral for my parents because, well, my parents couldn't exactly *be* buried, as their bodies had been burnt beyond recognition (not that I'd actually seen them; I couldn't even bear the thought), and who was going to pay for that? According to my uncle on the first night he brought us home, as he made us mac n' cheese from a box with the stupid SpongeBob characters on it, funerals were expensive and he couldn't afford one. But once we got some more money, we would do something special. As if doing something special would close the wide, gaping holes our hearts. Yeah, okay.

My uncle wasn't a bad guy. In fact, he was really nice to us. But he wasn't parent material. He was *nothing* like my father, which was probably why we'd never really seen him much over the years. Their relationship had been strained. My father had been the successful owner one of the best car dealerships in town, whereas my uncle was basically the black sheep of the family.

Uncle Timothy ended up getting me a job working at a pizza parlor, and thankfully my sister and I didn't have to finish the last couple weeks of school, given the circumstances. I just hated that everyone at the pizza parlor looked at me as if I was about to burst into tears at any given second.

Which would be accurate, if I'd felt anything at all.

My uncle had pulled me aside a day ago, while Mia was taking a shower, worry lines making permanent wrinkles in his forehead.

"Kid, you've gotta work on trying to cope sooner or later. I'm getting concerned."

I just looked up at him, not moving a single inch of my face.

He swallowed, looking away for a brief second. "I know it's hard, Ivy. I know this isn't ideal. You and Mia had amazing parents and now you have this..." His tanned arms fanned out around him, urging me to take a look at the house.

The kitchen was so outdated that it belonged in a 70's sitcom. Pale green countertops and dark wooden cabinets lined the walls. The floor was tiled with strange yellowish designs on every inch, making it almost painful to look at. My uncle barely knew how to make a grilled cheese sandwich and although he made enough to support us, he liked to gamble all his money away, which was exactly why he'd gotten me a job. I was going to have to start paying for stuff on my own, now that I didn't have my parents. It felt like a slash to my heart and that slash was opening wider each day.

He was right, though.

If there was anything I'd learned from the past three weeks, it was that life wasn't fair. Sometimes we were given certain circumstances that were almost unfathomable to deal with, but that's just the thing: you either deal with them or they'll just take you down in their midst. I was learning that pretty quickly. I felt like I was just constantly drowning, except instead of waving my arms frantically above the stormy waters for someone to save me, I was tying a ball and chain to my leg to drag me further below the surface. If I didn't deal with this profound hurt eventually, it was going to swallow me up whole.

My voice was no more than a peep. "Can I use your phone."

It wasn't even a question. Just a plain statement, lacking any kind of enthusiasm or hope.

"Of course," he said, almost excited that I was actually talking. "Just try to make it quick. It's a TracFone and I only have a few minutes left until my next paycheck."

I nodded as I dialed the only number I knew: Becca's home line. I instantly regretted using a cell phone and programming everyone I knew to their own special speed dial number because now I didn't know anyone's number.

And by anyone, I meant Dawson.

We rarely called each other, anyway. We were always together.

The phone rang and rang and rang and if I had been feeling any type of hope...it would have been long gone.

I left her a message, brief but to the point. I told her that I needed her to call me back, at my uncle's number, but more importantly, I needed her to tell Dawson that I was okay, and that I'd see him soon. My heart *almost* felt something, thinking about him.

As soon as I hung up, I glanced at the Playboy calendar hanging crookedly on my uncle's refrigerator. It was May. Becca and her family were more than likely on their summer vacation which they took every single May during the last week of school. They'd been doing that for years now, like clockwork.

I knew what I needed to do.

I knew what I needed to do in order to stop feeling like I was a hollow tree without any feelings at all.

I needed my best friend.

At least I didn't have to be strong around him. I could cry and weep and get all my feelings out in the open and then clear it all up before I came home to Mia.

She needed me and she needed me to be strong.

But right now, all I wanted was to be weak.

THE BUS RIDE to my not-so-hometown-anymore was awful. I was sweating because it didn't seem that the air vents worked at all in the back of the bus. We'd made a zillion and one stops, making this four-hour drive more like six and a half hours.

I didn't have my cell with me, since I no longer had one, and I couldn't afford one until I at least got my first paycheck from the parlor, so this time, I was on my own. If I focused my eyes hard enough, though, I could see the tiny digital clock up front where the driver sat.

There was no way I would make it back in time for my shift if I had to ride this bus back home, but I knew I wouldn't have to. Dawson could take me back. It was a four-hour drive. My shift started at six. We could make it if we didn't spend too much time at his house.

Finally, once the bus tires screeched and jolted us all forward, causing me to audibly groan, I shot up to my feet. My legs were wobbly from sitting for so long but for the first time in three weeks, I'd actually felt a tiny sliver of *something*. I wouldn't go so far as to say it was excitement, but maybe it was *hope*. Hope that seeing Dawson and being crushed in his arms would make me feel a little less empty.

It was probably a mile or two to Dawson's house from the bus station, but thankfully it was right in the middle of town so I knew all the shortcuts to get to where I needed to go. I definitely wanted to dodge anyone and everyone who surely hadn't forgotten my face in the last three weeks, because the only person I truly wanted to see...was Dawson.

I rounded the corner of the hardware store, glancing through the window for just a second, but something caught my eye, causing me to do a double-take. My stomach lurched and I felt a stabbing pain in my chest. It was so intense my hand shot up to rub my upper ribs underneath my skin.

There was a single piece of crisp, white paper with a black and white image of my parents on the front. I inched closer, my eyes locked on their happy faces, feeling myself gasp for air. There had been a memorial for them.

Last night.

In the park.

While my sister and I were four hours away, shut off from everyone and everything we'd ever known.

It had only been three weeks, but I felt like we were in a completely different world. Like the town of Oak Hill, Ohio no longer existed. Like the entire town was this tiny little blimp, floating away in the sky only to disappear and never return.

It hurt. It hurt me to know that this wasn't my town anymore. It hurt me to know that my parents no longer lived here.

My feet swayed underneath me but I reached my hand

out anyway, ripping the picture down off the glass. I folded it shakily and slid it in my jean pocket.

This was the only picture I had of my parents. Everything else had burned in the fire.

I shook my head out, trying to clear my thoughts and started to head towards Dawson.

If I could just get to Dawson, I'd be okay.

I'll be okay. With Dawson, I'll be okay.

I repeated the mantra in my head the entire way to his street. His house was only a few blocks from mine but I made sure to steer clear of where my house once sat.

Maybe someday I'd come back and be able to face it. I'd be able to face the fact that someone else would use that ground and build their dream home, just like my parents did, but not today. I couldn't do it today. I could barely *breathe* today.

My breaths were ragged as my feet propelled me down the sidewalk towards the two-story home that I'd spent my last night, in this town, at. I was so close to seeing Dawson that I thought I might combust. I got a glimpse of the old oak tree out front and it only made me move my feet faster.

I knew this was right. I just needed Dawson! I hope he's home.

As soon as I peeked around the tree, moving my feet a little closer to his side of the street, my heart stopped beating. Everything around me crumbled like buildings shattering during an 9.9 earthquake.

Dawson had stepped out of his house, his long brown hair flying away from his face. I almost yelled out to him with desperation but when I saw someone step out from behind him, I wanted to just disappear.

I recognized her right away.

Her blonde hair was piled high on her head in a cute

messy bun and her skirt was so short that I swore I could see her underwear. She squealed at something Dawson said and he nudged her with his shoulder.

The same shoulder he used to nudge me with, all the time.

My heart sank to my feet and my eyes instantly filled up as I watched them walk around the driveway so she could climb into her car. The stupid car she'd gotten from her stupid dad's car dealership. The stupid dad that *she* still had.

I quickly stepped backwards and half-hid behind an overgrown bush, feeling it scrape along my legs. My mouth opened and small puffs of air escaped me. I felt like I had just been hit by a bus, multiple times. Seeing him with another girl, *Breanna,* at that, three weeks after my life felt like it had ended, was the tip of the freaking iceberg and I was sinking way faster than the Titanic.

Part of me wanted to run over and scream at him and ask how he could betray our friendship like that, especially right after he'd kissed me and made me believe that he had stronger feelings than just friendship toward me. But the little bit of strength had me pulling rational thoughts of out the deepest parts of my brain and keeping me hunched behind the greenery.

It didn't matter if I ran over to him right now so he could give some sane, normal excuse as to why he was walking my worst enemy (whom I really didn't give two shits about any longer) out of his house, and to her car, which was parked RIGHT beside his Camaro. He could protest with some elaborate, amazing response that had me nodding my head in understanding; "Oh, Breanna was just here for," ... *yeah, I had nothing.*

But the reality of the situation would outweigh any

excuse he had. What the heck would Dawson do with me now? I was completely torn inside. *Broken.* And at the moment, I was feeling completely and irrevocably unfixable.

I thought he was the only person who would be able to put me back together but I was wrong.

I was going to have to do that on my own.

If there had been anything left of me still unbroken, Dawson had just finished the job. It was clear that he didn't need me as badly as I needed him and I wasn't about to pull him under, too. Seeing him with Breanna did do something for me though: it made me angry. So freaking angry that I felt my blood boiling underneath my skin. Like my veins were surging with fire.

And that was good.

Because anger was *something.* I could use it as my shield. I could use it as a lifeline, like I was using the burning edges of the rope to pull myself out of a certain Hell. I'd use the anger to pull myself out of this godawful mess.

I didn't need anyone to help me. I would put myself back together on my own.

Dawson and I had been right the night we'd kissed.

Things were definitely going to change.

PRESENT

NINE

Ivy

As I stood in front of my new (to me) home, I honestly felt at peace. It may have been slightly crappier than all the other homes that lined the street but at least it was mine, and at least it was in a town that I have been in love with since I was born.

I didn't think I'd ever be able to come back here. I hadn't stepped foot in this town for the last six years but then all of a sudden, when there was a job offer for me here, I didn't have a second thought about coming back.

It worked out perfectly. My old neighbor, Judy, who worked at the main bank in our town, had called and told me that there was an opening for an accountant. She knew that I would be perfect for it; I had graduated with honors from my community college and then gone on to complete my BA at an online school while I worked my way up in a bank up north. And not to mention all the practice I'd had with balancing money and figuring things out. I'd finally gotten my Uncle Timothy on his feet after a couple years of us struggling with his debt and gambling issues.

"Well, it looks..." I turned to glance at Mia who was standing with one eyebrow lifted and her mouth set in a grim line. "It looks... nice?"

I laughed. "Relax, I'm going to fix it up, as soon as possible. Just be happy that you can come here on your breaks instead of a tiny two-bedroom house up north with Uncle Timothy."

"His house wasn't *that* bad," she protested, looking back at my house again. "We're still going to visit him on holidays. Right?"

My heart softened. "Of course. He did take care of us..." I paused. "Well, I guess I should say that we all took care of each other during the last six years. He'll miss us more than he'll admit."

She chuckled. "Yeah, he'll miss the breaker always needing turned back on after we'd run our hair dryer and straightener at the same time."

I threw my head back and let out a loud laugh. Poor Uncle Timothy. He had gone from being a gambling, recovering alcoholic, living on his own as a gas station attendee, to raising two teenage girls who'd just lost their parents and were completely broken. He hadn't been the *best* guardian... but he definitely got an A for effort.

Mia and I both filled our arms with overstuffed cardboard boxes and heaved them through the entrance of my house. It smelled like dust and mildew, but I could work with that. *Nothing a little lavender scented Fabuloso couldn't cover up.*

Once we had all the boxes in the house (which took us a lot longer than I would like to admit, considering there weren't very many) we scattered them around my bare living room and both collapsed onto the ground.

"I wish you and Eric hadn't broken up. He could have carried all these in here while we stood mindlessly by the door, pointing in which direction they needed to go." Mia huffed, causing her golden-brown hair to fly up past her forehead.

I let out a sad sigh, thinking about Eric.

Eric was my boyfriend of two years. We'd met one day at a coffee shop while I was trying to work through my statistic homework. I ended up breaking my pencil in half from the sudden burst of anger I'd felt when I kept getting an equation wrong. The snapping of the wood wasn't all that loud but apparently, he'd heard it.

He turned around from the table in front of me and very slyly asked, "What did that pencil ever do to you?"

I was taken aback at how strikingly handsome he was. He wasn't the type of guy that I was used to...which would be *none*. Of course, my mind first wandered to Dawson. He was the last guy I'd even given a second thought to in a romantic way. Which was pathetic because all we'd ever shared was a kiss; he shouldn't even be in the boyfriend category, more just like a long-lost best friend.

Eric had jet black hair that was combed over just slightly to the right. His face was clean-shaven but even with his smooth face, I could tell he was older than me. He had sharp, dangerous features. His cheekbones were high and straight-edged, just like his jaw. The dark color of his eyebrows illuminated his baby-blues and I swore for a second, I could see the actual sky in them.

He was also *dripping* with money. His navy blue suit was pressed and starched so perfectly, as if he'd just pulled it off the dry-cleaning rack. He had on a checkered, red tie and when he smiled at me, my stomach flip-flopped. He was too attractive for his own good, and he knew it.

I didn't answer him when he'd asked about my pencil. Instead I only stared at him because my mouth had forgotten to form words.

"Ah, statistics," he clucked, looking down at my paper. "In other words, a big pain in the ass."

A small laugh escaped my mouth and it caused him to smile so widely, I could see all his dentist-approved white teeth glimmering behind peach-colored lips.

"That sounds about right," I answered, looking back from my laptop and then down to my notebook paper, scribbled with all sorts of equations.

"Do you want some help?" he asked, hope gleaming in his eyes.

I thought for a moment, trying to keep my expression even. Why would he want to help me? Surely, dressed like *that* he needed to get to some overly important business meeting.

"I'm okay, I think. You look like you're headed somewhere important." I glanced down at his attire and then back up to his chiseled face.

He bit back a smile. "I think there is nowhere more important than being right here, right now."

My heart jumped at his words. It'd been so long since I'd even given a guy a second look, let alone felt all swoony at a few words from his mouth. I couldn't hold back my smile, but what I did try to hold back were the thoughts of the last boy who had made my heart strum a little faster in my chest.

Dawson always crept into my head, even now, six years later, but I hadn't seen or heard from him since I'd ridden in that fateful bus for six hours only to find him standing on his front stoop with my one and only enemy. The only two people I'd kept in touch with since moving away was my neighbor, Judy, and that's because she helped me figure out some financial stuff over the years, and then Becca.

Becca was the only person who knew I had gone to see Dawson after I'd moved away. I'd thought she was going to blow a gasket when I told her about Dawson and Breanna. I was pretty certain that steam was going to come pouring through the phone from her ears. In the midst of her flipping out, which made me feel worse about the situation, I made her swear not to tell him where I was or that I'd ever come to see him. I didn't want him to know. I was angry. I was too angry for words and I hung onto that anger for as long as I could.

Becca kept her promise, even to this day.

Apparently, shortly after she'd gotten back from vacation that summer and after she'd called me back, he'd shown up at her house and asked if she'd heard from me. She slapped him in the face and told him to never, ever talk about me again. They got into a massive fight, one that they still haven't worked through.

She'd called the second he left her house and filled me in. It literally caused an ache inside my chest to know he was inquiring about me, and it swayed my inner turmoil slightly. But not enough to break down and have Becca give him my number. I just, couldn't do it. Too much hurt was still there, lying right below the anger, and although at one point in time Dawson had been one of the most important things in my life, it wasn't like that anymore.

Things had changed.

Too much had changed.

She's sealed her mouth shut, not giving up any bit of information on me (not that he still cared now) but he hasn't spoken to her since. It had been six long years, and he hadn't spoken to her *once*. Not even when they were both in the same bar (the only bar in Oak Hill), hanging with the *same* friends, or when they were sitting near one another at Wildcats football games.

He was still holding a grudge over it.

And I really couldn't figure out why that meant something to me, but it did.

A singsong voice grabbed my attention. "Earth to Ivyyyyy."

I blinked. "What?" I looked over at my sister who was eyeing me with such suspicion that I felt like I was in a room full of FBI agents.

"Where were you just then? I was asking if you wanted to unpack. I have to head back to school in a few days, so chop chop!"

"Oh yeah, let's get started. I'll order some pizza from Frankie's."

Mia stood up and came over to where I was. She bent down with her big, round eyes and droned, "I'm gonna bet my left arm... that you were thinking of a certain somebody with blue eyes." She grinned and then coughed the name Dawson under her breath.

"What? No I wasn't!" I acted like I was appalled, which only fed her more ammunition to use against me.

"Oh, whatever! You always look a certain way when you're thinking about him."

I turned away from her and shot to my feet, brushing off her accusation.

She didn't let my walking away stop her. "You're afraid to see him." Mia crossed her arms across her chest and quipped her eyebrow.

If she keeps prodding me, I'm going to eat all the pizza and give her none.

I rolled my eyes, snatching my phone to call in the pizza. "Pssh. No I'm not."

She smirked. "Whatever. You cannot lie to me. I know you better than anyone."

Yeah, so did he at one point.

I blew out a long breath, preparing myself to stay neutral. But even through my attempt to act nonchalant, my words came out all wobbly. "Fine. I'm terrified."

Mia's eyebrow lowered and her face softened. "It'll be fine, Ivy. You two were besties, and then you had to move away. He can't be upset with you over that. I mean, he has to understand that things were, like... crazy for us. It's hard to keep in touch when your entire life is spiraling out of control."

I breathed in and out, nodding my head up and down. I was nervous as shit. It had been a long, long time since I'd seen Dawson. It had been a long, long time since I'd even thought about seeing Dawson. I stopped with the "what ifs" awhile ago, too busy and smothered by life to really sit down and allow myself to wonder how things would pan out whenever we did eventually come face-to-face again. Would he hate me for moving away and never reaching out (minus the time I came to him and he was with Breanna) or would he act as if we were long-lost friends and envelope me into a huge, breath-stealing hug? *I wonder what the chances are of it being the latter...?*

Mia didn't know that I had come back here, to Oak Hill, to see Dawson after everything went down. It was the only thing that I had ever kept from her, which made me feel a little guilty, but it was something that I couldn't admit out loud for quite some time. It was hard enough telling Becca and having her freak out about it back then. I basically just wanted to hide under a rock, and never come out. It's a memory I'd been burying deeper and deeper, each time it tried to resurface.

Thankfully, Eric helped keep those thoughts of Dawson and our friendship – our short-lived kissing episode – buried. I probably wouldn't admit it to him, but I would consider Eric to be a sort of rebound, if that could even be a thing since Dawson was never actually my boyfriend. But Eric did help me. He kind of helped me feel alive again, and to be honest, he was a good boyfriend and I truly did care about him...until I learned his true colors. I was still trying to wrap my head around that issue.

I knew that I couldn't really be angry with Dawson just because I'd seen him with Breanna after my parents died. It didn't give me the right to hold a grudge against him, even if at the time, it destroyed me. It hurt me so deeply that I couldn't even grasp the idea of it.

And I hated declaring it, but every time I was brought back to that memory, it cut me all over again.

I sighed, finally coming up with a response to my sister. "Yeah. I just wish I knew a little more of what I was walking into."

"I know," she huffed, re-crossing her arms. "It's so annoying that he doesn't have a Facebook. Emmett does, but there's nothing really about his family on there." She tipped her head thoughtfully, staring at the ceiling. "Weird."

I knew that Dawson didn't have a Facebook and I also knew that Emmett didn't have any pictures of him on there. I looked, quite frequently.

Sounding hopeful, I said, "Well, maybe I won't run into him. Maybe he doesn't even live here anymore."

Ivy snickered, walking over to the kitchen to start unpacking the few boxes of plates and utensils that I'd obtained before moving here. "You know damn well he does. He took over his dad's business... or is about to... or something like that."

My stomach churned realizing that it was inevitable that I would run into him. His father's company was the only contractor in town, and I needed *a lot* of work done to my house. More than I could do, and I couldn't afford to hire someone outside of Oak Hill. I needed the work done and I needed to stay within budget.

I looked up at the popcorn ceiling, biting my lower lip.

Maybe Dawson won't be surprised to see me... maybe he'll wrap me up in his strong arms and welcome me back like I was still his best friend. Maybe he won't even recognize me and we can both pretend we weren't totally consumed by the other at one point and time.

That's what I'll keep telling myself.

TEN

Dawson

I fucking loathed my computerized schedule every time the stupid red circle appeared. The red circle meant I had a business meeting to attend, usually to discuss blueprints and costs with a client, which was fine, except it meant that I had to change out of my normal attire and layer on slacks and a dress shirt. I despised it. I was having to take these meetings more and more lately, due to my father's impending retirement. My days of working alongside the construction crew were numbered and my days attending business meetings increased by the week.

Like I said, I didn't mind meeting with clients; what I minded was having to dress up like I was some business schmuck who didn't know a fucking wrench from a hammer. Which I did. If I was being honest, I would work alongside the crew for the rest of my life rather than take over the "business" side of the company.

My mother insisted that I get a few good shirts and slacks to wear to these meetings. She had said the same thing to my father when they'd gotten married. If it were up to him and me, we'd both wear jeans and a construction t-shirt, maybe even paired with a dirty hard hat.

Voilà. Perfect.

I almost snickered at the thought of what my mother would say if I told her I was going to a meeting dressed in jeans and a t-shirt. She would probably fall over. Then I actually did snicker at the thought of what Breanna would say if I told her the same thing. She would gasp dramatically and cover her mouth with her dainty, manicured hand.

Appearances meant a lot to the both of them.

Looking back in the dirty mirror of the office bathroom, I adjusted my light blue collar so it was no longer suffocating me. I could hear my father talking to some woman out in the lobby but I wasn't paying much attention, not until his voice boomed with happiness.

"I almost didn't recognize you! Of course I remember who you are. How are you?"

I pulled back, still staring at myself in the mirror. I should have shaved this morning. My five o'clock shadow from yesterday made me look like I definitely should be wearing a hard hat instead of nice, pressed clothes.

Fuck it. No time to shave now.

My hand twisted on the cool doorknob and when I opened the door to walk through the lobby for my meeting, my ears instantly started burning.

I heard a low, feminine voice that caused my heart to thump. It sounded just like...

No. I've been through this shit before. It isn't her.

I knew it wasn't.

"Yes. Uh, I bought the house on Burbank," the woman's voice said. Although muffled, I could still understand her.

My father's voice was much louder than hers, so I could hear him clear as day. "Burbank?"

I walked a few more feet towards the lobby and as soon as I rounded the corner, I stopped dead in my tracks. *Holy. Fucking. Shit.*

Ivy's head snapped up to mine and those vivid green eyes, that I still very much remembered, shot right through my body. I'd felt like I'd just touched an electric fence. Even my legs were tingling.

"Hi, Dawson." *If thought her eyes shot right through me, what did her voice just do? Am I fucking dead?*

I said nothing in response, too shell-shocked to get myself to conjure up even a grunt.

After a few long, painful seconds had passed, I regained the ability to think again. At first, I felt like I'd just been given my life back. Like it had been stolen from me the moment she left, and she was so kindly handing it back over to me, saying, "Here ya go, Dawson, I'm back. Things can now resume to normal."

But, then... I felt angry. For so many fucking reasons I couldn't even pinpoint them.

Before I could say anything (which was probably a good thing), my father looked back at me, happiness covering his tanned face.

"Dawson, you remember Ivy Collins, right?"

My head bounced up and down but what I wanted to say to my father was, *"How the hell could I forget her? She was only my best friend for most of high school and she's the only girl who has ever broken my heart."*

"Yep," I answered.

The voice inside my head was on repeat; *What is she doing here, what is she doing here, what is she doing here? And my God, why is she so beautiful?*

I grunted, clearing my throat. I wouldn't look her in the face. There was no way that I could. If I looked her in the eye, I would wind up doing one of two things: crush my arms around her frame and never let her go, or, grab her by her shoulders and shake her, asking why she'd just up and left me and never looked back.

Both were extremely poor choices.

"I have a meeting," I said, casually walking toward the desk my father was sitting behind. Blueprints were spread across the top, along with pencils and pens, measurements on bright yellow sticky notes, and of course, his sunflower seeds.

"Dawson, Ivy bought Missy Holloway's house, over there on Burbank."

Jesus Christ. She's moving back? Why did that make my heart skip a beat?

Once again, I kept my mouth shut and I was hoping my father would get the fucking hint that I didn't want to discuss anything at the moment. He looked over at her, ignoring me while I searched around for the keys, and then rubbed the cleft in his chin, "So, that's close to your old house then..."

His words caused me to snap my head up in an instant. My pulse hammered in my wrist, blood rushing through my veins. *Did she know?*

She didn't meet my eye, thankfully. Instead, she brought her head down, her brown hair swaying in front of her shoulders. I hated that I could see the subtle way she flinched and I hated even more that it made my anger disappear.

Her voice was just as soft as ever. "Um. Yeah. It's a few streets over."

"So... you haven't been over to—"

"I gotta go," I said, stopping my dad from asking what I knew he was going to bring up. I snatched the keys from underneath his blueprints and walked past the two of them, keeping my gaze straight on the door.

My hand paused on the door handle when I heard my father tell her that I'd get back with her in a few days to talk about what she wanted done to her house.

There was no fucking way that was happening.

AS I PARKED the company truck in the parking lot, I felt myself getting pissed all over again. I was pissed for several reasons, the main one being the fact that Ivy had just showed up like nothing was wrong. Like she hadn't abandoned me six years ago.

What was she thinking? That I'd welcome her back with open arms and pretend like she hadn't fucking destroyed my heart so badly that I went an entire year without sex?

Me, Dawson Lanning, an entire year without sex.

Yeah, that's how you know I was literally fucked up.

Her voice sang in my head, "Hi, Dawson." *Like, oh, hey, long time no see there, ol' friend. How ya been?* There wasn't even a flicker of remorse or concern in her green eyes. She just seemed casual.

The gravel crunched beneath my leather shoes as I made my way up to the office door. The sun was setting behind the town's high buildings in the distance which meant I was late for dinner...meaning that when I got back to my place, Breanna was going to be annoyed.

She hated when I was late for dinner. Like she thought I was staying at work for shits and giggles. It was so petty and often had me reconsidering our newish relationship instead of the "just sex" that it had been.

"Hey."

The ghost of a familiar voice wafted around me and I clenched my eyes shut, not wanting to open them to find a pretty, amber-haired girl from deep within my past standing there.

But I opened them anyway and pretended not to notice the clench in my gut when I saw her. She looked so different from when we were younger...in the best way possible. She was captivating, almost glowing like an angel.

She had curves but her body was slim. Her features were more delicate than when she was a fifteen-year-old going through puberty. The pink blush on her cheeks stood out against her creamy skin and I knew that if I looked hard enough, I could see small freckles lining the bridge of her feminine nose.

Forest-green eyes stalked my every step, and I wanted to hold my breath so I couldn't get a whiff of her scent. She always used to smell so good...I could never pinpoint what the smell was and the memory of it had faded over the years, but now that she was standing within spitting distance of me, it was like I'd never even forgotten.

"Do you need something? I haven't had time to look at the plans for your house yet. I've been in meetings all day." My voice held a prickle of anger, but I was truly annoyed because I could already feel myself softening around her. I wanted to hold onto my anger for a long as possible because if I didn't, then I would start feeling all kinds of inappropriate things.

"I wanted to talk to you, privately."

Ivy stood awkwardly, her small arms crossed over her striped tank top. I could see the goosebumps along her skin and I wasn't sure if that was from the nip in the air or some other reason.

"Okay. Then talk."

I was painfully aware that I was being an ass and I couldn't remember a time in my life, ever, when I'd treated her poorly.

We never fought when we were best friends, ever.

I met her eyes again and they were glistening, just barely, but it was enough for me to look away. *Why did it still bother me that she was hurting?*

"I don't really know what to say. It's been a long time."

I scoffed, unable to stop myself. "And whose fault is that?"

She pulled back and winced, like I'd slapped her. I might as well have. I opened my mouth to apologize because she was right... it had been a long time. Why was I still holding a grudge? Why was I still pissed? Why was I still hurt?

I should be over this.

But I wasn't. I was the world's biggest pussy.

I held my tongue when I looked up at her again, because those eyes that were glistening just seconds ago? Yeah, they were basically simmering with fire. The green hues were sparking with anger and it set an undeniable thrill down my spine.

"I'm not sure why you're treating me so shitty. I mean," Ivy uncrossed her arms from her chest, where my eyes lingered for far too long, and then she placed them on her jean-clad waist. "I wasn't expecting you to be super happy to see me, but I didn't except you to act like such a fucking dick."

My mouth fell open for a second before I snapped it closed.

Did she just curse? Ivy, little Miss Follow-the-Rules, just said the F word.

I couldn't help it. I laughed.

I barked out a booming laugh, echoing through the almost empty parking lot, which only pissed her off even more. I could *feel* the boiling anger pouring off her body. Like if I were to reach out and touch her, I'd be charred.

"Is it funny when I'm mad? Because I don't think it's that funny, Dawson."

I laughed harder, running my hand through my hair. "It's funny to hear you curse, that's all."

She rolled her eyes so far back that I bet she could see her brain. "I'm not fifteen anymore, which means I'm no longer the girl you once knew. Saying 'fuck' isn't that big of deal."

That brought my laughter to an abrupt stop, reminding me that I was supposed to be angry and still holding a grudge.

"Yeah, I can see that." I almost growled, feeling all the hurt and despair that I felt so long ago creep up behind me like a stealthy cat. I instantly morphed it to anger. "I don't think I knew you very well back then, either."

Her mouth twitched and her eyes narrowed.

I hit a tender spot but that didn't stop me. I kept going, my voice becoming louder. "The girl I knew would never just leave like you did, without saying goodbye. Without somehow contacting me and letting me know you were okay. But I was obviously wrong."

Ivy bit the inside of her cheek, taking a step back. Her eyes welled up again and just like that, I was back to feeling bad. *My God, is this what it feels like to be a woman? One second mad, the next sad? Jesus Christ.*

She didn't say anything for a few long, painful seconds

and I was *this* close to taking everything back that I'd said but then she started to walk towards me, causing my entire body to go into panic mode.

We were only inches apart. My breathing was labored and heavy while my heart was thumping so loudly I could feel it pounding against my ribcage. I looked over her head, keeping my eyes trained on the glass doors to the office, when she whispered, "I *wasn't* okay, Dawson."

Then she sidestepped me and walked away, taking every bit of my anger with her.

ELEVEN

Ivy

I hated the way my eyes were puffy from crying last night. I hadn't cried in so long, but after seeing Dawson looking so... grown up, and then feeling the fury radiate off his body, because of *me*...I just couldn't keep it together.

I was happy to see him, elated even, and then he acted so cold towards me that it literally set a chill through my body. So, I waited. I waited for two hours outside his work to talk to him, to explain my side of the story, to clear the air.

I knew from the second I laid eyes on him that things would never be the same between us, no matter how badly I wanted them to be, but I definitely didn't want things to be so dicey, either. My God, he acted like I had ripped his heart out and fed it to the wolves. He clearly wasn't that upset that I'd left without any contact when I'd actually *had* come to talk to him. Why was he acting like he was so upset I left when he clearly was completely fine a few weeks later?

Like, it's been six years. Has he just grown cold and angry over time?

I wasn't lying to myself. It hurt my heart so badly that he stared at me with such distaste. If there were anyone I would want to make proud in this world today, other than Mia, it would be him.

He still meant something to me even after all these years. The bond we had wasn't just something that went away with time. No matter what happened between us, I still felt him in my very bones. Seeing him hurt and angry... made me feel sick, and empty. Seeing that small amount of pain on his face killed me. My heart had literally moved in my chest, like it was trying to dodge the hit.

I thought I'd done a good job burying all those unresolved feelings for him over the last six years, but the second I saw him, looking so attractively heartbroken, I realized that I had been so incredibly naïve thinking I could be around him without feelings from the past popping up.

I was so naïve. I was so trusting in myself to put on a brave face but I failed, miserably.

At least I had been able to keep it together until I got home.

That's when I let it all out. I cried so hard into my pillow that I woke up to my hair stuck to my face in a salty crust. It was lovely. So far, being back in my long-lost hometown kind of sucked.

Mr. Lanning, Dawson's father, told me that he'd have Dawson get back with me in a couple days to talk about what needed to be done to the house, and the price. But after our little spat last night, I wasn't sure that would be the case. He could barely make eye contact with me without acting as if he hated my very presence... so I needed to turn to plan B.

Which was to do the work myself.

I already had YouTube up on my phone this morning, teaching myself how to knock a wall out...which surprisingly looked really easy. *I could totally do it.*

I'd been surviving on my own for the last six years. I'd been working, going to school, taking care of my sister...and uncle, all while managing my money so well that I could afford my own house *while* helping pay for my sister's college.

If I could do all that, I could totally knock a wall out—no biggie.

I might even change my name to Joanna Gaines. I bet if we were friends, she would totally be cheering me on. Or probably even helping me.

I ran to my barely unpacked room, bypassing my mattress on the floor because I still lacked an actual bedframe, and yanked open my closet doors.

Smiling to myself, I grabbed a heather grey t-shirt and my thrift store, super-adorable, jean overalls. I braided my long, chestnut hair into a French braid and nodded to myself in the mirror.

Time to put on your big girl panties and get to work, Ivy the Builder!

I could do this. I could do anything I wanted. I'd proved that to myself over and over again. That was one thing I was sure of – I could definitely take care of myself.

Hopping down my cracked, concrete steps, I made a mental note to YouTube how to pour concrete next, or maybe I could splurge and pay a concrete company, because I was bound to break an ankle walking up and down steps that looked as if someone had taken a sledgehammer to them.

"Agh, shit!" I shouted while falling less than gracefully

onto my knees. My palms stung from the jagged concrete as I quickly hopped to my feet, staring down at the already bleeding slices in my hands.

"Yeah, I definitely need to fix those next," I mumbled as I looked down at my aching knees, thankful that my jean overalls had kept them somewhat protected. The jeans were worn a little from where I fell, widening the almost-tears, but at least that just made them look more *vintage*.

"Are you okay?"

My breath hitched as I flicked my head up to the one voice I did not expect to hear.

"What are you doing here?" I demanded, shoving my hands behind my back.

Dawson walked closer to me but I took a step back, eyeing him daringly. He looked much different today - not as put-together like yesterday. He had on worn blue jeans and a bright orange t-shirt with his company logo above the right breast pocket. His coffee-colored hair (which was so much darker from when he was a sixteen-year-old, sporting that surfer boy haircut) was tousled on top in a cute, messy way. It looked totally different from when I had seen it yesterday, all combed and slicked over.

Dawson's eyes narrowed slightly when he saw me step back, as if it surprised him that I would step back from him. He really shouldn't have been flabbergasted, though, as he was a complete dick to me yesterday.

"Let me see them," he commanded.

I muttered under my breath, "I'm fine."

"I see you haven't lost your stubborn streak."

My mouth twitched but I bit back my smile. "What are you doing here?"

He walked closer to me but this time, instead of stepping back, I stayed put. "I'll tell you as soon as you show me your hands."

A tiny sigh escaped my mouth but I eventually brought my hands around and flipped them up so he could survey the damage.

"Come on," he said, walking past me and around the broken part of the steps. I stood, just staring at him for a few seconds, but somehow my feet knew to follow him into my house.

His tall stature stood inside my living room, taking it all in before walking into the kitchen. I listened to the faucet creaking as he turned the knob and then the water flowing into the sink. As I walked into the kitchen I made sure to keep my distance from him. When he turned around and nodded for me to come a little closer, I took my time making my way over to him.

La-de-da, act normal, Ivy.

A shock of pleasure went through me when he wrapped his hand around my wrist and pulled it under the water. The contrast of his warm skin on mine and the cool water streaming over my hand literally made me dizzy. My heart started to beat erratically and I didn't know why. I felt energized but drained at the exact same time.

Suddenly, my feet swayed under my legs and Dawson's face twisted. He grabbed my arms to steady me and scanned my face. "Ivy, seriously. Are you okay?"

I swallowed my thick spit and tried to clear my head. *No. I think I'm having a fucking panic attack!*

I breathed, "Yeah, I'm fine."

He kept his sturdy hands on my arms and I stomped all over the thought of his arms wrapping around me.

I used to wish on every single star that I could have just one more hug from him. One more hug from my best friend...especially on those nights when I'd hear Mia whimpering in her sleep, or when I'd wake up from having a good dream about my old life, only to realize that it was gone. People were usually afraid of having nightmares, but not me. I'd stay awake as long as I could to keep away the good dreams, as they only made my real life seem that much worse when I did wake up.

But I had stopped wishing for hugs from Dawson a long, long time ago, right about the time that Eric had come into my life, yet here I was, desiring that very same hug that used to make me feel loved and safe, all over again.

And that probably had something to do with the fact that my boyfriend of the last year had dumped me the second I told him I was moving back to this "Podunk" town, as he called it.

Yeah, that's exactly why I feel like this. Because of my lack of Eric, not because of Dawson standing in front of me with those mesmerizing blue eyes.

"Are you sure? You look pale." Dawson's face contorted with concern and it was like getting a glimpse of the old him, the one I used to know; he seemed like he cared and it flooded my body with relief.

"I'm really fine. I swear. Just the combination of the fall and blood made me a little woozy. I'm okay."

He nodded, finally taking his hands off my arms. He reached over and turned the water off as I grabbed some paper towels off the counter. I started to dry my raw hands while trying desperately to calm myself down.

Dawson leaned against the counter opposite of me, looking relaxed with his arms crossed over his chest. His eyes followed my every move: the patting of my hands on the towel, the crumpling of the somewhat bloody material, and the walking over to the trash to throw it away.

I cleared my throat, bringing my attention back to him, my heart climbing in my chest. "Why are you here, Dawson? You made it pretty clear last night that you were... angry with me."

His face stayed even but his eyes spoke differently—he was definitely *still* angry.

"I just want to know why, Ivy."

I clenched my teeth, taking in a huge gulp of air. I could feel myself getting angry at the fact that *he* was angry. I was pretty sure my blood pressure was rising.

I blurted, "Why are you so mad, Dawson?"

His jaw worked back and forth before he pushed his body away from the counter. My eyes trailed his frame as he stomped back and forth in my kitchen.

"I'm angry because my best friend just up and left me six years ago. She was just gone and didn't even have the fucking heart to say goodbye. And now she's back, acting as if nothing even happened."

I sneered, rolling my eyes and slapping my injured hands on my waist. "You can't possibly justify being angry with me, can you?!"

His steely glare set forth a fire inside of me. Rage bubbling to the surface. "Yes, I can. I know it was six years ago but goddammit, Ivy. You had to have known that it would hurt me. You just fucking *disappeared*."

His voice trailed at the end and it was becoming raspier by the second. But it didn't matter, because I was still fuming. I was normally such an even-tempered person but right now, all I wanted to do was throw my toaster at his stupid face.

"You act like you know everything, Dawson." My voice was unsteady as its sound echoed throughout the kitchen. I walked towards him, pointing my finger in his face. "I know that you always used to beat me in *Jeopardy* and my God, I swear your head would grow ten times each time you did, but you don't know *everything,* so stop acting like you do!"

"Like what?" he shouted, bringing his hands out in front of him. "What changed that I don't know about? Did you go back in time just now and come see me to tell me that you were okay, or at least where the hell you where? The last fucking time I saw you was when you were crumbled in front of your burning house, crying your eyes out." He paused, breathing so hard his nostrils flared every few seconds. "And, I could still school you in *Jeopardy.*"

I would have laughed if he hadn't just implied that I had literally just skipped out on our friendship without even attempting to contact him.

I was pissed beyond belief. He had been holding a grudge for the last six years over the fact that I hadn't let him know that I was okay, and I had been holding a grudge for the last six years that when I *had* attempted to see him again, he was with stupid, slutty Breanna having a jolly ol' time.

What a freaking predicament we were in.

I backed away slowly, still keeping ahold of his eye. We were staring at one another so intently that World War Three could have been occurring around us and we wouldn't dare break eye contact.

"I don't have to go back in time, Dawson," I said, feeling my heart break a little in my chest as I replayed the memory in my head. "I did come back."

Then I spun on my heel and marched right through my front door, leaving him standing there to simmer in what I'd just said.

There! He can deal with that all by himself, jerk!

Unfortunately, before I could even make it down my

front steps, he'd grabbed my arm. My body spun around and he looked down at my face, still keeping his hand pressed tightly on my bicep.

"What did you say?" Dawson's voice was so low that I could barely hear him.

"I did come see you, Dawson. And you know what?"

His eyebrows furrowed, mouth softening into a frown.

"You were *fine*. You were fine without me, so don't you dare act like you're so angry with me for just "disappearing," because when I came back for you, you were with BREANNA, laughing, and nudging your stupid shoulder with hers."

Dawson let go of my arm as I hastily snatched it away. His lips parted as he stared down at me. He looked so confused and appalled, but I knew what I had seen all those years ago. I knew he was fine without me, and I knew that if I did go to him, in the state that I was in, he would just be stuck trying to put my broken pieces back together and he didn't deserve that.

"What? When did you see me with Breanna? That can't be right..." he pleaded, his eyes roaming around, like he was pushing through hazy memories.

I smiled sadly. "It doesn't matter, Dawson." He flicked his eyes up to mine. "I knew, after seeing you happy and laughing, that nothing good would come of me going back to see you."

The corded muscles along his neck flexed, as did his jaw, but he kept his mouth set in a grim line.

"Dawson, you were right that night."

His voice was strained. "What night?"

A blissfulness moved the muscles in my face, remembering the kiss we shared and the feeling of pure happiness I had, before everything *literally* went up into flames. "The last night we were together. We said that things would change..."

"I remember," he said softly, scrutinizing me, waiting for me to continue.

"Things did change. When I came back to see you, after everything, I wasn't the same girl I was that night in your room." My voice began to break at the end but I hurriedly covered it up with a small cough. "I was this hollow shell of a person, completely numb. I was so beyond broken that even *you* wouldn't know what to do with me."

He opened his mouth to say something, but I cut him off. "I'm sorry if it hurt you when I didn't say goodbye, but honestly, after seeing you happy and smiling with.... Breanna..." *God, even saying her name felt gross. Bleh.* "I knew I wasn't good for you. I came back so you could fix me. I went to you because you were my safe place. When everything came crashing down, the only thing I wanted was you." I looked away, feeling my cheeks flush. "And this had nothing to do with that one kiss... I don't know if you even really remember it."

Something resembling a laugh mixed with a sigh escaped his lips. "I remember."

Looking away, unable to keep my eyes trained on him, I finished what I started. "I just wanted my best friend, but everything was changing so quickly around me. I loved you so much, more than anything else in my life...and I loved you enough, despite the pain of seeing you move on with your life, to let you go. I needed to just... fix myself."

I hadn't realized it then, but I had done what I needed to do to in order to save the very last *good* part of my life. Over the last few years, and after some serious dissecting of why I hadn't just yelled at him from across the street, or why I didn't just run into his arms, even with Breanna there,

I realized that I was saving that little part of me that loved him.

He was the only part of my life that I didn't want to ruin. I just wanted him to be...him. Happy and carefree. I would have brought him down faster than my actual house when it burned to the ground.

"Ivy..." Dawson's tone was so full of hurt that I couldn't help but look up. I suddenly felt exhausted after putting everything out in the open like that.

I didn't expect to ever tell him those things. They were so imbedded in my heart that I was surprised I could even conjure them into words.

"You don't have to say anything, Dawson." I took a few steps back, leaning against my porch rail.

He looked like he wanted to say about a million things, but I didn't want him to. That's not why I'd told him. I actually didn't know why I told him. He always could coax secrets out of me.

Old habits die hard, I guess.

"I just wanted you to know that I would never not say goodbye for the fun of it. There was a reason why I did it. So..." I looked down at my Converse. "Just stop being so angry with me because I don't deserve it. Whether you think I do or not, I don't."

The sound of him gulping caused my gaze to leave my shoes. His eyes were clenched tightly and he was biting his bottom lip with his teeth. He used to do that when we were younger, too. Except now, instead of it looking adorable, it looked... *hot*. My face burned with the embarrassment of thinking something like that in such an awkward, intense moment.

Dawson didn't say anything to me. He pulled his head up and then looked me dead in the eye with such a powerful stare that I almost wanted to retreat backwards. His eyes traveled down to my mouth, then even further down to my legs, and then back up to my face. It was like he was really *seeing* me for the first time since I'd been back, without all the harsh anger clouding his vision.

A wave of heat gushed through my body and I instantaneously felt like I was sweating, even with the cool, fall breeze rustling leaves behind me.

I was about to say something, anything really, but he took his eyes off of me and walked down the porch steps. I watched him walk all the way to the end of the street and when he turned out of my sight, I lowered my head into my hands.

That was totally not the way I had that planned out in my head.

Not at all.

TWELVE

Dawson

After seeing Ivy again for the first time in six years, I was feeling all sorts of fucked up shit. I was happy, and pissed, and then upset that we'd fought and even more upset when I realized I'd hurt her. I was painfully aware of the hurt I'd caused by the way her face looked. She was good at hiding her feelings but not from me. Even after all this time, I could tell she was hurt, plain as day. I recognized it by the way her mouth pinched just slightly and the way her eyes crinkled.

And that led to me hurting, again, which just led to me being even more angry and confused. It was a vicious cycle.

When I got home that night, I expected Breanna to roll her eyes and scoff as soon as I entered the door. It was after eight, and she had come over at five to cook us dinner, which meant I was painfully late. Not that it would be a big surprise to her anyway, but now that we were trying this whole "boyfriend and girlfriend" thing, she would likely be pissed. But, I didn't even give her a chance to mumble a "whatever."

Instead, I pulled her up off the couch and slammed my lips onto her greedy ones. I buried myself so deep inside her, right there on my living room floor, that she couldn't even form a sound. I told myself I was trying to make it up to her, but deep down, I knew I was being dishonest.

What I was trying to do, was to forget the entire day. I pushed away every wicked thought as I wrapped my hands around her waist and plunged into her warmness, working her body until it blissfully fell into a puddle of mush. I thought it would clear my head. I thought it would just take away every ounce of anger and pain that I felt after seeing Ivy, but it didn't work.

I still thought of Ivy even with Breanna pinned beneath me.

It made me feel like shit. I felt so guilty afterward that I actually cuddled with her. We went back to the bedroom, landing softly on the bed, and I traced lazy circles over her bare skin as she fell asleep curled up onto my chest. God, I was so fucking guilt-ridden. I mean, I highly doubted that thinking of another girl while boning your girlfriend was cheating, but it sure felt like it. If Breanna had known I was thinking of Ivy, she would fucking gut me.

I'm not even kidding.

Breanna was so insanely jealous of Ivy. She always had been, even in high school. I can still remember very clearly how she had gone after Ivy's ex-boyfriend, Tyler, right after they'd broken up. Then, after Ivy had left and I was miserably pissed at the world, Breanna would constantly talk about how Ivy wasn't worthy of me and try to pick me up. Everything she ever said about Ivy had been conniving and it always led me to believe that she was simply jealous.

It was understandable for her to be jealous of Ivy. *Ivy was everything.* Beautiful, smart, funny, nice, caring. She was the only girl who ever truly broke me and the funny thing was, we never even dated. We kissed, once, but it was enough to hook me – as lame as that sounds.

I was truly messed up after she'd left.

She was my very best friend, the one person I loved more than I could even admit, and then she left and I was devastated.

Breanna was the first girl I'd hooked up with after Ivy. It was almost exactly a year after she'd left, and I was at the point of no return. I knew she wasn't coming back. I was trying to move on and Breanna all but threw herself at me any chance she got, so I finally took the bait. We spent a few years sleeping together randomly when she'd come home from college, and we had this friends-with-benefits, no-strings-attached type of relationship until a couple months ago. We officially started to "date," although nothing had really changed except for the fact that now we ate dinner together a few nights a week.

I sometimes thought I loved Breanna. I thought I had grown to love her because she helped me through a wicked heartbreak, but after just one tiny glimpse of Ivy at the office, I was thinking I may have been severely wrong.

Every feeling that Ivy had given me years ago festered and exploded right in front of my very eyes.

I was a shitty boyfriend.

And then the next day, after mindlessly fucking Breanna, all because I was flustered about Ivy, I grew even angrier about the situation. My fury intensified when I thought back to how I'd treated her just because of *Ivy*—the girl who'd left without any word, whatsoever.

Breanna might have been a little conniving and she

might have made Ivy's life a little rough in high school, but at least she never left me high and dry. She cared about me and that's more than I could say about Ivy.

I was becoming more irritated by the second, so right after lunch I stood up from my desk and stalked over to the crappiest house on Burbank. I was prepared to hash it out with her, demand a reason as to why she'd just... left.

Then she dropped a fucking bomb on me.

Now I couldn't even pretend that I was blistering with anger. I really hated that, because now all I felt was regret, and that's way, way worse.

I wondered while walking back to the office, after seeing Ivy looking so extremely adorable in her stupid overalls and pink-tinted cheeks, what life would have been like if she hadn't seen me with Breanna that day.

That's another thing that pissed me off. It wasn't like Breanna and I hooked up right after Ivy left. *I waited.* I waited for an entire year before finally letting some of my hope go. I couldn't remember the exact moment that Ivy would have seen Breanna leaving my house, but it definitely wasn't what she thought it was.

So what would have happened? Would we be together, today? Would our friendship have grown into something long-term? After kissing her that night, so long ago, I knew I wanted to have all of her. I didn't just want her friendship, I wanted her to be *mine* and I wanted everyone to fucking know it.

My mind kept drifting back to the way Ivy looked, standing on her porch, explaining her side of the story. Explaining why she'd left, and how she didn't want to burden me with her pain and sadness. Her posture told me that she was still hurting, and still festering over our lost friendship. I still meant something to her, and that did only one thing to me: it gave me the slightest bit of hope... and I had absolutely no business feeling something like that because I had a girlfriend.

Something I had to keep reminding myself over the last three days.

As each day passed, I kept wondering when I'd see her again. What I should have done was tell my father to handle the renovations of Ivy's house, because nothing good would come of me being so close to her again. I was already having very vivid thoughts about her and I'd only been around her *twice*. That's it. Only two times and she was already edging her way back into my head, as if she'd never left.

I had a plan, though. A shitty one and one that was probably going to bite me in the ass sooner or later, but I was raising a white flag—a truce. I would make it up to her. All the pain I had involuntarily caused her. All the pain that she'd involuntarily caused me.

I had the blueprints ready. I would show her what we could do to her shabby home (which by the way, I couldn't help but notice needed a shit-ton of work done to it) and then we could just go back to being... *friends*.

MY HEART WAS GALLOPING in my chest like an Arabian racehorse as I clutched the blueprints in my hand. I was standing just below her house, staring at the stupid, cracked, missing-pieces, concrete steps that she'd fallen down a few days ago, completely high with exhilaration.

I ground my teeth, reminding myself that I was here to fix her house and to be her friend. Nothing more. Would I love to go back to being best friends with Ivy? *Yes*. But I knew that wasn't possible.

Breanna would probably lose her shit, and although she

surprisingly hadn't been the jealous type regarding our sex-lationsip, I had a feeling that now that we were trying to make a relationship work, she'd show her true colors. Especially since it was Ivy and she and her family *loathed* the Collins, what was left of them, anyway. I didn't know the specifics as to why except for that Ivy once told me that Breanna hated her because their fathers were rivals in the car dealership industry.

Breanna wasn't even aware that Ivy was back in town yet. I didn't think many people knew other than my father and I. It seemed Ivy was secluding herself in her house, which made sense; it was probably a little difficult for her to be out and about in a town that she used to call home.

I was certain she hadn't been on her old street yet.

I definitely would have known.

As I walked up her front steps, I listened for a sound in her house, but the only thing I heard was the low rumble of a TV or radio.

I rapped my knuckles along the dull white, wooden door, which was in desperate need of a paint job, and paused. I clicked my tongue back and forth in my mouth, waiting, hoping she'd be just as down with being friends again as I was.

I mean, it wasn't like we were bouncing back from a long-term relationship full of sex and all that intimate stuff (let's pretend my dick didn't just stir thinking of Ivy and sex in the same sentence). We'd been really, really good friends back in the day. We shared one epic kiss, and that was it.

I was certain that we could *at least* be acquaintances again.

Finally, Ivy opened the door, but all I could see was a sliver of her shining face through the crack. Her emerald eyes widened, dark eyelashes fanning the skin below her eyebrows.

"Dawson," her voice was breathless, like she had been working out... or something else.

Hesitantly, I asked, "Is this a bad time?"

I turned my body slightly to peek inside her house but before I could, she placed her hand on my chest and shoved me backwards, following me outside and slamming the door behind her.

What the fuck? I'm aware that we had a little tiff and left things on a weird page but she wasn't allowing me inside now?

Then my blood started to boil.

...Does she have a man inside? That would make total sense. How could someone like her be single?

"Bad time? Should I come back?" I shut my eyes briefly, hoping she didn't notice the sharpness that fell off of every single word.

Ivy was quick to answer. "Oh no! It's fine, did you need something?" She crossed her arms over her white t-shirt and that's when I noticed the smudges on her face.

My mouth twitched as I reached my bare hand up to brush her cheek. Excitement hit my fingertips as I felt her soft skin and I unknowingly let my fingers linger for far too long.

"What's this?" I asked, finally pulling my hand back and looking down at the white dust on the pads of my fingers.

Ivy started to stutter so bad that I had to bite back a laugh.

"Oh! That? Ur... um, it's nothing!"

I quipped an eyebrow, watching her cheeks fill with a blazing red.

"Why are you nervous?" I pestered, voice full of laughter.

"I'm not!" she shouted.

I pulled back, a smile playing along my lips. "You are. I can tell you are."

Ivy placed her hands on her hips, sassy as ever.

"How can you tell?"

I snickered at her attitude. "Because even though it's been six years, I can still read you like a freaking book."

A conniving smile formed on her flushed face. "Oh, you learned how to read in the last six years? That's wonderful, Dawson."

As I scanned her face, I couldn't help but lose the hold I had on my laugh.

After my laughter subsided, I shook my head and I asked her again. "What's going on? Why did you push me out of your house?"

Her face dropped and then I remembered my earlier thought. *Fuck, what if there really is a guy in there?*

"Is there a guy in there or something?"

She gasped, bringing her hand up to her mouth. "No!"

"Then why can't I come inside?"

"Why are you here again?"

I pulled the blueprints up and waved them in front of her face. "I came bearing a white flag."

Her eyes slanted. "I see you learned to read but you forgot your colors. How sad."

I couldn't help it. I barked out another laugh.

"Someone has gotten quite sassy over the last six years."

Her soft giggle filled the air, and something inside me came alive.

"I thought maybe..." I pulled my lower lip in my mouth, feeling as nervous as I did the night I kissed her, which was completely pathetic that I still remembered how nervous I'd been, even this many years later. And Jesus, fuck, I was a man now; there was no need to be nervous around a female like I was still going through puberty.

"You thought what?" she asked, looking at me so sweetly that I felt my body visibly relax.

I let out a breath. "I just think we should start over. I don't want to be mad at you anymore..." I looked away for a second, then brought my attention back to her hopeful-looking doe eyes, "Actually, I *can't* really justify my being angry at you anymore. Not after what you told me. I don't know if we'll ever get to where we were before, as best friends, but I think we should probably try to let go of some of this anger and hurt feelings from six years ago. That's stupid."

Ivy nodded her head up and down and looked relieved. Did she really think I could still be upset with her after what she'd told me? It was just this giant misunderstanding. So giant that it had caused a lot of pain, but it really was a misunderstanding. I probably wouldn't have looked at it like that six years ago, but I liked to think I was a little more mature now. Even if I was acting like a dweeb with taped-up glasses talking to the most popular girl in school.

"That sounds nice."

Ivy's voice was a little wobbly, so I studied her face, and found my eyes getting lost in all the beautiful small curves, lingering on her lips for far longer than a second, and then landing back onto her big, green eyes.

"So, do you want to talk about these, then?"

"Um," she started, looking back to the front door and then back to me.

A nervous pit filled my stomach. "What is going on, Ivy?"

She timidly said, "Well…"

I'd had enough. She was hiding something inside and I wasn't waiting for her to beat around the bush. I took one more glance at her face before jostling around her and stalked to the door.

I sent a silent prayer up to God that she wasn't lying when she'd told me there wasn't a guy in there. It'd been awhile. The Ivy I once knew was long gone. Hell, for all I knew, she could be fostering a thousand puppies inside, or running a meth lab. I truly had no idea what I was dealing with.

I opened the door with her hot on my heels, preparing myself for the worst, and then my eyes took in the fucking warzone.

"What. Did. You. Do."

Ivy stuttered again. "Well, you see…"

I stepped in further and bit the knuckles on my hand. The scene in her house was fucking hysterical. It would have been even funnier if I weren't the one who was going to have to deal with the mess.

"Ivy," I stopped myself and her nonstop stuttering. I honestly had no words.

She took down a fucking wall.

No, let me rephrase that… she took down only *parts* of a wall. There were some random chunks of drywall hanging off the top part of the wall in between her living room and dining room, and broken wooden boards split down the middle. A sledgehammer was lying face up on middle of the floor, right beside her open laptop.

I walked in some more, careful not to trip over huge masses of the white drywall and glanced down to the screen, reading the title of the YouTube video.

"How to Take Down a Wall in Less Than 10 Minutes"

I couldn't control myself. I lost it. I threw my head back, laughing so hard my eyes watered.

"Stop laughing!" she hissed, which only intensified the hilarity. I bent down, placing my hands on my knees, and continued to laugh my ass off.

"Seriously, Dawson! It's not that funny. I can fix it."

My eyes almost fell out of my skull as I whipped my torso up. "Are you kidding!? I'm never letting you touch a tool, ever again. You are a hazard! Literally. Look at this place!"

Ivy bit the inside of her cheek, causing a little dimple to pop out. She looked out-of-this-world adorable with a pink hue dotting her cheeks and that pouty mouth, with white dust covering her forehead. Her lips instantly formed into a scowl as my laughter continued and she sent daggers at me with her eyes. I found it even cuter. She probably couldn't even scare a mouse.

"Are you finally done?" she asked, as I calmed myself down long enough to really take in the mess she'd made.

I sighed, "Yes, I'm back. Sorry, but this is fucking hilarious, Ivy."

I glanced at her, and she was finally grinning.

"Can I ask why you tried to take down a wall by yourself?"

She shrugged her shoulders, the grin on her face disappearing.

"Well... I didn't think you were going to work with me after our last conversation, and I can't afford to hire someone out of town, so I figured I would just do it myself."

"A little self-sufficient, are we?" I questioned.

Her eyes no longer held amusement and just like that, a flip switched inside of me.

"I've been on my own for six years, Dawson. I would say I'm very self-sufficient."

Abort mission, Dawson. Fucking change the subject so you don't allow her hurt to become yours.

"It's fine, I can fix it. And, since we're friends now... I'll even do it for free."

"No way! You do not have to do that, it's fine. Just add it onto the final price."

I brushed off her reluctance to let me help. "No."

She crossed her arms, ready to spew some type of argument but I stopped her. "Go order something from Frankie's. We have a lot to discuss and I'm certain we'll still be here when dinner rolls around." I waved the blueprints at her and turned on my heel, walking very carefully over all the debris, and into the kitchen.

I waited, listening to see if she'd followed my request and accepted what I was offering her, and when I heard her sing-song voice asking for a large pizza with extra pineapple on top (our favorite), I grinned.

She remembered.

THIRTEEN

Ivy

"Hello, my dearest sister," I said into the phone, slipping on my black pencil skirt.

Mia grumbled. "Why are you calling me so flippin' early?"

I laughed, shimmying the pencil skirt up and over my hips. "It's 8. Don't you have class soon?"

A loud, muffling sound hit my ear and I pulled the phone away from my face. Mia groaned and then I laughed again.

"I give myself exactly ten minutes to throw clothes on and rush to class in the morning. I should still be sleeping for another fifteen minutes. Don't you know anything about being a college student?"

Not really.

"Okay, fine. I'll let you go back to sleep, sleeping beauty."

I walked over to the mirror and ran my hand through my curled hair. Today was my first day at the bank, and I was more than ready. It wasn't what I wanted to do for the rest of my life, but it was a really good job until I could score enough private businesses as clients.

I loved being an accountant. I loved working with numbers, which most people find extremely odd, but numbers never change. They're a constant thing and I found that very comforting for some reason. But really, what I truly wanted to do, was be an accountant for small businesses. I didn't necessarily enjoy working for bigger financial groups but right now, it was a steady income, and I needed that.

"No, no! I'm up now. I want to talk."

I smiled. "Okay, so how was the first week of school?"

I heard Mia sigh. "Boring and tiring. How many pies have you gotten?"

"What? None."

"Liar."

A smirk crept onto my face. "Fine. Four."

"YES!" I laughed out loud at my sister's sudden burst of excitement. "I freaking knew I would win the bet."

My sister bet me that I would get at least three pies when people got word that I'd moved back to town. I told her I'd get one, maybe two if I was lucky, but she only rolled her eyes. In a small town like Oak Hill, it wouldn't be long before people learned the Collins girls had moved back home; I just wasn't sure what they would say. Did they care? My parents hadn't had a plethora of friends or anything, but my father had run one of the biggest car dealerships in town, so our name was known...as was our history.

"You were right, whatever," I mumbled, slipping on my heels.

"So, have you been down... you know." A frog lodged its

way into my throat as soon as the words left Mia's mouth. I knew *exactly* what she was getting at.

She was wondering if I'd gone past our old house (or lack thereof). I wanted to. I wanted to put on a brave face and walk over there and see my childhood street, but I just wasn't ready yet. I knew someone had bought the lot that my parents had also purchased, long before Mia and I were even born. It was where they had built their dream house, their house for life. Which was why I hadn't gone to look yet. I knew that as soon as I rounded the wide, green bushes on the corner, I would be flooded with a lot of awful memories and I just wasn't really ready for that.

It had been six years since our parents had died and although it still stung, I had grieved and moved on. I no longer thought about what could have been, but more like, what *was*. I only reflected back on the happier memories of my parents now and that was much healthier than avoiding any thought of them whatsoever.

But, still, I was well aware that when I saw where our house *used* to be, what my life *used* to be, it would rip off the band-aid.

"I'll go soon," I answered, beelining to the kitchen to grab some coffee before I headed into the bank. Thankfully Dawson had cleared up some of the wreckage from my failed DYI wall knock-down until the crew could come over and start working on all the things that needed fixed.

"I saw Dawson," I said into the phone, while inhaling the aroma of warm coffee.

"SCREEEECHHHHH." I pulled the phone away from my ear and yelped.

"Mia! I am now deaf. What the hell was that?"

She laughed. "That was me putting the brakes on. Why didn't you say something earlier? What happened? He was fine, right? I knew he wouldn't be upset with you after leaving."

I forced out a laugh. "Ha, yeah. He wasn't upset..."

"See! It's fine. I bet you two will be best friends again in no time. But before I get off here, is he hot?"

My breath hitched. "Um..." *Saying Dawson is hot would be the biggest understatement of the year.* Dawson Lanning was strikingly handsome, and rough around all the right edges.

"I freaking knew it; he's sexy, isn't he? Emmett is so hot with those tattoos splayed all over his chest. My God, have you seen his pictures on Facebook? I always wondered if Dawson had them, too. Does he?"

I started to stutter. "No, I don't think so... I didn't see any."

Heat filled my lower section at the mere thought of Dawson having hidden tattoos on his body somewhere. *I wonder what he's hiding underneath his clothes?*

I shook my head, blowing out the trapped air in my chest. "Look, I gotta go."

"Me too, have a good first day of work. I'm coming home this weekend, okay?"

"You are? Yay! I love living this close to you."

I could tell she was smiling as she said, "Me too! Oh, and I told Uncle Timothy we would video chat him!"

I laughed. "Okay, sounds good. Love you."

"Love you, too!" Then the phone went dead.

I knew, after hearing the joy in Mia's voice, that I'd made the right decision moving back here to this sleepy ol' town. Eric was wrong... I *could* be happy here. Even if it was without him.

. . .

WORKING AT THE MAIN BRANCH, right in the center of town, taking over Judy's job, was literally perfect. She was so excited to see me this morning that she took me along, her wrinkly hand clasped in mine, and introduced me to every single person who was now considered my new co-worker.

She was showing me off like I was her daughter who had just announced she was pregnant or something. She'd say, "This is her, the brilliant Ivy!" I laughed the first couple of times, feeling embarrassed, but then I just grew to adore that fact that everyone already knew who I was.

She must have been gushing about me for quite some time now, as everyone (including the big boss) was waving and smiling at me like we were all long-lost best friends.

Which only reminded me of Dawson.

He'd texted me while I was working at the bank and told me he was coming over after I got off work to take some measurements. My finger hovered over the "send" button after I'd typed up a text explaining that there was a spare key underneath the floormat that he could use, if he wanted to head over now, but I just couldn't bring myself to push my finger down on my screen.

I didn't hit send because the thought of seeing him after work made me as excited as a child going to the zoo for the first time. I was semi-embarrassed that I was already looking forward to seeing him since we could barely even be considered acquaintances at this point.

Sure, we shared a large pizza the other night and I felt like I was fifteen again, throwing pineapples at his head when he wasn't looking, causing us to crack up, but that didn't mean we were best friends again.

I couldn't consider us best friends again after sharing one pizza and falling into easy conversation. Aside from going over the blueprints of the house, we'd filled each other in on the last six years, skimming over what we had been up to: his business college experiences and what it was like living with my uncle and Mia. We didn't touch any of the awkward "Are you seeing anyone" kinds of questions or the "How are you since your parents died" segment but nonetheless, I couldn't deny that things felt right. I felt like... the old Ivy, for the first time in six years.

Not even Eric could get me to feel like my old self the way Dawson had the other night. I thought Eric had lessened the hard shell I had formed around myself since losing my parents, but I was wrong.

And what did I expect? Eric and I seemed so *real* and like the perfect couple on paper, but he never made me feel the way I *should* have felt. And I obviously didn't make him feel those things, either, considering he dumped me over one fight about moving back here.

Eric didn't fight for me, but I couldn't really blame him. I wasn't sure I would have fought for him, either.

As soon as I got out of my car, I rushed around the front bumper so fast that I actually scraped my calf. I ran up the porch steps, eager to get inside to at least wipe off the layer of grease my face had probably obtained from being stuck in an office all morning, but a voice caused me to shriek and fall backwards.

"Oh my God!" Becca laughed as she tried to pick me up off my wooden porch. "I'm so sorry!"

I quickly got back to my feet and threw my arms around Becca's neck. "What the hell are you doing home!?"

"Well, I'm glad you're still happy to see me after I just made you fall."

I pulled back. "It's not that hard to make me fall, Bec."

"True," she said, thoughtfully. "I came home a little

early to set up my classroom and wanted to surprise you! I still can't believe you moved back home. It's like... my childhood dream coming true."

"I can't either," I said as a matter-of-fact.

"How was work? Do you like it?"

Becca started to follow me inside as I answered her. "I do. Judy is staying an extra week just to train me before she retires fully, but—"

Becca gasped, interrupting me. "What the hell happened to your house, Ivy?! It did *not* look like this when you sent me pictures! Oh my God!"

I chuckled. "Well, you see..."

My door opened just slightly and I saw Dawson's head peek through. "Hey, Ivy? Can I come in?"

Becca's jaw fell to the floor and her eyes blazed into mine.

"What is he doing here?" she mouthed, her lips pulled into a straight line. I laughed out loud.

"Yeah, come on in," I yelled back to Dawson.

Becca looked as if she wanted to kill me. She spun around and crossed her arms over her chest, just waiting to give Dawson a dirty look.

I should have told her that Dawson and I had kind of made a truce. I briefly texted her about the fight we'd had but I didn't follow up with what happened afterward (aka Dawson and I eating pizza in my kitchen with me feeling light as a freaking feather all night).

"Oh. I didn't know you were going to be here," Dawson murmured as he made his way through my door. I stared at his scruffy jaw and messy hair for a moment too long. I found myself licking my lips and falling into a dream-like state.

He was really hot. Like, gives you instant butterflies hot.

There was no way around it. The Dawson that I used to visualize in my head on those rare, unstoppable moments, was a teenage boy with wild hair and a cheesy grin. But Dawson was no longer a teenager and I no longer had the hormones of a fifteen-year-old girl. I now had the hormones of a woman who was currently looking at her ex-best friend like he was dessert. A naked dessert. A naked dessert with a cherry on top.

My legs tingled as the thought slipped through the barriers of my brain. If I didn't get my mind out of the gutter regarding Dawson, our friendship would never work out.

And I so desperately wanted it to.

Becca snarled. "So he does know how to speak to me. Hmph."

I had forgotten all about Dawson's little no-talking-to-Becca rule until right now. I almost laughed, but I didn't because Becca was becoming awfully good at sending death glares my way.

"I'm learning to let go of grudges," he said, only eyeing her for half a second.

"Are ya now? Not mad at me anymore for keeping a secret *she* made me keep?" Becca pointed back to me and I dropped my head.

Can we just move past this whole thing already?

"Okay, you two. This is neutral ground," I said.

"Whatever," Becca groaned, rolling her hazel eyes in my direction. She glanced at Dawson, who was standing awkwardly by the door and gave him an eye-roll, too. Dawson and I made eye contact and a small smile traced his lips. I smiled, too, and then ruined everything when I raked my eyes down his torso and all but salivated at the mouth.

Bad Ivy!

Becca turned around to face me, uncrossing her arms.

"I'm going home. You're going out with me Friday and don't even try to argue with me."

I held my tongue and gave her a tight smile. She narrowed her eyes at me before walking right past Dawson, who had sidestepped out of her way. I knew that she would no-doubt be calling me in a few hours to scold me for not filling her in on whatever happened with Dawson and I. But that was something future Ivy could worry about.

When she was out the door, Dawson turned towards me, eyeing me with just as much suspicion as Becca had a few seconds ago.

"It all makes sense now," he whispered, walking further into my house.

"What does?"

I trailed after him, willing myself not to stare at the way his jeans hung so perfectly on his hips.

"Why she hated me after you left. I *knew* that she knew where you were, but she was so fucking angry at me. Did she tell you she slapped me?"

I choked out a laugh and then threw my hand over my mouth to silence it. Then I mumbled, through my fingers, "Yes. I'm sorry."

Suddenly he paused, his face actually twisting like he was in pain. He roughly ran a hand through his amber waves and locked his blue eyes onto mine. "I'm sorry I hurt you, Ivy."

My heart stuttered in my chest as I stood and stared into them. How could six words affect me so deeply? Like they had some magic healing power.

Maybe it wasn't exactly the words that affected me so much; maybe it was just the person speaking them. I faked a smile although I knew he could see right through it.

"It's fine. It was just a big mess. All under the rug now."

"Yeah..." he said, and then he quickly turned around and started to dig into the bag he had been carrying.

After he'd dug out some plates and I'd found what was inside the mystery bag (chili fries from our all-time favorite restaurant, Ronnie's), Dawson got to work on measuring some of the projects in my house. They were fixing the wall, starting tomorrow, to open up the living room and dining room, and then they'd work on the master bath and putting in new floors everywhere. It wasn't all of the work I wanted done, but in order to stay in my budget I needed to take baby steps.

"Hey, I've been meaning to ask..." I piped up from sitting Indian style on my hardwood floor, watching his jaw tick back and forth as he jotted different notes and dimensions.

"Yeah?"

"How are your parents? I know I saw your dad, but how is your mom?"

Dawson's eyes flew up to mine, a pencil tucked behind his ear and a tape measure in one hand. "I keep forgetting that you've been so shut off from this town that you know, like, nothing." His eyes swayed from mine a bit, showing he was conflicted about something. "My parents got divorced a few years back."

Oh shit. Way to go, Ivy. Should have just stayed with the easy topics like last week.

"Oh, gosh. I'm so sorry, Dawson. I didn't know."

He waved his hand. "It's fine. It actually worked out. They're better apart than they are together..."

I scrunched my eyebrows. "How so?"

I studied Dawson as he scribbled something down on his notepad and then as he tucked the pencil back behind his ear. The muscles in his forearm taunted me, as they moved swiftly with each motion he made. In my head I wiped the drool off my chin.

"Hey, come here for a sec. I need you to hold something while I measure."

I jumped up from my feet, eager to be closer to him... I mean, eager to *help*. Help. *He just needs some help, Ivy.*

"And to answer your question," he stated, "my mom and dad are just more present now. Like, when they were married, they were so focused on their jobs and beating one another at being successful that they forgot they had kids." His soft chuckle filled the room. "Once they got divorced, they seemed to have more of an interest in Emmet and I than fighting with one another."

I nodded my head understandingly. "That's great, Dawson. I can remember that they weren't home a whole lot when we were younger."

"Yeah. Here, hold this up there."

Dawson laid a yellow tape measure at one end of the wall that was still standing (even after I'd tried to take it down, adding that to my DYI fail list later) and then had me hold it up while he ran it across to the other side. I watched him the entire antagonizing time.

The way his tongue darted out to lick his lips while he was concentrating. The way his brow furrowed as he scribbled a number down on the paper. Then the way he sauntered over to me, stopping only inches away from my body. I turned my attention forward, looking past the single piece of wood that was still left, and stared into the darkened dining room.

I could feel the heat radiating off his body, bouncing right onto mine. I could also feel the racing of my heart from our close quarters. I tried not to smell him, but I did. I smelled that familiar scent of Axe deodorant and it made a tiny smile spread along my cheeks. It was so familiar, and it was so nice to not have to push away an unwelcome memory of him.

Still standing beside me, Dawson reached his hand up and touched my two fingers, holding up the tape measure. It was barely a nudge, but the feel of his fingers on mine set my entire hand on fire. I jolted my head to where he stood and met his intense stare.

His Adam's apple bobbed up and down and then he opened that beautiful mouth. "I just need to see the two numbers that your fingers are covering." Dawson's normal tone was long gone and in its place was something along the lines of raspy and husky, all wrapped up into one hypnotic sound.

That's what I was. Hypnotized. Like I couldn't even understand what he was telling me to do because his voice had my nerve endings standing straight up, razor sharp.

Dawson licked his lips and a source of eagerness crawled down over my shoulders, all the way to the heels of my feet.

My eyes fell to his lips, and my mouth opened in response. *Wow*. It'd been six years and just the mere sight of him licking his lips, standing *this* close, instantly had me reliving my best fifteen-year-old memory all over again.

Dawson jumped away from me when his phone started ringing loudly in his pocket. We both dropped our hands, causing the tape measure to smack me right in the forehead before it clattered to the floor.

"Ouch," I huffed while hunched forward. I brought my hand up to the painful spot, humiliation flooding my body.

"Shit, are you okay?" Dawson asked, bending down alongside me to look at my head.

"I'm fine," I grunted over the still ringing phone. "Your phone."

"What?" he asked, confused. Like he was in a daze.

"Your phone is ringing."

Surprise flickered on his face when I glanced down to his pants and then he hurriedly snatched it from his back pocket and pulled it in front of him.

Call it curiosity or just a coincidence that I'd looked down to see who it was, but I instantly wished I had a time machine to redo the last few seconds.

The throb on my head no longer bothered me.

What bothered me was the name "girlfriend" flashing right above a picture of someone I recognized immediately.

I quickly snapped my head forward as I saw Dawson hit "Ignore" on the screen.

I hurriedly bent down to pick up the tape measure while willing the simmering resentment that lay so quietly in my lower stomach to go the hell away, and asked if he was finished taking measurements.

He answered, "Yeah, I think I've got it," and then swiftly grabbed the tape measure out of my hand and headed to the door.

I stood back beside my half-wall, waiting for him to turn around and at least mumble a "goodbye" to me, but he didn't. Instead, he pulled the door open and walked out without saying another word.

That's when the realization hit me.

I shouldn't even be talking to Dawson if Breanna was involved. If she hated me back in high school, for absolutely no good reason, what would she do now if she knew I was having dirty thoughts about her boyfriend?

Kill me. That's what she would do. She'd sever my head and feed it to the freaking wolves.

FOURTEEN

Dawson

Ivy was taking up space in my mind that was no longer reserved for her. I used to think about work, Breanna, and my next beer at the Sailed Ships but now all I could think about was when I'd get to see Ivy again. Which was not how a *friend* should be thinking, and I was pretty sure it wasn't how someone who already had a girlfriend should be thinking.

Breanna called me when I was mere seconds away from dipping my head down and crushing my lips to Ivy's the other night, which was so out of line that I could barely form words afterward. The only thing I could focus on was the way that Ivy's mouth had parted and how she had sighed when I moved closer; as if she were tempting me... as if she really wanted me to kiss her.

Then the switch was flipped. The second my phone rang, the realization that I had almost just cheated on my girlfriend, with my childhood best friend, hit me like a 7-ton semitruck. I knew that Ivy had seen Breanna's picture flash on my screen; she'd inhaled a sharp breath and her voice was unstable afterward.

Apparently, there was a lot that she needed to get caught up on.

Me dating Breanna.

The house I currently lived in... I couldn't wait until she saw that. That would open up a whole new can of worms.

Breanna thought it was weird that I lived there. She said it was creepy, but she knew very well that I wasn't going to move. She wouldn't get her way with that.

She got her way tonight, though.

The second she got to my house after working at the dealership, the one her father owns (the same one that was always neck and neck with the one Ivy's father had owned) she plopped herself in her tight, little dress down on the couch and ran her fingernails over my bare arm.

"Let's go out tonight, babes."

I groaned, running my hand through my hair. "I'm kind of busy, Breanna. I have a lot of work to do."

She pouted so hard that I could *hear* it. Breanna was the *queen* at pouting to get her way. She was like a three-year-old trapped in a very attractive woman's body.

"You're always busy. You've been slaving away lately on whatever it is you're working on. What's keeping you up at night? The last few nights I stayed here, you've crept out of bed to work...we're boyfriend and girlfriend now, remember? We're supposed to go out together every once in a while."

I wasn't aware that she noticed me casually rolling out of bed and going into my office, which then led to me working for hours and crashing on the couch.

"Just this one house that needs a lot of work."

This one house = Ivy's.

"Well, take a break and let's go to Ships. There's a band tonight and I'm pretty sure Max is going and, like, more than half our friends. Pleaseeeee."

The whiny part of her voice made me cringe and honestly had me contemplating why I was even with her in the first place. Oh, that's right. Because *she* was the one who was there for me when Ivy left.

I sighed, slipping my reading glasses off. "Okay, sure. Go get ready."

A smile spread along her face, showing off her bleached teeth and pink lipstick.

"Maybe we can slip off into the bathroom while we're there, like old times..." Breanna winked at me and the suggestion had my balls tingling but only for about three seconds because another pretty face crept into my mind, which only made me feel like the worst boyfriend in the entire fucking universe.

What the fuck was I doing?

WHEN I WALKED into the Sailed Ships, I was relieved to have a beer placed in my hand almost instantly by Max. I knew he'd gotten word that Ivy was back in town and I was literally counting the seconds on the clock, waiting for Breanna to find out. I wasn't sure how she didn't know yet, but I knew for a fact that she didn't because she'd be all over it like there was a sale going on at the local beauty store.

The second Breanna interlocked her arms with one of her stuck-up friends, whom Max had been trying to shag for months, he pulled me aside.

His jaw slacked when a shit-eating grin molded to his face. "You're in over your fucking head, aren't you?"

I tipped back the longneck, allowing the ice-cold beer to

coat my throat, temporarily stunning any words that wanted to spew out of my mouth.

"I have no idea what you're talking about," I muttered, moving my eyes around the bar. Ships was moderately empty but I knew that within an hour or two, people would be hopping on the dance floor with copious amounts of alcohol swishing through their systems.

Sailed Ships was the only bar in our town and since we were considered a small town, there literally wasn't anything better to do than to come here. Friday and Saturday nights were for drinking at Sailed Ships – at least that's what it said on the wall above the bar.

"I know you've seen her, I can tell. You just have this glow..." Max cackled as the words left his mouth.

I rose an eyebrow. "What the fuck are you talking about, Max?"

He smiled before tipping back his beer. I did the same, needing more alcohol in my system to deal with the thoughts swimming through my head of how I was the world's worst boyfriend and how I couldn't stop wondering if Ivy was going to show up.

"She has you by the balls already and she just got to town."

"Dude, no. We're friends. If you can even call it that. I'm working on her house and that's it. We cleared the air a little, and now we're just on neutral ground."

He barked out a laugh, throwing his head back. Breanna caught my eye from across the bar, and she winked.

My stomach twisted. If I wanted Max to believe me, and even more importantly, *Breanna*, whenever she did catch wind that Ivy was back, I needed to make *myself* believe it.

I pushed past Max and his howling laughter, striding

past a few already tipsy people who were dancing to an upbeat song in the middle of the poorly lit dance floor, and snuck up behind Breanna, where she waited for her low carb beer. I spun her around fast and she let out a piercing yelp.

My hands roamed over her curves as my mouth captured hers with a low growl. It took her no time to wrap her arms around my neck and push her full breasts up against my chest. Breanna nipped my lip before I let go, and her eyes twinkled with the sexy, mischievous, little glint that she'd always worn whenever I'd given her my upmost attention.

"Shall we head to the bathroom now... or later?" I asked, bending my head down to nip the skin just below her ear.

Breanna laughed softly but then her entire body went dead-stiff in my arms. I pulled back slightly and the second I saw her face, I knew.

I glanced to my left and then to my right. Almost every single person had stopped talking, stopped drinking, stopped paying attention to whatever was around them, and their stares were all directed to the same place.

I didn't even have to turn around to know that Ivy had walked in.

The parted mouths on every single man's face and the questionable expressions on all the females told me exactly who they were looking at.

Breanna's tone was like fingernails on a chalkboard. "What the fuck is she doing back here?"

A surge of protectiveness flashed through me, causing my hands to leave Breanna's hips. I turned around slightly, ignoring the way her eyes flashed with hate, just enough so I could get a glimpse of Ivy. That was a wrong decision on my end.

Ivy flipped her glossy brown hair behind her shoulder and laughed softly at something Becca had said. Her pretty green eyes swept the room, first landing on Max who was waving like a fucking maniac, then to the people on the dance floor, until they finally landed on me. Her smile fell instantly and the disappointment in her emerald hues was plain as day.

It was as if she was asking me what the hell I was doing with Breanna... and I was beginning to wonder the same exact thing.

FIFTEEN

Ivy

I had been waiting the entire, antagonizing week to lay into Becca. After she grinded *me* about not filling her in immediately about the whole Dawson and I making up, she turned around and didn't tell me that he and Breanna were a *thing*!

I wasn't certain exactly how intense of a relationship they were in but I could only assume it was on the higher end of that spectrum considering he'd run out of my house like a bat straight out of hell after we stood, alone, faces only a few inches apart. I've been wondering and simmering all week; were they serious? How long had they been together? Did he *love* her?

After trying on the third outfit Becca had thrown at me, and explaining whatever it was that had occurred between Dawson and me, I started to prod her.

"Are they serious?"

Becca's head slowly inched upward and I knew right then that I wasn't going to like her answer.

"Why didn't you tell me?!" I exclaimed, pulling off the stupid sheer tank top she'd tried to get me to wear. It was too cold for a tank top. We were in Ohio and it was September: too chilly for no sleeves.

"Are you serious?" she asked, throwing off the tank that I'd chucked at her.

I stomped over to my closet, even more pissed than I was before because now it was confirmed that he was dating Breanna and it was also confirmed that it bothered me beyond explanation.

"Yes! How could you not tell me! Why is he with her?! God!" My words were coming in spurts and I literally had to reel myself back in before I got so worked up that I started to cry.

I was a crier when I became angry, which was infuriating because then people never truly knew that you were angry. They just thought you were sad when you were actually *boiling* inside.

"I didn't tell you, because we agreed to never talk about Dawson again."

I spun around towards Becca, my eyes skimming over her strawberry blonde hair and cheetah-print silk top. "When did we decide that?"

She rolled her eyes, standing up and coming over to help me pick out yet another outfit.

"It was an unspoken agreement. You never asked about him and I didn't want to bring him up because I didn't want you to go back into your shell."

Shell? Like I'm a freaking turtle?

"I knew it would bother you and I knew it would make you upset. Even if you didn't have these secret, lustful feelings for him." I gasped, appalled that she thought I was lusting after him. "You and Dawson were super freaking close. Closer than us, closer than me and Casey. You and Dawson were like Siamese twins, except you two were a very rare form because you were, like, in love with each other."

I laughed out loud but I didn't deny it.

Becca quipped a well-manicured eyebrow at me and handed me my next outfit without saying another word.

I slipped on a sheer white blouse that I had originally bought for work, but without pairing it with its blazer, it looked casual enough for Ships. Becca threw a pair of dressy, closed-toe shoes at my head, which bounced off and hit the floor. I snatched them up and placed them on my feet, tying the black leather strap around my ankle with as much force as possible.

I was bitchy and pissed, all because Dawson was dating Breanna.

Or was I acting that way because he wasn't single in general? Maybe it had nothing to do with Breanna.

"Are you ready to be welcomed back into our sleepy ol' town once again?" Becca asked, not even laying a pinky toe on our previous conversation.

I grinned, thinking back to when Eric called my favorite place in the entire world a Podunk, stupid, sleepy-town. I almost wanted to take a picture of myself in my super-hot outfit at the bar, having fun with my old friends, and send it to him.

I wanted to pair it with a middle finger emoji and tell him he was missing out.

"DAWSON'S HERE," Becca whispered, grabbing my hand and placing it in hers.

"How do you know?" My heart jumped for two completely different reasons; I was overly excited to see him but also totally nervous that Breanna would be with him.

"That's his truck," Becca threw her head in the direction of a navy blue GMC Sierra truck that looked brand new. It had the famous Lanning Construction logo plastered on the side.

My stomach twisted and lurched like I was going to puke up the Ramen noodles I'd scarfed down after work (don't judge, I may be twenty-five and have a well-established bank account, but I still lived like the college-student I never truly got to be).

Becca pulled open the door to Ships and I was immediately greeted with neon signs glowing on every single wall. My eyes swept over the bright lights overhead and then made their way around the establishment, looking for only one person in particular.

Becca giggled. "I feel like I should lay out a red carpet for you."

I laughed at her, hoping it would make it seem like I was totally at ease.

At first, I spotted Max from across the room, standing near a pool table. I couldn't help the cheesy smile that molded to my face. He waved so frantically at me that I actually started to laugh. I gave him a small wave and then moved my attention apprehensively to the bar.

Dawson's sculpted face was hidden underneath bleach-blonde hair but I knew it was him. My body reacted before my brain even registered it; a tingle of excitement came over me only to be quickly shut down when Breanna's head popped up.

I felt like I'd been cut.

Am I bleeding?!

The jealously that sparked from deep within caused me to grind my teeth.

My God, I was acting like Dawson was my ex-lover and I had just seen him fucking some other girl. Jealousy reared its ugly head and I wanted to duck out of Sailed Ships immediately.

But then he turned and flicked his eyes up to mine. I only held his stare for a few seconds if that, but I swore he was telling me something with his eyes.

I wasn't sure what, but he was definitely trying to convey *something* to me at that moment.

Breanna pulled his attention back, causing my gaze to lock onto her platinum-colored hair and slutty, pink dress. Then when I found her narrowed eyes, she was glaring at me with such distaste that I was almost convinced I'd done something terrible to her.

Had I run over her cat?

Had I wrecked into her car?

Had I murdered her best friend?

The world may never know because I was about three seconds away from being murdered by a pair of mascara-laden blue eyes.

Maturity would probably have been a better tactic for me to take, as I was literally looking into the future and seeing my own death at the hands of a manicured Barbie, but the jealous fifteen-year-old girl inside of me emerged and I narrowed my gaze right back at her and smiled widely. I also waved, my fingers twinkling towards her opened mouth.

I could have sworn I saw Dawson's lip twitch, but his

face was quickly out of my sight as Max appeared in front of me, holding his arms out for a giant hug.

"I can't believe you're back, Ivy!" Max pulled me up and swung me around the bar.

"I'm glad you're happy to see me," I giggled as he put me back onto the sticky bar floor.

Max grinned. "Come on, you two. Come sit with me back here. It's quieter and... less catty."

I snickered as Becca and I followed him to his booth. I looked over at her, making sure she was following and suddenly she looked nervous and a little bit frazzled. Her cheeks were a little darker than normal, too, but maybe it was just the weird way the bar lights made everyone look like Avatars.

As soon as we were tucked back in the booth, Max threw his head back and erupted with the most ridiculously loud laughter. Becca and I shared tiny smiles but it clear with our deer-in-the-headlights looks that we had no idea what was actually going on.

"I can't believe you fucking..." Max laughed again. "I can't believe you fucking waved at her."

I bit my tongue to stop myself from also cracking up.

"I know, I... I don't know what came over me."

Actually, yes, I do. The Charlie's Angel inside of me wanted to fucking karate chop Breanna away from Dawson. I was channeling my inner Lucy Liu.

"I don't know, but I loved it. The old Ivy never would have done that. She would have retreated back into her little mouse hole."

My shoulders slumped. So far tonight I'd been called a turtle and now a mouse.

"I've done a lot of growing up over the last six years," I stated.

"Yes... you have."

"Gah, keep it in your pants, Mr. Adams."

My head shot over to Becca, whose cheeks were no longer flushed. She looked steely and cold, angling her body toward Max.

"Mr. Adams?" I questioned, looking back and forth between the pair of them.

They were staring at each other with an intense hold, so intense that I bet if I waved my arm in front of their faces, it wouldn't even phase them.

A few more seconds passed, along with some thumps of a microphone toward the front somewhere, then they finally broke their stare.

"Yeah, that's my last name."

I rolled my eyes at Max. "I know, dummy. But why so formal?"

"We work together," Becca mumbled under her breath, seeming completely unhappy about the predicament. "He's the P.E. teacher at the high school."

"Oh, nice!" I cooed, but Becca huffed from beside me.

"So, what'll you be having, dears?" Max asked, sliding out from the booth. "Drinks are on me for the two prettiest ladies in here tonight. We've gotta welcome Miss Ivy back like she'd never left."

I giggled because Becca had said the same thing.

As we relayed to Max what we wanted from the bar, a small town band started to play some of their cover songs, blaring acoustic music through the speakers. My attention was momentarily glued to the stage tucked away in the corner, but soon I turned my head around, looking Dawson and Psycho (I mean Breanna).

I saw Max, grabbing our drinks while also flirting with a girl displaying a lovely tramp stamp from beneath her hot pink tube top. I snickered and Becca groaned in disgust.

I asked, "What's going on between you two? You seem tense."

My eyes roamed the bar, looking for a tall, dark, and handsome guy and his bleached blonde minion but... Dawson and Breanna were no longer in sight.

I searched frantically around the bar, but once again, I came up empty-handed.

Great, I've run them out of the bar just by my mere presence.

I would have been happy about that if it had just been Breanna who had left but of course, Dawson being the great boyfriend that I'm sure he was, probably went with her.

"Nothing," Becca answered, her voice a mixture of contempt and outright anger.

I crinkled my eyebrows, preparing to coax a better response out of her, but I heard a familiar voice boom up ahead.

I gasped with surprise when my gaze landed on another familiar face: Emmett.

Emmett and Dawson didn't really look alike, although they both had dark hair and jaws made of steel. They both resembled male models, like the type you see in cologne ads, but they were also extremely different. Dawson would be featured in a more sophisticated cologne ad, like Calvin Klein, but Emmett would be seen in something similar to Gucci with his mysterious vibe and sexy, unshaven face.

"Wow, Emmett looks..." I started, looking at Becca and then back to Emmett.

He finally caught my stare and his eyes widened at the same time his mouth did. He formed a cunning smile and started to make his way over to me.

"Yeah, he's fucking hot in that dangerous, might-fuck-you-in-a-dressing-room kind of way."

I laughed, watching him stumble over to our booth.

"Is he drunk?" I whispered.

"Looks like it..."

I could smell the tequila on his breath as he reached for me, pulling me to my feet and draping an arm over my shoulder. He squeezed slightly and slurred, "Wow, I can't believe my brother's girl is home."

My breath caught but before I could say anything, he lightly shoved me back into the booth and then climbed in beside me, causing me to squish Becca against the wall. She was hiding a smile behind her hand and I gave her a "help me" look, but she only chuckled.

"I think Breanna would disagree that I was your brother's girl, Emmett." I tried desperately to change the direction of the conversation. "How are you? It's been a really long time since I've seen you in person."

He leaned back, placing his arm around the top of the booth behind my head. "Me? I'm just fucking dandy."

I couldn't tell if he was being sarcastic or not. I didn't know Emmett very well when I was younger. He'd been absent for most of my friendship with Dawson, since he'd been sent to a military school for his bad-boy behavior. And now, he was more like a complete stranger to me. He didn't seem to think I was a stranger, though. He brought his arm back down, resting it slightly on my shoulders again.

"Better not let Dawson see you with your arm around her like that, Emmett," Max warned as he came back to the table and handed Becca and I our drinks – a beer for Becca and a whisky sour for me.

"What, think he'll get his panties in a wad? Good."

Max looked uneasy as he observed Emmett slurring his

words and swaying back and forth in his seat. His dark eyes were red and glossy, and he could barely keep them open.

He was drunk as a skunk.

Apparently bad-boy Emmett hadn't changed all that much.

Before I could even sip on my drink, Emmett snatched it out of my hand threw his head back, gulping the entire thing in one single swallow.

My mouth dropped as he slammed it back down on the table.

"Thanks, babe," he said and I literally laughed out loud.

"Thank him." I ushered to Max who was all but glaring at Emmett. "He bought it."

A huge smile covered Emmett's face and then he rested his heavy head on my bare shoulder.

The entire situation was weird. I kind of felt like I was in the middle of some wicked acid trip. Emmett was acting like he and I were the best of friends, and the full weight of his head was so heavy on my shoulder that it was starting to ache.

"You're all grown up, Ivy," he slurred, his alcohol-laden breath almost stunning me into a daze.

I breathed out a small sigh, suddenly feeling a little sad for him. He was truly drunk off his ass and I was pretty sure people didn't get this shit-faced this early in the night just for the fun of it.

Okay, maybe they did, but I had a serious hunch that Emmett was troubled and that was why he was so inebriated.

I leaned my head over on top of his and patted his arm a few times to make sure he wasn't about to pass out on me, and then I heard the bar door slam shut. I peeped my eyes upward and I was met with the coldest stare that I'd ever seen.

Dawson's narrowed gaze was trained on his brother's head, resting on my shoulder, and even from a distance I could see the rage swimming in his icy blue hues. It seemed that Dawson did *not* like seeing his brother with me...and that sent a shock of excitement down my limbs.

SIXTEEN

Dawson

I saw red. Pure red.

I'd never wanted to fucking hurl my brother across a room before but I was mere seconds away from adding it to my bucket list and crossing it off all in the same night.

He was touching Ivy. *My Ivy*.

I paused on my way over to the table. *My Ivy? Jesus Christ*.

Breanna had one of her friends take her home after screaming at me in the parking lot (classy). She was livid. No, she was beyond livid. She wasn't even screaming proper insanities at me. Something about me knowing that Ivy was back and how I didn't deny it.

She wanted to know why I hadn't told her, and I couldn't give her a truthful answer. Deep down I knew why I didn't tell her, because she would forbid me to talk to her and I wasn't going to do that – which was sure to put a wedge in my new-ish relationship with her.

I told her that I'd talk with her after she calmed down a

bit and she rolled her eyes and stomped off with her friend, saying she'd talk to me when she felt like it.

Okay, then. I'm sure she wanted me to chase after her but after knowing Breanna for years, I knew that it was better to talk with her when she had a level head. She was slightly less crazy that way.

I probably should have gone after her; that's what a normal boyfriend would do, but as soon as I saw my drunken brother resting his dumb head on Ivy's delicate shoulder, all thoughts of being a decent boyfriend flew out the fucking window.

My eyes fell over the long curve of her neck, all the way to the slope of her collarbone and then to his stupid, fucking head laying there.

I was only a few feet away, keeping my eyes trained on him, when I noticed that his eyes were closed.

I stopped, squinting my eyes. *Is he passed out?*

I flipped my attention over to Ivy and her face was a mix between remorse and concern and then I instantly realized that he was probably drunker than drunk, and *was actually* passed out on her shoulder. Ivy's eyes softened, as if she was portraying how sorry she was that he was drunk and it was like my heart was torn inside my chest.

Ivy had nothing to be sorry about. But I knew exactly who should be.

His fucking girlfriend, or maybe ex-girlfriend, Carrie. They'd broken up and gotten back together so many times over the last few months that I couldn't keep up. When they were broken up, it was so embarrassingly obvious to everyone because Emmett would drown himself in liquor and then sober up for work, only to be face-to-face with her again because she worked at the tattoo shop, too.

Why didn't he fire her? I had no idea. He owned the business, he made the rules, yet he just couldn't do it.

"Emmett," I hissed, but he didn't move an inch. I walked over and a hush fell over the table. I could see the penetrating stare from Max and I was absolutely sure that Becca was scowling at me because, well, she hates me.

I brought my clenched fist up, opening it, and nudged his head with my hand. I wanted to smack the hell out of him, but since he was leaning on Ivy, I tried to be gentle.

Fucking shit.

Emmett moaned but that was it. He didn't move an inch which meant I was going to have to carry him out of here.

I didn't have time for this shit. I had a girlfriend who was fucking pissed at me, and then I had Ivy who looked at me like I'd run over her puppy moments ago when she saw me with Breanna, and unfortunately, that was my biggest concern.

I looked back at Max. "Help me carry him to my truck."

Max slid out of the booth, his weight causing the leather booth to squeak. I reached towards my brother and pulled his arm to slide him out. His head wobbled off of Ivy's shoulder and hit the back of the booth with a loud thud.

As soon as I had one of his heavy arms draped over my shoulders, Max did the same for the other. I paused and looked up at Ivy, who was biting her fingernail, staring at the three of us.

"Ivy..." I started, feeling totally unsure of myself, which seemed to be a common thing when I was around her. "I know you're pissed at me, but can you go see if he has an open tab and come out and let me know so I can pay it?"

Her face faltered for a second, small creases forming around her eyes, but then she gave me a curt nod.

I swallowed, feeling my pulse hammering underneath

my skin and then started to drag my brother out of the bar. No one even paid us any attention, which meant one thing: this had happened way too often and it was becoming a problem.

The chilly autumn air cooled my glistening skin as I leaned against the fender of my truck after Max and I shoved Emmett in the back. I honestly felt a little unstable. Things were getting out of control.

Breanna was pissed (I gave fewer fucks than I should have).

My brother was a mess, just after he'd gotten his shit together (that bothered me more than it should).

Ivy was probably upset with me (and I cared about that more than anything in the world).

And now I had Max looking at me like I was about to bust a gasket. *Fuckin' rad.*

"What?" I snapped, meeting his amused face that also held a glint of caution.

"You okay?"

No.

"Yeah, I'm fine. I just want to kill Carrie."

Max sighed. "That's not what I'm talking about and you know it."

I didn't answer him because as soon as I opened my mouth, I heard the bar doors opening and found Ivy shyly walking over to us.

I watched her the entire time and it was almost an instantaneous feeling of relief. Like just seeing her face made me feel a little less suffocated, like I wasn't actually being pulled in ten different directions.

Her voice was soft and hesitant. "There were only a couple drinks on his tab. Apparently he came with the band."

Max started to back away, to give her and I some privacy but before he got too far, he looked over his shoulder and said to Ivy, "I'll see ya in there and I'll have a new drink made for ya." Then he winked, and I actually growled out loud.

I instantly wished I could take it back, but it was only a natural reaction. *One of a wild animal, that is.*

Ivy turned around, squinting her eyes, and when I looked back at Max his eyes were widened and his arms were up in surrender. I knew he didn't mean anything by winking at her, but the thought of her in the bar with Max, coupled with the thought of every other guy who was checking her out from head to toe, put me right back into the frenzy I'd been feeling seconds ago – out of fucking control.

"Can we talk before I go in and pay and then drag this sloppy mess home?" I asked, hitching my thumb back to Emmett.

She smiled softly. "I already paid; it's no biggie."

And just like that, my heart was climbing out of my chest and reaching out for hers.

"You didn't have to do that—I'll pay you back. How much was it?" I asked, pulling out my wallet from my back pocket.

She landed her hand on mine and I froze. She pulled it back quickly and then peered up at me with those long eyelashes brushing against the tops of her eyelids.

"It's fine, it was only ten bucks. What are friends for?"

Friends. *Why did that one little word irritate me so fucking much?*

I leaned back against my truck, peeking a glance at Emmett, who was curled up like a baby in the backseat.

"Are we okay?"

Ivy adjusted her feet on the gravely parking lot, kicking up a few rocks in her wake. "Why wouldn't we be?"

I almost smiled because even by the way her voice stayed neutral, I could tell she was beating around the bush.

"Ivy," I protested. "If you're mad, then just tell me."

Ivy's brows furrowed as her light pink lips formed a straight line. "I have no idea why I would be mad at you, Dawson."

I exhaled. "Because of Breanna and I dating."

She let out a nervous laugh. "Dawson, I know you and I had a mind-blowing kiss when we were teenagers, but I didn't expect you to carry a torch around for me the entire six years that I was gone."

Oh, but the thing is... I *had* been carrying a torch around for her. It had been hidden under a ginormous amount of lust for Breanna, burying myself between her legs to try to stifle the hurt, but deep down, I'd been waiting.

I'd been waiting for her.

Ivy spoke up again, using that nervous, tiny voice that had never left my memory. "But why her? You could do *so* much better."

I blurted, "She's changed." But even as the words left my mouth I knew they were a lie.

Ivy's perfectly arched eyebrow rose. "She still seemed pretty dead-set on hating me from the look she gave me." She laughed.

I wanted to move past this conversation and go on about my way because I knew that nothing good was going to come from it. It would be wrong of me to agree with her because Breanna was still my girlfriend, whether my mind frequently wavered from the idea or not.

The thing with Breanna was, I knew we didn't have this amazing relationship built on love and all that mushy shit. I knew deep down that I'd never feel for her what she probably wanted me to feel, but... she really did help pull me out of a massive slump. She helped get me out that dark place I was in after Ivy left, and I grew so comfortable with her that I thought us being in a real relationship was inevitable.

I owed it to her. Right?

"She's just jealous of you. Always has been. Her entire family has been."

She shrugged. "Nothing to be jealous of." Then she chuckled. "I mean, I'm a twenty-three-year-old woman who has worked her life away to save up just enough money to move into her own house while also supporting her sister because her parents died in a house fire. Oh, and let's not forget the fact that I've only had one serious boyfriend my entire life. What is there to be jealous of? I'm like a forty-year-old living in a twenty-three-old's body."

So much. There's so much to be jealous of my sweet, naïve Ivy.

"Had?" My heart suddenly felt like it was slowly falling down a jagged, rocky cliff. Colliding with each and every bump.

"Huh?"

"You said you had a boyfriend. You don't anymore?"

Ivy's face turned a little pink and even under the night sky I could see that she was suddenly embarrassed. She started to kick the rocks with her foot again, all while not meeting my face. *What did he do to her? Because I'll kill him.*

"Oh," her voice was weak. "Yeah, we broke up right before I moved here."

"Why?" I inquired.

"He told me he would break up with me if I moved to this 'Podunk town.'"

"So you did anyway?"

A harsh laugh fell out of her mouth. "If someone is willing to let me go because I wanted to move to my hometown, the only place that actually held good memories of my parents, then fuck him."

A smile grew on my face. *My God, I love how strong-willed she's become.*

"So that was it? He just said it was over, and then you moved?"

She shrugged again. "Yeah. Well, no. He's called a few times, but I usually ignore them. Today he left a voicemail. He said he wanted to talk because he missed me."

Fire went through my veins.

"Are you going to talk to him?"

She inhaled a deep breath and I couldn't help but stare at the way her chest expanded. If I looked hard enough, I could see the black, lacy bra under her white shirt and that only made my guilt intensify.

"I don't know," she finally answered and all the hope I had inside my body evaporated.

My phone started vibrating in my pocket. Ivy's eyes glanced down at the noise ricocheting off the side of my truck. I pulled it out and saw Breanna's icon flashing.

I rolled my eyes but muted a groan.

"You better get that. I'm going to head back in."

I hit ignore as she was walking away.

"Hey, Ivy. Wait." She turned around and looked at me with wonder in her eyes. "Um, you're here working at Belton Bank, right?" She nodded slowly, probably thinking back to our past conversation on why she'd moved back. "Have you ever thought of taking on small businesses for accounting? That's what you are, right? An accountant?"

The green in her eyes sparkled like I'd just given her a

diamond ring. "Actually, that's my career goal. I'd like to take on small businesses and handle their accounts. Why?"

I edged my chin towards my brother. "Do you think you could take a look at Emmett's accounts? I don't know if you know, but he owns the tattoo shop uptown and he's been having some issues. Which is why he's drinking." Her chin rose as she lifted up onto her tiptoes to look at Emmett's dense, sleeping body. "Carrie, his 'sometimes' girlfriend is in charge of all the billing and ordering of supplies – she basically handles all the money, but we've got a pretty big hunch that she's skimming it."

Ivy's mouth opened as she let out a huff. "Of course I'll take a look. I'll do it for free. That's crazy."

I smiled. "No, he'll pay you. I'll make him."

"That's not necessary, Dawson. I'm your friend and he's your brother. Bring the files over tomorrow... unless you're not coming to work on the house again? You can always give the files to John or Garret; they can give them to me."

I could have sworn I heard disappointment in her voice. I'd been having our two best men work on her house instead of me because I knew I needed to keep my distance. For the love of God, I tried to *kiss* her last time we were alone. Like, my body couldn't help it. The attraction I had for her was almost too much for me to handle. And now that we were alone right here, her being so genuine and sweet and looking sexier than I'd ever seen with those tight jeans hugging each of her curves, and the way her creamy skin was exposed, just above her breasts, I wanted to kiss her again.

I want to do more than just kiss her.

I worked a swallow down my throat and brought my eyes back to hers. "I'll be there."

Then I turned around and climbed into my truck,

because if I didn't get away from her in the next second, I would do something I regretted.

I knew how to treat a woman and Breanna was the woman I was currently bound to. I wasn't a cheater... but my God, Ivy made me want to be.

SEVENTEEN

Ivy

My heart was frantically beating in my chest like I was creeping up a rollercoaster, ready to fly over the edge into a surge of excitement and panic. This was the third day in a row that Dawson said he was coming over to work on the house and it literally had me basically flying through my day like I'd grown fairy wings overnight.

There was still quite a bit to do in the house, but the guys that Dawson had put on the job were always working diligently when I returned home from work. I got off at four but they always stayed until six, hammering, drilling, putting up drywall. Fixing the ceiling. It was comforting having someone to come home to, even if they were sweaty men who liked to chatter too much.

This was the first time I'd ever lived alone. After my parents had passed away, I was either with Uncle Timothy or Mia, and then when I moved out of my uncle's, and into Eric's fancy townhome in the city, I still always had someone near. I never realized how lonely it was not to have someone around, until recently.

So, even having forty-year-old men around who rubbed tobacco and showed their butt-cracks every time they bent down was nice. But what was even nicer was that the last three days I'd been coming home to a familiar face, one that made butterflies erupt in my lower belly the minute it flashed in front of me.

Even the thought of seeing Dawson got me completely giddy, and it shouldn't, because we were friends and he had a girlfriend.

The first night he was already here when I came home. It was only him; he let the other guys go early. He looked even more attractive to me that night because he was totally in his element. He was casual and relaxed, chuckling at me every so often when we'd have a conversation about something simple.

That was the thing with Dawson. Things were always so easy with him; he grounded me with such an ease that I wished he'd been with me the year after my parents had died. I could have used him to pick me up every so often.

I'd spent most of the evening sitting at my kitchen table, looking through some of the documents that Dawson had given me from Emmett's business. There was definitely something fishy going on, and I had yet to figure it out all the way. I should have been able to get this figured out within a day but with Dawson working a hammer in my living room, I couldn't focus.

I could only see a sliver of him from my where I was sitting. Just his arm, or the occasional sight of his edgy jaw bone. I found myself staring at the way his arm muscles flexed with each pound of the hammer. Back and forth, back and forth, like they were provoking me. I think I even thought, na-na-na-boo-boo while mesmerized by the sight.

You can look, but you can't touch, Ivy! That was my new mantra any time he was around.

He was taken.

You're too late.

The second night, I casually moved into the empty living room. I hadn't purchased a couch yet because the floors still needed done and it just seemed easier. It wasn't like I had a ton of people over at my house anyway. No one needed a seat.

I plopped myself down on the hardwood floor, comforted by the sight of Dawson's tall stature, working meticulously on the crown molding that he was putting up above the new archway that the other workers had done the previous day.

My mouth went dry the second he lifted his arms up above his head and I was met with his toned stomach. I only saw the lower part of his torso, but let me tell you, I could be 100% certain that he had washboard abs underneath his black, Lanning Construction t-shirt.

I was completely distracted most of the evening, trying to focus on the numbers blending together in Emmett's business account, but anytime Dawson would strike up a conversation with me, I would be totally consumed by it. Then, when he wasn't talking to me, I was too busy squeezing my legs together to ease the dull throb that had made itself very, very known.

We talked about the past a lot, and about how our lives were when we were apart for those six years. It was never an unsettling conversation when we'd fill each other in on our past, but we always skidded right over the pain that had driven us apart.

I was happy not talking about it; I just wanted to move past it. If that was possible.

Taking a deep breath, I looked at myself in my rearview mirror, making sure that there wasn't any smeared lipstick near my mouth, or that my hair didn't look like I'd spent the day standing underneath a sprinkler.

My mocha-colored locks were falling out along my face from the topknot that I'd worn to work and there was a coffee stain on my light pink blouse, but there wasn't much I could do about that now. It didn't matter anyway, Dawson probably wasn't even paying attention to how I looked.

Then again...my mind drifted to the last two nights when I'd caught him staring at my legs as I spread them out while propping myself against one of the walls, and how his eyes lingered a little too long on my lips.

I was quite possibly making all of this up in my head. Yes. That was it. I was so desperately attracted to him that I was imagining that he felt the same.

God, what I would do to hear that he still thought I was beautiful. He always told me I was beautiful when we were younger, and it always made my heart full.

Always. Even when I thought he was joking, it still made me happy.

Just as I was getting out of my car, his truck pulled up behind me.

I hadn't even realized that he wasn't already inside working. I slumped my shoulders. I could have totally run inside and at least spritzed some perfume on myself before he got here.

"Hey, you're late tonight," I said as he got out of his truck.

He pulled his dark sunglasses up and perched them on

his head. He quickly glanced down to my outfit and then clenched his jaw.

"Yeah, I got... caught up."

"Doing what?" I questioned.

"Fighting with Breanna."

Oh.

I didn't say anything because... what was that old adage? If you can't say something nice, then don't say it at all. Yes. That was going to be my new rule when I was around Dawson and he brought up Breanna, because I would never have anything nice to say. She could be the Queen of fucking England and I would still hate her.

The next hour flew by. Dawson and I barely spoke, and I could tell that his shoulders were tense anytime I glanced up at him. He was standing on a small ladder, putting up the last of the molding. The lights were dim in the living room, and as it was nearing October, the long light of summer was slowly disappearing and darkness was coming sooner and sooner every night.

Dawson was standing underneath a light that he'd hung up above his head and it literally looked as if he was in a spotlight, illuminating his handsome features that much more. I took in his every attribute, the shine of his golden-brown hair, the straightness of his nose, how his lower cheeks had that edible little bit of scruff lining them.

Suddenly, Dawson turned his head and found me staring at him. I snapped my head down so quickly that it popped. It popped loud enough that he probably heard it from across the room. A flush started to creep up my neck and I basically wanted to die.

Does he know how attractive he is? Does he know how attracted I am to him? He's grown into such a steely, handsome man that even straight men are probably in awe of him.

Breanna is a lucky, lucky girl. I hope she knows that.

I hurriedly put my attention back onto Emmett's paperwork for the next few minutes.

"Aha!" I shouted.

I peered up at Dawson and a sly smile formed on my face.

"What?" he questioned.

"Come here, I'll show you."

I wanted to jump up and down all around the room as confetti fell from above, because I had put it all together. I found where they were losing money and I knew exactly who was taking it.

Carrie.

It was obvious. She thought she was being slick with adding the wrong deposits into the bank, but she was clearly lacking knowledge as her numbers didn't match up at all. I'm not sure if she was truly stupid or if she didn't think anyone would notice, but after comparing the last several bank statements until my eyes bled, it was obvious.

Dawson strode over to me and slowly lowered his body to where I was sitting. He pushed his shoulders and back along the same wall that mine was leaning against and angled his head down to the paper in my hand.

I began showing him how the numbers didn't add up correctly and where Carried just so happened to stop marking the correct amounts onto the deposit slips. He inched a little closer and I could smell the soap he'd used; I could smell the last little bit of shampoo still lingering in his hair.

His jean-clad leg rubbed against the little sliver of skin on my bare thigh from where my skirt had risen and I gulped. I knew my voice would be shaky if I spoke, but he'd asked me a question and I couldn't feign becoming a mute in a matter of a few seconds, so I answered anyway.

I opened my mouth, trying to calm my heart. "The first time she did it was over five months ago, and then..." He adjusted his leg against mine once more and I literally had to catch my breath. I swallowed, clearing my throat. "Ur, um..." I took my finger and pointed to the increasing amount of times that she'd marked the wrong amount. "Right here, and then right here again... and then—" Dawson took his own hand and placed it in the spot that I was about to move to.

Our fingers brushed and a surge of pleasure went down my spine. If he could elicit such a feeling in me with the brush of one of his fingers, I couldn't imagine what they'd feel like all over my body.

Or, maybe I could.

Goosebumps broke out along my skin and I turned my head over to his. He was only a few inches away from me, but it was close enough that I could feel his breath.

I flushed from head to toe, staring directly at his lips. Almost begging them to just touch mine.

Just kiss me. Please.

I wasn't thinking about a single thing in that moment other than *him*. His body heat, the way his bottom lip was slightly fuller than his top, the way his azure eyes almost called out to me.

He looked at me and I looked at him and the entire world melted away. Dawson's hand reached up and tucked a loose strand of hair behind my ear, and my heart swelled. His eyes traced my face, leaving a blissfulness after every single movement.

Suddenly, I was back in my fifteen-year-old body, staring at the one boy I'd ever truly felt connected to, the one boy I'd ever truly loved, and I wanted him to love me back so badly I could taste it. It was like the last six years were nonexistent. We were back in his bedroom, many moons ago, about to have the best kiss of our lives.

But then he backed away.

Dawson looked absolutely mortified, like he couldn't believe we were just that close for that long. Reality smacked me across the face and I felt my eyes instantly welling up. Such a strong force of hurt went through me that I could barely stand it.

"Um," I muttered, my voice along the lines of breaking in every way possible.

My body was still reaching out for him, but my mind had thrown up defenses. Dawson was taken, and I wasn't fifteen anymore. I shouldn't still have this massive crush on the guy I considered my best friend once upon a time.

This was wrong on so many levels. If I were Breanna, I would hate me, too.

"I'm sorry," I whispered as he was pulling himself away even further to stand up.

"Don't be. I crossed a line."

I was quick to get to my feet, adjusting my pencil skirt along my hips. "No, you didn't. Nothing happened."

Oh, but so much did. Even though Dawson and I barely touched, other than his finger accidently skimming mine and tucking a strand of hair behind my ear, and even though we didn't kiss... anyone with a ten-foot pole could feel the pull that was occurring between us. It was evident that we very well could have gotten swept up in those long, lost feelings.

Because they were there, as if they'd never left, and in fact had only grown stronger.

Dawson's eyes locked onto mine and they were full-on

feverish. They were so heated looking that I could almost see the thoughts whirring through his head.

Then he opened his mouth, regret clinging to his voice. "No...but I wanted something to happen, and that's just as bad."

Dawson walked over to his ladder and started to pack his stuff up. I hated the feeling that was edging its way into my lower stomach. A feeling that he was about to put a lot of distance between us. It was inevitable, though. I mean, he had Breanna and she hated me. As long as they were together, Dawson and I could be nothing more than a simple "hello" here and there, and that might even be pushing it for her.

Dawson had all the construction equipment put to the side in less than three seconds flat and then he finally got the nerve to look back up at me. I tried to pretend like I wasn't hurting or disappointed in some way or another but I knew the barely-there smile on my face couldn't fool him.

"I'm sorry," he droned, looking down at the floor and then back up at my face. My heart wrenched because he appeared so troubled.

"For what?"

"For allowing you to believe that we could be friends again."

And just like that, my stomach plummeted to the ground and I felt my heart shattering into a million little pieces.

I was horrified at myself. I was completely stricken with pain over the fact that I allowed myself to believe that Dawson and I could ever be like we once were. The last three days of shared laughter and easy conversation, like I was getting to know him again, had felt like standing under a nice spring shower on a record high day, but now, with him staring at me with guilt written all over his face, I felt more like a volcano had erupted behind me and I was being scorched with hot, simmering lava.

My voice broke. "It's fine."

But it wasn't. I felt sick to my stomach. I'd gone six years without him by my side and in a matter of a few nights together, I was right back to feeling that same, damn, devasting heartbreak I'd felt back then, when my entire life had flipped upside down.

"Ivy..." he started, watching my face fall and tears form behind my eyes. For a second, I felt relieved because I could tell the way his face twisted that he still cared about me. That at least, for a split second, he didn't want to see me hurt. He inched his way toward me, and then it was as if a brick wall had been thrown up in front of us.

Instead of taking a step in my direction, he took a step back. Further and further until he was at the door. He locked onto my face one more time before he spun around and stomped away. I stood in the same spot until I heard his truck pulling out from behind my Camry. That's when I let the floodgates open.

I was openly weeping for a friendship that I didn't even think was possible a few weeks ago.

And if I wanted to be truthful to myself, I was openly weeping for more than just a broken friendship.

EIGHTEEN

Dawson

"Breanna, there is nothing going on with Ivy and I. We aren't even friends."

God, did that hurt coming out of my mouth. Like a repeated punch to the gut.

Breanna and I had been going back and forth about Ivy, nonstop. She was pretty adamant that something was going on between us and I wasn't sure if I was really that obvious or if Breanna was just *so* obsessed with hating her that she'd hang on to any good reason to fight about it.

I told Ivy on Monday that we couldn't be friends, and the look on her face almost sent me straight to the grave. But that night with Breanna stuck with me.

Before I left to go work on Ivy's house, we'd been bickering, as she still wasn't over me not telling her about Ivy in the first place. The last words she said to me had my steps faltering at the door.

She yelled, "Just remember who picked you up when you were down, Dawson. She hurt you, and *I* was the one who picked you up. I was the one who waited around for you to get over it. She didn't come back here for you."

I didn't say anything because she was right. Ivy did hurt me, and even if it was inevitable at the time, I still couldn't deny the pain.

I knew very well that she'd had to leave. I was aware that she had to go live with her uncle because her parents had passed away in the fire. Of course, at the time, I'd thought she just left without a single goodbye but even if she'd told me goodbye, it still would have hurt just as much.

The feelings for her that I'd developed through our friendship never really left. They ran deep, deeper than anything I'd ever felt. Breanna was a great numbing agent. She numbed the pain for so long that I finally just gave in to her. I ignored all the unresolved emotions still swarming around for Ivy in my head...out of sight, out of mind, but now that she was back, those feelings were popping up in every fucking direction. The second I pushed one down, another one popped up.

And Breanna wasn't numbing them anymore and I knew the more time I spent around Ivy, the more they would emerge, and it would be too late.

I would be consumed by her and then I'd be fucked, because if she could hurt me that badly, six years ago, before we even started a real relationship... I couldn't even imagine the pain that I would feel now if she were to leave.

I knew she was also feeling some type of attraction or lust. I would catch her stare every few seconds and each time it would send a wild thrill through me. The way her body reacted when I was close, the way her laughter was so easy and free. I had a pretty big feeling that she still felt what we'd both never really openly admitted years ago, and that had me on the edge of my seat. But, I could be wrong.

And I hated admitting it but I almost didn't want to give her the power to hurt me again. I was better off with Breanna, in my safe-zone. It wasn't a bad safe-zone by any means; in fact, I hadn't even had these thoughts pushing up against my skull before Ivy came back to town. Which was just another reason that I should probably stay away from her.

I should leave the past where it was.

But I wasn't quite sure I could.

Breanna's shrill voice broke me out of my pathetic, repetitive thoughts. "That's not what I heard!"

My brow furrowed as my chest heaved. I took in Breanna's posture; her exposed shoulders were pulled back slightly so that her breasts were pushed up towards my face. Usually, I would have stared and felt some arousal, but not right now.

She was acting absolutely crazy.

I stalked over to her so quickly that her annoying cat ran and hid. I give her props: she didn't even bat an eyelash. She crossed her arms over her work shirt and huffed.

"I'm telling you right now that I told her Monday that she and I couldn't be friends, so lay off, Breanna."

"Don't talk to me like that!" she yelled in my face.

I reeled myself in, trying to calm down. It wasn't even worth it. I wasn't even angry that she was yelling at me. I was angry because I was upset that I hurt Ivy. It was sickening.

"Why are you so angry?" I asked, voice back to normal. "Why do you hate her so much? You're acting *crazy* about this."

Her eyes narrowed. "I just don't like her. Never have, *and* I don't want her to hurt you again."

"I appreciate that, but I'm a big boy and I can make my

own decisions. I'm trying to make this 'relationship' work with you, but I didn't expect to see an entirely different side of you all because Ivy came back to town."

She placed her hands on her hips, clearly irritated. "So you think I'm crazy now? See! She's already swaying your opinion about me!"

I huffed out a laugh. "If you were to act like this, even before Ivy came to town, I would have still thought you were being irrational and possessive. We've been dating for a couple months and all of a sudden, you're acting as if you own me. Ivy and I aren't friends. I'm working on her house, and that's it. Breanna, when I told you I would try a relationship with you, I wasn't expecting you to do a 180. I don't like this drama."

And I don't even think it's worth it.

Her eyes grew large. "So what are you implying? That we break up because I'm angry about Ivy? I'm allowed to get upset, Dawson! I'm your girlfriend now—did you think we would never fight?"

"I'm saying that I need you reel in your crazy, because I didn't sign up for this."

Breanna didn't answer me. I wanted her to simmer in that for a little while. Ivy aside, I wouldn't be able to deal with this for much longer. Even if Ivy weren't back and Breanna was acting like this about something else, I'd be long gone.

And I was certain that Breanna wouldn't act like this with anyone else; it was just Ivy. She had hated her for as long as I could remember. And as of right now, I couldn't even blame her for feeling insecure because whether I admitted it aloud or not, Ivy was a threat. Even if I never saw her again, she'd be a threat because I loved the simple *thought* of Ivy more than I could ever love Breanna and that... that was absolutely *terrible*.

Why am I even still with her?

Because I felt like I owed it to her? Or was it just fear?

I LEFT Breanna's on semi-okay terms. She was leaving for a car auction with the dealership in the morning and she'd be gone until Sunday. I hated to feel thankful, but I was. We needed some space. She needed to think about what I'd said and I needed to get my shit together.

I had a feeling that she was still going to continue to think that there was something up with Ivy and I, even if we didn't speak. Breanna had known me for a long time, and we've grown closer over the years. Nothing like Ivy and I had, but we spent a decent amount of time together. Whether that time was spent having sex was beside the point. We still knew each other pretty well. I think she knew deep down that I still had something lingering in the background for Ivy.

If she knew me like I thought she did, she probably had at least an inkling of validation.

I almost felt stuck, like I was frozen. I didn't know which way was up. Stay with Breanna in my safe place, try to make her happy in the long run, or...

I didn't even want to think about it any longer. I couldn't. I hastily shook my head, clearing my thoughts as my truck's tires crunched over the loose gravel in front of Ships. I quickly shut it off and hopped out, my mouth instantly watering for a beer as crickets chirped in the distant hayfield. At least that would help ease the tension crawling over my shoulders.

The second I stepped into the bar, I knew that Ivy was

somewhere near. Every male had his attention elsewhere, even guys who that were with a date. We lived in such a small town that when a newbie sauntered in, especially one as attractive as Ivy, people noticed.

My eyes followed everyone else's and when I found her, I almost died right then.

It was a heart-stopping moment. She threw her pretty head back and laughed and I swore I could feel it on my skin. But the happiness I felt, seeing her so carefree and beautiful, quickly dissolved when I took in the rest of the scene, which involved her sitting in a booth with my brother and one of his employees.

Jealousy tore into my chest and pulled out my heart. My ears flamed and my fists clenched at my sides. I almost walked over to them and ripped my brother out of the booth for letting her sit so closely to that piece of shit employee who was leaning his head down so far that she could probably smell his alcohol-ridden breath.

I stood, ramrod straight, staring at them for so long that people started to turn their attention to me.

Ivy didn't even glance at me though, and that was probably better for the both of us. I had told her we couldn't be friends, so me staring at her like a fucking dipshit wasn't going to help matters.

But she was sitting beside Kip. Fucking *Kip*. He smoked weed in his spare time and banged more than one chick a night.

She had no business being near him.

I was going to fucking kill my brother. *Kill*.

I let out an uneven breath and walked over to the bar, so fucking angry that I was almost foaming at the mouth.

My thoughts were only on Ivy and Kip, like I had

complete tunnel vison...they were the only two in the room. That's why Max's voice startled me.

"What?" I snapped, whipping my head over to him and Becca.

Becca wasn't even looking in my direction, but Max was eyeing me cautiously.

"Sorry," I mumbled, raising my hand at the bartender. I needed a drink and I needed it now.

"You okay?" he asked, but I didn't answer. I looked back over at Ivy and Kip, and then at my brother who was sliding out of the booth.

Good, come over here, fucker, so I can plummet my fist into your fucking head.

I ground my teeth as he approached. He smiled at me with a shit-eating grin and then peeked around and winked at Becca, who was apparently watching the scene unfold.

My finger stabbed his chest and he looked down briefly before bringing his stupid grin back up to meet my face.

"What the fuck are you doing bringing Kip around Ivy? What the fuck are you even doing with Ivy?"

He chuckled and it only heightened my rage. "I will fucking put you through a wall, Emmett, and you know it."

He sobered up quickly. I may be younger than Emmett, but I was stronger and faster. He knew that.

"I'm with Ivy because she came by the shop earlier to tell me about Carrie stealing the money, and then I told her I'd buy her something to eat tonight since she refused when I offered to pay her, then Kip saw her..."

My nostrils flared as I moved my body around his and looked back at their booth.

Ivy was smiling, then she glanced up lazily and found me staring. Her eyes went wide and her face blanched. I felt sick. I felt sick because I knew that I hurt her feelings the other night and I couldn't do a damn thing to fix it.

What I could do, was pull Kip out by his greasy hair and threaten him never to lay a fucking finger on her.

Yeah, that sounds like the perfect idea.

I went to stand up as my eyes made their way over to him. He was staring right at her breasts and I felt a chill go through my body.

My brother put his hand on my shoulder to stop me. "Dude, calm the fuck down. What is your problem?"

"He isn't good enough for her!" I shouted, but thankfully, there was so much chatter in the bar that no one heard other than the few people surrounding me.

"So, who is?" Becca asked. I whipped my head over at her and glared. "Surely not you..."

I opened my mouth to say something but Max gave me a dark look, raising one eyebrow as if warning me. It stunned me for a second. Last I knew, he and Becca didn't quite see eye to eye and they bickered constantly.

"I'm certain you don't think *you're* good enough for her, because from where I'm standing, you're not the best option either... considering you have a girlfriend who probably wouldn't be thrilled that you're so caught up in who Ivy is talking to."

Becca's words made sense.

The entire world felt like it was shifting around me. I didn't say a word. I only stared at her and then I looked at Max, who was staring at me, waiting for me to say something.

But the truth was... I couldn't argue.

She was right.

Kip wasn't good enough and neither was I. Hell, I had a girlfriend and here I was, only concerned about Ivy.

What the fuck am I doing?

I snapped my head over to my brother. "Don't let her go home with him, because if she's going to be with someone... it shouldn't be a fucking, doped-up walking STD."

My brother gave me a knowing grin and tipped his head down, as if complying with my demand.

I watched him walk away and then I took the beer I'd ordered and chugged it, all while Max and Becca drilled their stares into the side of my head. I didn't speak another word to either of them. Instead, I stood up and walked out of the bar, not even looking back in Ivy's direction. I knew if I did, it would only end badly.

NINETEEN

Ivy

I hated getting flowers. I knew I was an enigma. Bright, iridescent roses were delivered to me today by a young delivery boy, and while all the older women awed and oohed at the flowers gracing my desk at work, I was rolling my eyes.

Eric was like a little gnat. He wouldn't leave me alone. He had called me several times since I'd moved back to town and I had ignored every single call.

The truth was, I was still overly pissed (and a little hurt) that he broke up with me on such a whim and now, I was even more pissed that he was filling my inbox with unnecessary text messages and leaving me voicemails out the ass.

Like, helllllooo. I don't have time for your stupid "I miss you" texts and "Call me back, baby" voicemails. I was too wrapped up in my depression regarding Dawson.

Even the thought of Dawson made me bitter.

I hadn't seen him since the bar the other night, and that

was torturous enough. He took one look at me and then left. Like he couldn't even stand the sight of me.

That went really well with my barely-there confidence.

The only good thing was that Breanna wasn't with him and I really did end up having an okay night with Emmett and his friend, Kip. Although Kip was a bit handsy, we still had a good time. I danced with both of them and they bought my dinner and all my drinks, so that made up a little bit for the hurt I'd felt when I locked eyes onto Dawson.

He looked angry.

I wasn't sure if he was angry because of what happened the other night or if he was angry because I was sitting with his brother and Kip. I doubted it was the latter, because how could he possibly be angry when *he* had a girlfriend?

Beats me.

I was huffing and puffing, carrying my enormous bouquet of nausea-inducing roses up my front stoop. I put them down on the porch and reached inside my purse for my keys.

No one would be working on my house tonight. Mr. Lanning had called and said they were waiting on a part for my bathroom, which was finally getting some TLC. The part wasn't scheduled to get in until the following week.

The night after Dawson told me we couldn't be friends was the last night he'd worked on my house. He sent back the other men the following day, and the disappointment made me eat an entire pint of Ben and Jerry's. This is how the night went:

Me: I need ice cream because I'm depressed over a boy I used to be best friends with, who no longer wants to be my friend at all.

Also me: You're borderline lactose intolerant, don't do it.

Me: I'm depressed.

eats pint

Me one hour later: Why the fuck did I do that? Now I'm depressed and harboring a fatality-inducing stomachache.

Yeah, so I was basically pathetic. Whatever.

Just as I was putting the key into the lock on my front door, I heard footsteps behind me. I quickly spun around and my sister appeared out of thin air, her usually bright and happy face pale and drawn.

"Mia? What's wrong? I didn't think you were coming until later?"

I looked around for her 1999 Honda and saw it across the street. My brows furrowed as I met her solemn-looking face again.

"Mia, you're scaring me."

Mia didn't even make a peep. She walked up my broken steps and took my wrist in her sweaty hand and started to drag me down the steps. I tripped, but her grip on my arm held me upright enough that I didn't completely fall.

"Mia. Stop!" I yelled, but she didn't comply. Her grip only hardened on my arm.

I was honestly scared and at a loss for words. My stomach twisted, thinking something terrible had happened.

She pulled me down the rest of the street in the one direction that I hadn't gone yet. I avoided it at all costs.

Its name came into view on the bright green street sign and I planted my feet firmly on the ground.

"Mia, no," I tried to say, but she dragged me even further, ignoring me.

My feet were aching in my black work heels, but I knew I couldn't take them off because she would probably just pull me along even harder.

Once we rounded the corner of my old street, I felt my insides turn to mush. Everything I'd eaten that day threatened to come up and although it was far from hot outside, I was full-on sweating.

My heart rapidly beat in my chest because I knew we were headed to my old house, the one that burned down and probably had some other stupid house in its place.

I avoided it like the fucking bubonic plague. I couldn't stomach seeing another house standing upright, growing happy children with parents who weren't *gone*.

My eyes clenched as soon as Mia stopped walking.

Her distraught voice had me peeling them open in an instant. "Look. Just look."

I slowly rose my head, preparing to swallow bile, and what I saw was so much harder to actually take in than what I'd expected.

Greif struck me so hard that my hand involuntarily went to my stomach. It clenched and turned in such a vicious way that I felt like an actual knife was cutting into me. Goosebumps broke out along my arms.

What stood on my street, in the same place that my home once stood... was a house that looked identical to mine.

Even down to the white siding and navy blue shutters. Almost everything was the same, except for the vehicle in the driveway.

That's when my heart and tears fell simultaneously.

A blue GMC Sierra with a logo on the side reading, "Lanning Construction" was parked in the concrete driveaway.

A muffled cry came out of my mouth and Mia was instantly there, wrapping her arms around my body.

I had to get away. I had to get away before Dawson saw me standing here like a complete lunatic, losing her mind.

Every single scar on my heart was suddenly aching.

Memories flew at me from every angle and not only did that hurt, so did the fact that Dawson was there at the house.

Does he live there?

What the hell is this? Some twisted version of The Notebook? Was he about to walk out of the house with a handful of letters? Professing his love for me?

Probably not.

I somehow managed to get myself together and grabbed my sister's hand and dragged her back all the way to my house.

Once we reached the security of the porch, we sat down on the steps in silence.

I was trying to sort through my thoughts, but the only thing I could focus on was the *how*. *How had my house been rebuilt? Did Dawson do it? Did Lanning Construction do it? And when? And why?*

So many questions.

"So, I take it you didn't know?" Mia asked, finally breaking the silence.

A choppy laugh fell out of my mouth. "Trust me, if I knew... you would have known."

"Who the hell built our house exactly the same? That's kinda creepy."

I bit the inside of my cheek. Mia didn't know much about Dawson and I, and I supposed that now would be a good time to fill her in. She was an adult, so that awkward "I'm kind of trying to be your mom," thing didn't really apply any longer. We'd talked about guys before, and sex – and although our relationship in the past was mostly me trying to be a good guardian for her, attempting to make up for the shitty hand we'd been dealt, we'd grown out of that phase and now were more like best friends.

So for the next twenty minutes, I told Mia everything.

From the kiss Dawson and I shared, many moons ago, all the way to our last encounter at the bar. She didn't seem surprised, which unnerved me. Maybe I wasn't quite as good at hiding my feelings as I thought.

"So, like... did he build that house for you? Was that his truck?"

I breathed out a bundle of air while unstrapping my heels. I wiggled my toes once they were free and placed them back down on the cool concrete. "Your guess is as good as mine."

"I bet he did."

I scoffed. "Doubt it. He basically hated me for leaving without saying goodbye. He didn't really understand the situation until a few weeks ago, and I highly doubt he built it in that time."

Mia's dark eyes met mine and they twinkled, as if she knew something I didn't.

"Are you going to ask him?" she asked.

I shrugged, scanning all the pretty bronze and crimson leaves littering the ground below us.

"Maybe, if I ever get a chance. I don't think we'll be speaking much anymore."

Even as I said it, I could feel my heart deflating.

My sister snickered. "Okkkkayy."

"What?"

She only shook out her brown, honey-colored hair. "Nothing." Then she paused, clasping her hands together in her lap. "I miss them still, ya know?"

A small amount of pain slithered around my heart. "I do, too. Everyday. It's been six years but somehow, one little reminder makes it seem like yesterday."

Mia nodded her head, looking out at the desolate street. I studied her profile, the way her button nose turned up slightly and the way her long, pretty eyelashes curled upward, making her eyes appear even brighter. Even though Mia and I shared the same pain of losing our parents, I still felt even worse for her.

I wasn't sure why. Maybe it was the motherly instinct that I took over the second my parents passed away, or maybe I'd just grown to recognize someone else's pain before mine, but it made me feel empty and lost.

Like I was back to being that scared fifteen-year-old, with the weight of the world on her shoulders.

Alone.

Mia turned her head to mine, locked onto my eyes, and let out a small sigh. "Enough of this sad shit, I'm starving."

I laughed. Mia had always been one to use food as a buffer. Food makes everything better, she'd always say. I mean, she wasn't wrong.

"Mia Marie, when was the last time you had a decent meal?"

She rolled her eyes, her normal smile creeping back along her face. "I'm in college... my meals consist of snack cakes and copious amounts of coffee."

I groaned. "Well come on, I'll make you a hearty meal."

She snickered. "I can't remember you ever making a hearty meal that wasn't boxed mashed potatoes and canned vegetables. Please tell me you remember when you tried to make Uncle Timothy and I a meatloaf one night..." she snickered again, which really just turned into a fit of laughter.

I couldn't help but laugh along with her and it felt nice. It felt nice to laugh after being in such a strange and unnerving situation – one that I was going to try and forget. Although, I had no idea how I was going to forget that there was a replica of my old house down the street, and the person living in it was someone who wouldn't leave my brain, no matter what I did. No amount of Ben and Jerry's could take the sting out of Dawson's words...not even when accompanied with a massive stomachache.

I swiftly got to my feet and opened the front door with Mia still laughing and going on about how my meatloaf tasted like feet, and then that's when I heard it.

It sounded like a waterfall.

My first thought was, *did I leave the faucet on?* Which didn't make any sense because even if I had, the men who were over at the house taking a few last-minute measurements of the pipes (according to the voicemail I'd received earlier from Mr. Lanning) would have turned it off.

I'd assume. But you know what they say when you assume something.

When I fully opened the door, my mouth fell to the floor.

The very, very wet floor.

"Holy fuck!" Mia yelled. I couldn't even yell at her for using such a dirty curse word because I was frozen.

My entire house was full of water. Like, not just a little bit damp... there was water *everywhere*. It covered the tops of my feet when I walked in. Water poured over my toes and crept out onto the porch. The weather strip at the bottom of the door had been keeping it inside.

I quickly ran into the living room, dropping my purse on the porch first, and went straight to the bathroom. Water was spraying everywhere.

It hit me in the face so hard that I had to take a step back to catch my breath. It was like walking up to a spewing fire hydrant, spraying rapidly in every direction possible. I was soaked from head to toe and there was no fucking way I could tell how to turn the water off. The only thing I could tell was that water was squirting from an exposed pipe behind my no-longer-there shower.

They were replacing it and had taken the old one out earlier in the week. Apparently, something had gone very, very wrong.

I hurriedly ran out of the bathroom, dripping with icy cold water. Mia stood back with wide eyes, taking in my appearance.

"Holy shit! What do we do?"

Build an ark and tell people to call me Noah? I have no fucking clue.

Instantly, I thought to call Dawson. I pulled my phone out of my bag, hearting racing from stress, my bare feet squishing on my now wet rug, but then my shoulders slumped.

I didn't have his number! *Oh, my God.*

Shit.

"I'll be back," I yelled, running down my concrete steps.

I knew that if someone had seen me running down the street in a see-through blouse and skirt sticking tightly to my lower body, bare-footed with stringy, wet hair, they'd probably call the police.

Or a psych ward to come collect me and throw me in with the loonies, but I truly didn't know what to do and I knew he would.

I rounded the corner to my old street and zeroed in my gaze onto the blue truck that was still parked in the driveway. My heart lifted.

Praise!

I didn't have time to hesitate as I climbed the familiar porch stairs. I didn't have time to absorb the pain that I'd felt when walking along the wooden porch and up to the navy blue front door that looked exactly like the one I'd opened and closed so many times in my youth.

Oh, but I definitely had time to worry that Breanna would answer the door.

I knocked anyway. No, wait—I didn't knock; I fanatically pounded my wet fist on the wooden door.

It opened quickly. Dawson stood there wearing only jeans. Let me reiterate that: Dawson stood there wearing *only* jeans. There was something mouthwateringly edible about an attractive man in dark blue jeans, no shirt, and bare feet. I praised God again, for the beautiful sight.

The dark jeans hung low on his hips, just below those lick-worthy abs that I just *knew* he'd have, and then my eyes traveled down to the bottom of his pants, where his bare feet stood out. I licked my lips. Literally. The sight of him snatched words right out of my mouth. In fact, the sight of him snatched any other thoughts right out of my brain. When I finally brought my eyes (that no doubt had *"fuck me"* written all over them) to his, he locked onto my face for a split second before raking his own eyes down *my* body. They moved so slowly that I felt like time had stopped.

A distant throb ached between my legs and my mouth went dry. My heart squeezed in my chest and I was instantly turned on. One look from him and I was drowning in a puddle of swoon.

Wait, that's water.

Oh! My house!

"Need a towel?" he asked in that overly cocky voice that I hadn't heard since we were teenagers.

"My house..." I shook my soaked hair, still unable to put a proper sentence together. "Water."

His dark brows furrowed and he bit his lip. The blank

expression on his face told me that he had no idea what I was mumbling about.

I grabbed his hand, ignoring the stupid, giddy feeling inside my body and pulled him towards my house. We basically ended up jogging our way over there, me pretending that my feet didn't hurt from running on the sidewalk and him questioning what the heck I was doing.

"Ivy, what's going on?" he demanded the second we got to the bottom stair of my porch.

Mia was sitting on the porch, completely content with the fact that my house was literally flooded. It was actually *almost* funny.

"Ivy!" Dawson said again, but I just pulled him up further into my house.

He muttered, "What the fuck," as we maneuvered through the living room and down the hall.

"Wet," I croaked and he took in the spraying water with wide eyes.

Dawson quickly went into action. He took in the situation calmly (unlike me) and ran out of the bathroom into my living room, intently searching for something. He found what he needed and ran over to the toolbox that the workers had left. I had told them they could keep it there instead of dragging it in and out of my house every day, and I was thankful because Dawson grabbed what I guessed may have been a wrench, and ran out the front door to my small front yard.

I followed him briskly and watched as he lifted some lid-thing that was in the grass and lowered his long-limbed body down onto the ground. He took his one hand holding the wrench and shoved it down into the hole.

I heard the water stop spraying instantly and I had never been more confused in my entire life. *So, that's how you turn the water off? Some hole in my front yard? Who would've guessed?*

I also had never been more aroused in my entire life. Dawson's entire bare chest was glistening with water, and the way his muscles moved so languidly with the tool, I was pretty sure I'd gone to heaven. Picture Michael Phelps emerging from an Olympic pool, swishing out his damp hair, and his very toned torso shining with little beads of water. Just replace the speedo with low-rise jeans and boom – perfect visual.

If I died right now, I think I'd be okay with it. Wet house and all.

"What the hell happened?" Dawson asked, walking up to my porch and heading back into my house.

I followed after him, my wet feet slapping on the slippery floor.

Before I even made it into the living room, I'd slipped and fallen. I almost wanted to say "Ta-da!" after I fell because that's how graceful the fall was, but the sudden tear of my groin muscle had me spewing a line of curse words instead.

Dawson flipped around quickly, his eyes wide. I fell onto my back, stunned because I was pretty sure I *heard* the ripping of my muscle.

Loud laughter came from behind me and I tilted my head back, my hair sliding on the floor. I stared up at my sister, who was laughing so hard her face looked like a freaking tomato.

"Shut up," I grumbled, trying to sit up. A small grin formed on my face and before I knew it, I was laughing too.

Mia had one of those laughs that resembled a hyena (that was, when she *truly* thought something was funny. I'd heard her laugh in front of a cute boy before and it did not sound anything like it did right now). I reached my hand up, still laughing, and let Mia pull me to my feet.

"Seriously, that actually hurt. I think I ripped my vagina muscle." My eyes grew large because with my back turned, I'd forgotten that Dawson was only a few feet behind me.

Mia's mouth gaped and then she laughed even harder, her entire body shaking in front of me.

"How is it possible that you've become even more clumsy over the years, Ivy?"

I slowly turned around, still embarrassed, and smiled innocently up at Dawson.

"It's a gift."

The apples of his cheeks lifted as he threw his head back to laugh. I stared at him, basking in how my heart lifted at the sound of it. He had a nice laugh. Like you didn't even have to know what he was laughing at to join in.

"Okay, before I ask what the hell happened to your house, are you okay? I wouldn't want to overlook the fact that your *vagina* muscle may be injured."

My face flamed.

Was he flirting?! God, this is taking me back to high school when I couldn't decipher between him flirting with me and him just being... Dawson.

I coughed, clearing my throat. I nudged Mia with my elbow when she snickered. "I'm fine, and I don't know what happened to the house. I came home and water was everywhere."

Dawson rolled his eyes and then mumbled, "Fucking idiots."

"Who?" I asked, following him back to the bathroom.

The floor was the worst in there. Soaked wasn't even an adjective I could use to describe it. The entire thing was up in shambles before, and now... it looked unsalvageable.

"I had the guys come over here to get some measurements for the pipe... this one right here." Dawson's bare foot stepped into the no-longer-there shower and then he pointed to the pipe that had water droplets slowly dripping off it. "They must have hit it or something on accident and it burst, causing your house to look like a fucking lake."

I pursed my lips as I looked around my destroyed bathroom.

"It's fine. I'll just use the other bathroom until we can fix it. How much will it cost? Do you have a ballpark figure?"

Dawson's head snapped over to mine, his eyes blazing right into me. "What? You're not paying for this! Are you crazy?"

I shot back a little. "Huh?"

His eyes crinkled. "Ivy, you're not paying for this. I wouldn't let you pay for this even if I didn't own the company. But standard protocol calls for *us* to pay for the damages and repairs since it was something *we* did."

That was a sudden relief. The only thing I could think when I had first seen the water gushing through my house was how I would have to do some serious skimping to afford it *and* Mia's next tuition bill.

"Oh."

I glanced over to the right when I saw Mia walking down the hallway. "I managed to save these, where do you want them?"

Ugh. The stupid flowers with the stupid note tucked inside (that I still hadn't opened). "I don't care," I answered, backing out of the bathroom and toward her. I needed to be worrying about how the hell I was going to get my house dry so I could walk around it without my toes shriveling up like raisins, not about flowers. "Give them to the bees if you want."

"Who are those from?" Dawson asked from behind me.

I knew who they were from, Eric, duh, but I suddenly felt awkward telling him and with my sister's cocked eyebrow, I *really* didn't want to answer.

I lied. "I don't know."

"Well then let's just open up the note. Oh, and hi, Dawson. It's been a long time since I've seen you," Mia called back as she walked to my somewhat dry kitchen.

"I know, kiddo. How ya been? You're going to St. Joseph's, right?"

She smiled when she turned around. "Yeah, I love it. I just came from there... I was gonna stay with my sister tonight, but..." she gestured toward the living room, "I think I'll head back and let you two deal with this..." Then she laughed.

Before I could say anything, she started to rip open the small card that was tucked into the flowers, which were lying on the counter looking much more wilted than earlier. I hurriedly walked over to her to snatch the card out of her hand, but she lifted it high above her head, out of my reach.

Mia got my father's tall genes, whereas I got my mother's short ones. She was much taller than me and she was totally using that against me right now.

"Stop, just throw it out."

She crinkled her perfectly plucked brows. "Why don't you read it? We both know who it's from."

Because suddenly, since moving back, I couldn't care less about Eric.

"Who is it from?" Dawson asked, leaning his still-naked torso against the wall. His arms were crossed over his chest, making his pectorals look that much more delicious.

"Give it to me!" I shouted, jumping up on the balls of my feet and reaching my hand to snatch the card out of her hand. My sore groin muscles protested, but I kept at it.

Mia formed her I-can-get-anything-I-want smile and then jolted around me, past Dawson and out to the front porch. While running, even on the slippery floor, she pulled open the card and started to read it.

I was only a few steps behind her, and I noticed that Dawson had also followed us, as if he really cared what the stupid note said.

"Ivy-cakes," Mia had started. *There goes my face, fifty shades of freaking red.* "Please forgive me and call me back. I want to talk to you and I'm sorry for my hasty reaction to you moving away. I love you."

Ugh! I ripped the card out of her hand, fuming not only from her reading it aloud in front of Dawson (*why do I even care? I don't know*), but also pissy because Eric was becoming more annoying with each passing day.

Did I miss him? A little, but only after Dawson had told me we couldn't be friends.

Was I still hurt by Eric's rapid decision to break up because I was moving to Oak Hill? Kind of.

But I definitely didn't need anyone knowing that, and I definitely didn't need to call him back so I could hear him ask me to move back in with him *again*. He wanted me to cave in to his sweet calls and notes, and I wasn't going to.

I had too much going on to deal with that.

"He's not going to give up. You know that, right?" Mia said, raising her eyebrows at me.

"Don't you have, like, a paper to write or something?" I asked, crossing my arms over my damp shirt.

She rolled her eyes at me. "Yes, and I was going to bum

off your Wi-Fi while you made me that 'hearty' meal, but I didn't bring my bathing suit."

I laughed out loud. "Well, just go back to campus and come stay next weekend. Hopefully it'll be dry by then?" I turned and looked to Dawson at that last sentence. He was grimacing, looking from me and then to Mia's hand (still clutching the stupid note) and then back to me.

"It'll take at least the weekend, if not longer, for us to clean this mess up. It's best if you go stay at campus, and then..." His eyes bored into mine. "You can just stay with me."

I wanted to throw my hands up in protest. *Stay with him! What!?*

"What! No! I'll stay with Becca."

Dawson's eyes narrowed. "And you'll spend, like, an hour driving to work on Monday. That's stupid. Just stay at my house. I don't bite, Ivy."

This is what I pictured about staying at Dawson's (aka replica of my old house...a little issue upon which I would most definitely have to touch base if I stayed there): Breanna coming at me with some type of weapon (in my head it was a very, very sharp pair of tweezers that she had previously used on her stupid, skinny eyebrows) and plunging them into my eyeballs, trying to scratch them out. *No, thank you.*

"No. I really don't want to be roomies with you and your girlfriend, *Banana*..." I cleared my throat. "I mean Breanna."

Mia laughed from behind me and it caused me to grin.

Dawson didn't laugh. Instead, he wore an expression one might if they'd seen a monkey talking. "What? Brenna doesn't live with me."

Oh, thank the freaking Lord. I almost couldn't handle the thought.

"Oh, well, still. I don't think she'll like it if I'm there, Dawson. I'll stay with Becca or at the motel down on Curtis Ave."

"EW! No," Mia shrieked. "I can hear the cockroaches crawling from here!"

I ignored her and looked back up at Dawson.

"You're staying with me, and that's final. It's the least I can do since my guys were the ones who destroyed your house."

"Dawson, I don't think that's a good idea. Seriously, Breanna *hates* me."

His cheek lifted up on one side as he pulled out his phone. "You leave *Banana* up to me, Ivy. You're staying and that's final... Come on, it'll be like old times."

I bit my tongue so incredibly hard that it could have fallen off.

Dawson didn't take his eyes off his phone. "Now, I'm going to go make some calls about this. Pack some stuff."

Then he turned around, naked torso and all, and stormed back into my house.

I looked back at my sister, who was grinning like a Cheshire cat while holding up Eric's note. She took her fingers and ripped it in half, allowing the paper to fall onto the floor. "Bye-bye, Eric."

I gave her a knowing look, but the truth was...I didn't know *anything*.

TWENTY

Dawson

What in the ever loving *fuck* was I doing?

I just told – no, I *demanded* – that Ivy stay with me, at my house, for the entire weekend until we could get her house fixed. If I thought that Breanna was pissed at me before, now she was likely to actually grow horns and *kill me*. She'd probably send me straight to hell, but my heart had spoken before the rational part of my brain could catch up, and now I was stuck.

Not that I was really complaining.

Ivy and me, at my house, like old times...yeah, I was more than eager.

When I opened my door earlier and saw her standing on my front porch with wet hair and clothes clinging to every curve of her body, I almost passed out. My dick all but jumped to action and my mouth was as dry as the Sahara Desert.

She was beautiful, but also looked so sexy that she could have been on the cover of *Sports Illustrated*. Her brown locks were darkened and framed her heart-shaped face; her emerald eyes were wide and pulled me in so fast that I couldn't have held onto anything to keep me from being swept up in their twinkle. My eyes traveled down her body and I could see every single round curve of her body. I could see the color of her bra through her soaked, sheer blouse, and the skirt she wore...it was hugging her hips like a boa constrictor cutting off someone's circulation. Gorgeous tan legs led down to her cute bare feet with toenails painted purple...she was adorable.

She was this perfect, beautiful, sexy woman who was standing on my front porch, soaked from head to toe.

I wanted to wrap her in my arms and drag her back into my house and never leave again.

Once I'd snapped out of my daydream, I managed to climb back into rational Dawson's body and figure out what the hell was going on.

Which is what I was still doing.

Sure, I had a moment of relapse when I'd asked her to stay at my house, but I sent her on her merry way so I could get some of my employees over here to set up fans and start cleaning up their mess.

If I was jerk, I'd fire the men I'd sent to take measurements earlier, since they were the ones who'd made this mess, but I wasn't an asshole.

They'd have to work after hours to fix the problem, but I realized that everyone made mistakes and that everyone deserved a second chance, so their jobs were safe – for now.

"Okay, I'm going to head back home," I yelled back to the guys wringing out sopping wet rugs and angling fans towards Ivy's soaked floor.

I was still only wearing jeans and although I was a hot-natured guy, I was beginning to feel cold. Oak Hill's fall was always crisp and chilly, just the way I liked it, but standing here almost naked, my nipples could cut through glass.

On the walk back over to my house, I tried to come up with a rational explanation to give Breanna regarding the fact that Ivy – the person who drove Breanna into acting like a possessive psycho – would be sleeping in the same house as me.

Our last conversation was me basically informing her that we needed some time apart to think, and here I was, doing the complete opposite of thinking. I was *doing*.

I brought my gaze to my porch before even crossing to the right side of the street.

Ivy was sitting on the front stoop of my house, still wearing the same clothes as earlier, and although they weren't hugging her body any longer, she was still just as compelling.

My brows crinkled the closer I got to her. Her head popped up when she heard my scuffle on the sidewalk, and her eyes grew wide.

"Why aren't you inside?" I questioned, closing the distance between us.

She said nothing. She only drove those forest-green eyes into me.

"When did you do it?" Her voice was as soft as a whisper but still demanding.

"Do what?" I asked, eyeing her suspiciously.

Ivy stood up and crossed her arms over her chest. She walked over and leaned against the porch pillar and then jutted her head at the front of the house.

"Did you do this? Did you build this house? Did Lanning Construction build it?"

So, my suspicions *were* correct. She really hadn't seen it yet. I figured she hadn't, or she would have said something, and I honestly could not believe that Becca had never told her. But, then again, Becca lived on the complete other side of town. She might not know, either.

I climbed the steps and leaned against the rail on the other side of the porch, crossing my arms over my bare chest, still feeling the cool evening air brush along my exposed skin.

I narrowed my eyes. "How have you avoided this street for so long? Have you been taking the long way into work since moving back?"

She swallowed and averted her eyes down. My heart ached a little in my chest but I pushed it away.

"Yeah..." she whispered, then looked back up at me. Her eyes burned with such heavy truth that it rocked me to the core. The hurt was still there. It'd been six years since her parents passed but it still hurt her just as deeply. Which hurt *me*. "I know it's been awhile, but the pain is still there. Just because I'd grieved and moved on, that kind of pain doesn't leave you, ya know? I just didn't know if I could handle seeing some different house in the spot that my house used to be. I didn't want to put myself through that."

I looked away because I honestly couldn't stand seeing that much pain in her eyes.

"When did you do it?" she asked, voice low.

I swallowed down my need to look away and glanced back at her face. She was staring at me intently, eyes full of need.

"The summer after my senior year."

I paused, thinking back to when I'd *begged* my father to buy the lot and build her house again. He'd surprised me when he agreed. He said it was a nice house, and that the neighborhood just didn't seem right without it.

Thinking back, he must have known that I needed some

type of closure for that part of my life. As if somehow, building her house would help me heal.

It didn't necessarily help me heal, but it did bring new clarity to the situation. I was hurt when she left, and so confused. The little boy inside of me wanted to rebuild that house so that maybe... things would go back to a normal. But after we finished, a man emerged, and I realized that she was gone.

I also realized that nothing would ever be the same.

Her house had been rebuilt, but she never came back, and her parents...they would forever be gone. The family that once lived there was no longer.

It had been a turning point for me – and it was about that time I started to climb out of my cave, and I started to be the Dawson that everyone knew again.

Not fully, because I'd never truly felt like the Dawson I was when I'd had Ivy by my side, but I was better. Semi-healed.

I thought I'd closed all the gaps in my heart through Breanna but the truth was, I hadn't. They were sealed, barely, but now that I was standing here looking at Ivy, the girl I'd been chasing for most of my life, those gaps were laid wide open.

And I knew, deep down, the only person to close them all the way, as in pour-cement-over-them closed, was the girl standing only a few feet away from me with tears glistening in her eyes.

Her bottom lip trembled. "But why?"

My heart pounded in my chest because I'd never admitted the truth aloud. Never.

My voice was hoarse and strained. "Because I thought it would bring you back to me."

Ivy's mouth parted, just barely, but it did. I swore I heard her take a sharp inhale of breath, too.

I kept my stare on her as her eyes roamed around the porch floor. She was deep in thought, as if trying to come up with some response to what I'd said, but she came up empty-handed.

"Ivy?" I asked, walking the short distance over to her tiny body being held up by the pillar.

She slowly brought her face up to mine, her lip tucked between her teeth.

"I'm sorry," I said.

Her brow crinkled. "What? For what? You're saying sorry for building my exact house because you thought it would bring me back to you? How could you say sorry about something like that? It sounds like it's from some amazing, romantic movie – like, *The Notebook,* or something."

I chuckled but quickly replaced my half-smile with a realness that I felt all the way inside my chest.

"I'm so sorry about your parents." Her brow twitched and her mouth formed a straight line. "I never got to tell you that, and I'm sorry."

She swallowed, searching my face. "It's fine..."

I placed my hands on her shoulders, feeling the dampness of her shirt along my palms. "Nothing about that situation was fine. Not what happened to your parents, not the fact that you had to up and move within a day – without being able to say goodbye to your friends—and not the fact that when you came to see me when you needed me most, you saw me with another girl...and it wasn't fine for me to think that you just up and left, without even trying to come back. I'm just sorry for it all."

A lone tear fell down her face, slowing sliding over her

high cheekbone and all the way to the bottom of her delicate jaw. I took my hand off her shoulder and swiped it away with my finger.

She brought those green, tear-filled eyes up to look at me, and the only thing I wanted to do was take away the last six years of her pain, the last six years of her hurt. She was so strong, I knew that, but no one was *that* strong.

My heart stretched in my chest as the words poured out of my mouth. "I know you felt like you were alone in it all, but you weren't, Ivy." My eyes bounced back and forth between hers, hoping she could understand what I was trying to tell her—what my heart was trying to tell her. "I was right there with you, every step of the way. I never stopped hoping that you were okay, I never stopped missing you, and I never, ever, replaced you."

A sob escaped her throat and her shoulders fell as her head dropped. I pulled her body into mine and wrapped my arms around her slim torso. Her entire body relaxed into mine, her wet cheek resting along my bare chest, and I knew, right then, that I'd been chasing Ivy since the day she'd left.

I'd thought I'd been chasing away the memory of her, my feelings for her, but I wasn't. I was just chasing *her*.

And now she was back.

And I was in over my head.

Finally, after what seemed like an hour of me holding her on my porch, the sun had started to set and reality came crashing over our bodies.

She pulled back slightly and angled her head up to mine. Her eyes were puffy, but there was a ghost of a smile along her lips.

"I'm sorry I just cried for that long on your shoulder."

She laughed and turned her head away, hiding the little blush that spread along her cheeks.

I laughed, too. "Some things never change..."

She pulled back even further. "What! I've never cried on your shoulder before..." Then she looked away, the wheels turning behind her eyes. "Okay, fine. Maybe a couple of a times I cried on your shoulder, but I'm still embarrassed that I just did it again."

A chuckle escaped my mouth. "It's okay. I felt like it was kind of a breaking point for us, don't ya think?"

She smiled brightly this time. "Yeah, but...uh...should we talk about the fact that the last time we talked, you told me we couldn't be friends? Or..."

Ah, right. Back to reality.

Breanna.

I stood and walked over to the front door, opening it and looking back at Ivy, standing awkwardly, alone, still in the spot I left her. Her black bag that she'd packed earlier was still by her feet.

"I spent six years without you... I'm not spending another six in that same boat because my kind-of girlfriend wants to dictate my life."

Her eyes flicked to mine, as if she wasn't sure if I truly meant what I'd just said.

I meant every last word. Ivy and I were friends long before Breanna was even a thought in my head. I felt bad realizing that, but the truth was, I couldn't seem to care. I cared about Ivy too much to let her go. I was losing the battle between my heart and my head, and unfortunately, I was pretty sure that Breanna was going to be the casualty.

Ivy's face faltered as she bent down for her bag. "Okay... but seriously, what about your 'kind-of girlfriend,' whatever the hell that means? Because I'm going to go out on a limb and say that she's not going to be okay with me staying here, ever."

I sighed. "Like I said, let me worry about Breanna, okay?"

Ivy looked skeptical, but she walked toward me anyway.

The little voice in the back of my head told me what I was going to have to do.

I was going to make room in my life for Ivy, regardless of what Breanna said...and that, my friends, was the biggest issue of all.

TWENTY-ONE

Ivy

What am I doing in Dawson's house?

What am I doing in Dawson's bathroom, changing out of very uncomfortable, damp clothes and into my pajamas? Three weeks ago, I would have doubled over and laughed my ass off if someone told me this was where I would be right now.

My face shined brightly in the mirror above his sink. I tried not to notice the glimmer in my eye and the small smile creeping along my lips, but I couldn't deny it. The last time I'd talked to Dawson, he'd looked me right in the face and told me we couldn't be friends.

It felt like someone had carved my heart right out of my chest and then stomped all over it.

But now, here I was, a week later, standing in his bathroom, feeling my hidden fifteen-year-old self emerge like I'd traveled back to the past to relive my favorite night all over again.

I couldn't wrap my head around his reason for building

this house. I mean, honestly, people should just start calling me Allie. He could go by Noah and I could go by Allie. Except that I looked nothing like Allie from *The Notebook,* but Dawson...he could definitely give Ryan Gosling a run for his money, I'm telling ya.

Besides the fact that I felt like Dawson and I were like Noah and Allie (we totally weren't), I was totally, one hundred and fifty zillion percent ignoring the whole Breanna issue. Dawson said he would handle it, and I'd let him.

It still ate away at me, though.

Especially right now, as I spied the girly shampoo and conditioner in his shower.

Freaking, stupid, expensive, good-smelling shampoo, too.

I almost poured it down the drain, just to spite her, because just as much as she didn't like me, I didn't like her equally as much. But I lifted my hand off the shampoo bottle, mainly because I couldn't fathom wasting an $80 bottle of shampoo, even if it was Breanna's, and honestly, if I knew that someone had thoughts going around in her head about my boyfriend the way I did right now to Breanna's, I wouldn't like me, either.

Giving myself one last look in the mirror, running my fingers through my air-dried hair, I puffed my cheeks and then let all the air out.

Dawson was my friend.

That's it.

He wasn't single, even if he did say that Breanna was his "kind-of girlfriend" (like I'd missed *that* little bit of info; it was a like neon sign flashing in my brain), but I had to put my game face on and I had to behave myself. Not that it was totally hard to behave myself. It wasn't like I was going to sneak into his bed, wearing nothing but a lacy pair of under-wear (not that I hadn't imagined it), but I did have a hard time not staring at him for too long.

Any girl would openly stare at him because it was hard not to. He was a masterpiece; like his masculinity drew you in, inviting you to stare. It was his fault. Not mine! But I knew I needed to get myself together. I'd done it back in high school and I could do it now. Although, truth be told, I did *not* have *these* hormones in high school. I didn't even know what an orgasm was.

Now I knew. I knew what it felt like to ride on top of someone, scratching an itch that needed to be scratched in the best way possible. I now knew what it felt like to have a man push his body up against mine and make me forget the entire world existed. I was well aware of what it felt like to crave a man, and desiring Dawson was like craving a margarita when you were also being offered an endless bowl of salty chips and spicy salsa.

You just *had* to have it.

Just like I *had* to have him.

"Behave," I muttered, puffing my cheeks out once more before opening the door to the bathroom.

The house that Dawson had built with his father looked exactly the same on the front as it did when it was mine, but the inside was so much different, and I was so thankful. I highly doubted I could have kept it together if the inside of his house had been the same as mine when I was younger.

The walls were mainly bare and painted a soft, grey color. It was all very bachelor pad-ish with modular furni-ture and it held nothing at all "homey." I was almost surprised that it wasn't more girly inside – I had imagined that Breanna would have decorated at least a little, even if she *didn't* live here, but I'd guessed wrong.

I was relearning a lot about Dawson and one thing that I'd noticed, point-blank, was that he didn't let Breanna walk all over him. I got the vibe that he told her what was up and that was that.

Which I liked.

She had been so domineering in high school, and not just with boys. She had told her friends what to wear, how to do their hair, who to be friends with, etc. So, knowing that Dawson didn't let her dictate his life; that made me happy.

Too happy.

Rounding the corner to the stairs, my feet stopped moving. I wiggled my toes on the soft, nylon carpet and craned my head to the master bedroom, just off to the right.

I swallowed and held my breath, knowing very well that I shouldn't be eavesdropping like I was currently doing.

Dawson's voice was flat and irritable, lacking any of the happiness that I'd heard earlier. "I just don't know, Breanna. I just don't think it's fair to you or me."

My eyes widened. I really, really shouldn't be listening.

So I went ahead and listened some more, adjusting my body so I was closer to the cracked door.

"I know I said that I wasn't going to be her friend anymore, but how can you even ask me that? After everything?"

Huh? What does that mean? I wish he'd put it on speak-erphone. *Like, hello, I'm trying to listen over here!*

"Breanna, I just think—" he paused. *Why did he pause?*

"Fine, we can talk when you get back. I'll give you that much, but right now, I think you know how I'm feeling. I think we both knew in the beginning, even before all of this blew up that things probably wouldn't—"

Feeling what way? How has he been feeling?

My heart pounded in my chest, full of eagerness and wonder. Whatever he was talking about with her, wasn't good. I knew that much. His voice was, for lack of a better word, monotonous.

He sounded like our old U.S. History teacher in high school—the man was, like, 75 years old; I literally had no idea how he was still teaching us back then.

Mr... Mr. Peters was his name. He was no taller than I was right now (5'4"), and he wore the blandest looking cardigans over his checkered dress shirts every day. His glasses sat perched on the end of his nose and he always carried a briefcase with him.

Do you want to know what was in his briefcase? A crossword puzzle.

That was it.

That's all Mr. Peters carried in his overly expensive briefcase.

"What are you doing?"

"Aagh!" I yelled, jumping so high I could have beaten the Olympic high-jump standing record.

"Goodness!" I yelled again, placing my hand over my heart and feeling its rapid beat against my ribcage. "You scared me!"

Dawson's dark brow rose upward while his mouth twitched.

"What were you doing?"

He knows.

I stuttered. "Nothing. Just thinking about Mr. Peters."

"Thinking about Mr. Peters? The history teacher?"

"Yep!" My voice was in full-on cheerleader mode: high-pitched and ridiculously annoying.

Dawson laughed but eyed me with utter cynicism. I didn't give him a chance to ask me what I was doing again, and I technically hadn't lied to him. I truly was thinking about Mr. Peters!

Skipping downstairs, suddenly feeling super awkward that I was in a house that I wasn't really comfortable in, I paused at the entry way to the living room.

I turned around slowly, watching Dawson walk down the stairs as graceful as an angel, his breathing not labored at all, unlike mine.

"So, how much did you hear?"

I sucked in my bottom lip as he descended the final stair.

"Just bits and pieces. I didn't mean to pry." *Yes, I did.*

My ears quickly felt hot and I almost reached up to cover them, but instead I clasped my hands behind my back.

"You're lying," he grinned.

"How can you tell?" I pried.

He smiled wider, showing his heart-stopping smile. "Your nose does this little twitch thing when you lie. Well, it did back when you were younger and trying to hide something from me," he paused, flicking his eyes from my nose to my eyes. "And it just twitched."

My hand flew up and I grabbed my small nose.

"Whatever," I mumbled.

He laughed. "You're cute, Ivy."

My heart hiccupped and at the same time a rush of heat covered my body. Thank goodness I was semi-tan, or else he would have seen just how much those words had affected me.

Slowly lowering my hand, I asked, "I'm causing trouble with Breanna, aren't I?"

Dawson's mouth formed a straight line. He turned on his heel and walked towards the kitchen, avoiding my question.

I followed after him, my bare feet smacking against his weathered-wood floor.

He must have sensed me behind him, as he glanced at me out of the corner of his eye while bending down and looking in the fridge. I couldn't help but let my eyes travel over his butt.

Dark grey sweatpants hung loosely from his hips, just below his white t-shirt, and even though they weren't fitting him tightly like the jeans from earlier, his butt looked *just* as good. If not better.

"Things with Breanna aren't... good."

I walked over to the island and rested my forearms along its marble top.

"And I'm making them worse," I stated.

He shut the fridge and walked over to the island, placing his palms flat along the top. I finally brought my eyes up to his and waited.

"You're making them *real*," he answered, driving his dreamy blue eyes into mine.

What the hell does that mean?!

"Dawson," I started, backing away from the island. "Maybe I should just go... I don't want to make things worse for you two, even if I don't think she's right for you."

My heart climbed up to my mouth. *Why. Did. I. Just. Say. That.*

"You're not going anywhere, and you don't think she's right for me?" he asked, perplexed, a smirk growing on his face.

I laughed. "Of course not, and I bet everyone agrees with me."

He turned away for a second, showcasing his jaw that looked as if it had been chiseled from stone. I knew what he was thinking; he was probably going through all the times someone had said the same thing that I just did.

She wasn't right for him. She didn't make him happy; anyone could see that.

I've barely seen them together, but the one time that I had, he had literally looked pained and she... well, she'd looked like she was going to kill me.

"Then who is?" he asked, turning his chiseled face back to me.

I gulped.

I felt flutters deep within my stomach, and looking directly into the beautiful, dark-blue hues of his eyes honestly stole any coherent thought out of my head. His eyes were heated, pupils dilating...like they were begging me to say the right words.

And then, I heard a faint male voice say "Hello?" from my pocket. I opted to ignore it, choosing to stare into Dawson's eyes instead.

They had me caught up in thinking all the wrong things.

I'm right for you.

But I wasn't.

Or was I?

"Is your pocket talking to you?" he inquired, his gaze never leaving mine.

"Huh?"

His cheeks lifted and then he finally released my stare. I let out a held breath that I wasn't even aware I'd been holding.

If I could get that engrossed in Dawson from just a lengthy stare, I couldn't even imagine what else could turn my world upside down and make me forget to breathe.

"Your phone. You pocket dialed someone, Ivy." Then he chuckled and embarrassment hit me head on.

My hand fumbled with my phone, pulling it out of my pocket. I was still flustered from the uncanny, intense moment with Dawson that it didn't even register that I'd accidently called someone. The second I heard his voice, it was like getting my hair stuck in a fan, jerking my head so hard I wanted to cry out.

"Wow, she finally calls me back..." Eric's voice was smooth, and it used to be the one voice I enjoyed hearing but right now, staring at Dawson's tall and broad frame as he surveyed the contents of his pantry, I loathed it.

"Oh, I didn't mean to call you. Don't get too excited, Eric."

Dawson's head snapped to mine, but I averted my eyes, trying to focus on Eric's voice.

I heard a muffling on the other line. "Ouch."

Yeah, it was kind of mean, but so was breaking up with me just because I wanted to move back home.

"Sorry," I said, both of us well aware that I wasn't truly sorry.

"I've been trying to reach you for a long time, Ivy. Did you get the flowers I sent to your work? How is that going? Do you like it?"

I snapped. "I got the flowers, but I didn't read your note."

Not a total lie. I didn't really read the note—Mia did.

"Ivy, I think we should meet up and talk. I made a hasty decision and took my fear of losing you and turned it into anger. I was stupid."

Dawson glared at my phone and I was pretty sure he cursed under his breath.

I turned my back to him, taking the time to figure out

what to say to Eric. Meeting up with him wasn't the worst idea he'd ever had. It would probably be nice to get some closure, but was it really worth it? Because I was pretty sure he didn't want closure.

"I don't know, Eric."

All of a sudden, I heard something strange from behind me. I glanced back and saw Dawson standing only a few feet away, with a devilish smile forming on his mouth. My brows crinkled as I listened to Eric ramble on about why it was a good idea for us to get together.

Dawson's smile grew bigger, his straight, white teeth shining brightly between his lips as he pressed a button on his phone. All of a sudden, pornographic noises started to play in the background. My mouth gaped and Dawson laughed silently.

Moans and screams from a woman were playing loudly, so loudly that Eric had stopped talking on the other end of the phone.

If I hadn't been enjoying watching Dawson laugh silently, his face turning red with a smile reaching all the way to his ears, then I'm sure I would have felt embarrassed.

"What the hell is that?!" Eric bristled through the phone which only made a laugh bubble up out of my mouth.

Dawson's eyes glittered. "Hurry back, Ivy! We miss you..." he said in a voice dripping with sex.

"Ivy?! What the hell?" Eric yelled again and then I hit end on my phone.

Dawson's and my laughter echoed throughout the kitchen. I had to bend forward, still clutching my phone in one hand, and placed it over my stomach from the dull ache left behind from the ridiculous amount of amusement.

"You should have heard him!" I said, through my giggles.

Dawson's face was red with watering eyes.

"I wasn't sure if you'd be pissed or not, but I couldn't resist. You looked leery when you were talking to him and once I heard that it was your dumb-as-fuck ex, I couldn't stop myself."

I laughed again. "Hilarious. He sounded *so* confused!"

"I can't even imagine the amount of jealousy he was feeling..." Dawson's voice trailed, which only perplexed me further.

Suddenly, my phone started to vibrate again.

Eric's name flashed on the screen and I was torn: Should I answer it? Or should I let it go to voicemail and let *him* feel abandoned for a while? I wasn't really a mean-natured person so I veered toward answering but then again, he shouldn't have broken up with me in such a "hasty" way, so... I decided I'd let him wonder.

I hit ignore on the phone and peeked back up at Dawson. A barely-there smile crept onto his face.

"So... tacos and movies?" he asked, and my heart all but exploded.

"Just like old times," I whispered, smiling from ear to ear.

"Lead the way, *Ivy-cakes,*" he said through a muffled laugh.

A gasp escaped my mouth. I reached up and smacked him in the arm. "Shut up!"

Walking out the door to his house, grabbing our shoes and still laughing, he said, "Seriously? How could you let him call you that! Ivy-cakes? I almost died when I heard Mia say that earlier. Fucking Ivy-cakes."

"Says the guy who's dating Breanna..." I rolled my eyes and he nudged me back.

A playfulness fell over the both of us as smiles almost engraved themselves onto our faces. I couldn't help but notice just much I relished this easy moment with him.

I also couldn't help but notice just how happy I was. Even if every ounce of happiness I'd felt in the last six years were all smooshed together, it still wouldn't even come close to how I felt right now. Like every single time I'd thought I was happy, I hadn't really been.

But right now, I *was* truly happy...and I wasn't sure if that was going to bite me in the ass or not.

TWENTY-TWO

Dawson

I should be given an award for last night.

A medal? A trophy? A marking of some sort.

I kept my hands off Ivy, all night long, with her sitting beside me on my couch. Her little feet, curled up underneath her body, a cotton blanket covering her lower half. She was so adorable and beautiful, even more so when she'd laugh at the movie we'd picked out.

She wanted *Charlie's Angels*; I told her no.

I couldn't believe that she was *still* obsessed with that movie, and she couldn't believe that I hadn't watched it once since she left.

I didn't tell her the actual reason as to why I hadn't watched it. It made me angry and a little envious for that last moment with her. The night her parents died was the last time I watched it (well, part of it...the other part I'd spent staring at her sleeping on my bed and then ended the night with a life-shattering kiss).

We spent most of last night talking and laughing at

older movies, and it was honestly one of the best nights of my life. Which sounds so fucking lame, considering all we did was sit in my living room, not touching, staring at a TV screen, but that's how it'd always been with her.

Back when we were teenagers, we'd drive around in my Camaro for hours, doing nothing but listening to music and slurping on milkshakes, and it was honestly more fun than anything else I could have been doing. Time spent with Ivy had always been fulfilling.

It didn't matter what we were doing. I could sit on my couch with her, every single night, for the rest of my life and be happy with it.

I'd probably have the biggest case of blue balls in the world, but I would rather sit with her, not touching, than be with someone else, buried in between their legs.

Which brings me to my next rant: Breanna.

The realization came over me quick and hard after the whole crushing-a-crying-Ivy-to-my-chest moment. I had to break up with Breanna and it wasn't fully *because* of Ivy. I mean, there was definitely something going on with us (I hoped, or else I was reading all her signals wrong) but I wasn't necessarily on the end game with Breanna because I wanted to replace her as quick as possible with Ivy.

Ivy had just made things a little clearer to me.

Breanna and I weren't in love. Breanna's and my relationship was based around sex and a poor attempt at being in a committed relationship.

We didn't go on dates, we didn't laugh for endless hours on my couch while watching a movie. We barely even cuddled.

I didn't love her and I wouldn't love her, not in the way that I should, and how could I stay with her if I didn't love her?

I was using Breanna to protect myself from ever getting hurt because I knew, very well, that Breanna could never hurt me.

She could break up with me, right now, and I'd say, "Okay."

I just wasn't in love with her, and she knew that. She'd have to be blind not to know that. *Did she love me?* I doubted it. I think she just liked the fact that she'd scored me, finally, after years of trying.

I tried to end it with her last night, while on the phone. I told her what had happened with Ivy and although I'd assumed she'd blow a fucking gasket, she didn't. She stayed eerily calm on the other line and shut me up when I was close to saying, "I think we should part ways."

She said I owed it to her to talk to her, face to face, if I wanted to "discuss our relationship," and she was right. I did owe it to her. I just needed to learn how to keep a cap on my attraction to Ivy until then.

Like right now, sitting on the end of the couch, with Ivy's toes brushing along my thigh, while I stuffed my face with a gigantic bowl of cereal. She was mind-blowingly sexy even while asleep. Her touch was innocent, but it sent some interesting signals to my dick.

I offered her my bed last night and she very abruptly shot up on the couch and yelled, "Absolutely not!"

I was taken aback, and asked her why the hell not.

Her voice was slightly wobbly. "I'm not sleeping in a bed that you fuck Breanna on: no, thank you."

I could sense the jealousy on Ivy, even if she didn't openly say anything. Her nose turned up, scrunching just a little, and her entire body tensed.

It caused such a strong sensation to go through me that I had to adjust myself before getting up off the couch to refill our popcorn bowl. The thought of Ivy being envious of me having sex with someone else just fueled my fantasies of getting her underneath me.

Sex with Ivy would be different.

Sex with Ivy wouldn't just be sex; I knew that just by staring at her calm, sleeping face this morning.

Yeah, I needed to end it with Breanna. As soon as fucking possible...before I did something I regretted.

I chomped down on my Cap'n Crunch louder than before, no doubt trying my hardest to wake up the angel curled up with a grey blanket tossed all around her body.

Her legs were peeking out from below the blanket, her leggings ridden up further than I'm sure she'd like. Tanned calves stuck out underneath the black, spandex-like fabric and although I tried, really, really, really fucking hard not to look, her ass looked like the most perfect, round peach.

I chomped even harder on my cereal then, turning my gaze away from her and clicking on the TV.

I sensed her stirring before I glanced over, silver spoon still sticking in my mouth.

Ivy shot up quickly, brown hair spilling out from her ponytail, and grabbed the blanket to wrap around her body. She'd thrown her jacket off sometime in the night, I assumed, so the only thing she had on were her black leggings and a skimpy tank top.

A skimpy tank top *without* a bra.

Small buds were poking through the almost see-through, white fabric and I all but grunted aloud to keep myself from bursting.

I could literally feel my dick straining against my tight boxer briefs.

Focus on the Cap'n Crunch. Focus on the Cap'n Crunch.

My ears flamed and I clenched my eyes shut when I felt

the shift of the couch and heard her moan, while stretching her arms above her head.

"Holy crap!" she shouted, turning her gaze to my lap.

At first, I thought she might have seen my salute to the devil, but I instantly relaxed when I saw that she was staring at the giant bowl in my hand, full of cereal.

I don't care what type of man you are, cereal is the *best* meal.

"What?" I asked, perplexed. "Do you want some?"

"That's huge!!" she said, pulling the blanket tighter around her body.

A sliver of a smile formed on my face as I tipped my eyes down to her. "That's what she said."

Ivy rolled her eyes as a grin stretched along her cheeks.

"Seriously, though. How can you eat all of that?!"

I smiled again. "That's what—"

Ivy's cheeks turned an adorable shade of pink. "Stop it, Dawson!" Then she laughed.

I laughed, too, shoving more cereal in my mouth.

"How long have you been sitting there staring at me while munching on cereal?"

I shrugged. *Not long enough.*

"Long enough for me to attest that you don't snore."

Ivy snorted. "You do."

I pulled back, angling my torso towards her.

She rolled her eyes again. "Well, you used to."

Chuckling, I put my (mixing) bowl up to my mouth and gulped the leftover milk from my cereal. I slowly lowered it, wiping my mouth on the back of my hand, and flashed her a smile.

"I don't snore anymore."

She snickered. "That you know of."

Changing the subject, I got up from the couch (now

thankful that my Viagra lookalike erection had finally cowed) and jumped up and down on the balls of my feet a few times. "So, what's the plan for today?"

Ivy scanned her eyes down my naked torso, all the way down to my bare feet poking out from under my Nike sweats. She gulped and, on the inside, I smiled naughtily...until that little voice in the back of my mind whispered, *Breanna.*

Right. *Behave, if only for a few more days, Dawson. You can do it.*

I made a mental note to take an ice cold shower before spending any more alone time with Ivy – that would surely take the edge off, right?

When was the last time I'd had sex?

Oh, that's right. The night Ivy blew into town and rocked me from the inside out.

Her voice shook me straight. "I'm not sure. I don't work on Saturdays and Becca hasn't tried to drag me out, yet, so I guess I'm free."

The wheels in my head only spun for about three seconds before I knew what we were going to be doing today.

"Wanna take a drive?..."

Ivy's face brightened. "Like old times?"

I nodded slowly, clasping my hands together to steeple them. "And do I have a surprise for you..."

Ivy hopped up off the couch, adjusting her black leggings so they were straight on her body. My eyes drove into her chest, only for a second and out of simple reaction, but she noticed.

I heard a small breath before I snapped my eyes back up to her face. Desire filled her green irises and I knew instantly that I hadn't imagined all the signals pouring off her body.

She was definitely into me, too.

Ivy quickly went into action, bending down and grabbing her light grey, cotton jacket off the floor, slipping her arms inside the sleeves gingerly. Once she had her jacket zipped up, she cleared her throat, bringing her attention back up to mine.

Reality must have hit her because the desire I had seen in her dilated pupils and wild, feral stare, was no longer there.

"What surprise?" she asked, sucking in her cheeks slightly.

I smiled, ignoring the lust swimming around us. "Follow me..."

Ivy's footsteps were light against my wooden floors as she trailed behind me, all the way to the door right off the kitchen, leading into the garage.

Once I opened the door and flipped the switch, Ivy squealed!

She quickly ran past me and into the garage. Her hand trailed over the top of my old Camaro, the one that I *still* had.

"Oh my GOD!!! Red Rocket?! You still have her?!" she shouted, flipping around to stare at me.

I grinned, leaning against the door jam.

"Like I could get rid of my first love? Are you kidding me?"

She smiled again, flipping her tiny body around to stare at the red Camaro again. The one she had spent so many days inside, riding in the passenger seat until dusk overcame the town.

"We're TOTALLY going cruising today!" Ivy turned around and smiled so cheerfully that I almost fainted.

I hadn't seen her smile like that for so long that it almost didn't seem real.

And *I* was the one who put it there.

That was all on me.

"Well, go get ready, sleepyhead." I said, inching my brow up.

She squealed again and started to run past me, right through the threshold, and typical Ivy, her jacket pocket got caught on the doorknob, causing her body to swing around and hit the back of the door in a loud whoosh.

She grunted as I moved my hands around and grabbed onto her body. She was all tangled up in the door, breathless and wide-eyed. I stared down at her, my hands covering her small biceps.

"You are the clumsiest person I have never known, Ivy." *And it's damn cute.*

She let out a held breath, staring up into my eyes. "I know."

Then it was like another realization hit her because she quickly diverted her eyes to my kitchen floor. I slowly released her arms as I felt the sudden impact of awkwardness floating around us.

Ivy got herself untangled from the door, also noticing the sudden shift in the air. Then she peeked up and looked at me through her long lashes. "When does Breanna come back from her trip?"

"Tomorrow sometime."

Ivy locked her eyes onto my face and then slowly nodded her head, relief passing across her features.

Was she also counting down the days until I officially ended it with Breanna? So that way we didn't have to deny the attraction and happiness we both felt when we were around one another?

I could only hope.

"I'll be ready in a few," she whispered, backing away from me.

I stood at the door, watching her walk through the archway and to the bottom of the stairs.

I was almost angry that I wanted to be a good person and break up with Breanna face to face, because I felt like I was missing out on something in this moment. As if I was missing out on feeling something *more* with Ivy. Something that I'd been chasing all my life. Breanna was like this giant roadblock, standing in my way.

My head whipped upwards when Ivy yelled from the stairs, "We're making a pitstop at Ronnie's! It's not a real cruise if we don't have our milkshakes!"

And just like that, I was back to chuckling, and all thoughts of Breanna disappeared.

Which was so fucking dangerous.

Because the bottom line was that I was still in a relationship. Even if only for another day.

TWENTY-THREE

Ivy

He has a girlfriend. He has a girlfriend. He has a girlfriend.

I'd told myself that so many times today, I'd lost count.

I'd say it had to be somewhere in the hundreds, but I lost count after fifty-seven.

I even had Becca text me occasionally throughout the day to remind me that Dawson had a girlfriend, she was NO help at all.

These were her texts:

Dawson has been in love with you for so long, go for it.

Breanna is evil, and even though I don't think anyone should be cheated on, she is E V I L.

Then, moments later:

Should I remind you about the time she took all your clothes freshman year during gym? You

had to wear a size XL smelly old gym shirt that Mr. Birks gave you. NOT OKAY. EVIL.

I laughed out loud on that one, remembering the awful day and how Dawson had pulled me aside to ask me why the heck I was wearing such a large shirt.

My head fell, just as my shoulders did. I was completely defeated and wanted to cry. Breanna always hated me. She always tried to make my life a living hell. I truly had no idea why, that just how it was back then.

Once I told Dawson what had happened, he skipped his second period class (yes, I had gym first period – how rude of the school to make me preform physical activity so early in the morning... Oh, and not to mention having gym-hair all day long) and he made Emmett drive him to my house to grab me a shirt and pants.

As soon as they arrived back at school and snuck back in, he pulled me aside just as I was walking to English. He smirked as he handed me my favorite blue polo and a pair of jeans.

I was completely shocked to the point that I couldn't form words.

Neither could Breanna when she saw me walking into English wearing normal clothes.

She didn't admit to taking mine in gym, but I knew she did it. The redness of her ears and angry lines around her eyes told me so. It was definitely one of my better memories of high school...all because of Dawson.

I hurriedly texted Becca back, telling her that she was absolutely no help, and then moved onto my sister's text:

How was it staying with your old pal?

I replied, **Fine.**

Dawson glanced over at me and smiled, causing my heart to flutter. Yeah, my "fine" was a big, ol' lie.

Mia's text made my fingers still on my phone.

Have you told him that you're still crushing on him, even six years later?

Am I that obvious? My God.

I texted her back: **I have no clue what you're talking about.** And then I shoved my phone back in my bag and leaned against the cool, leather seat of Dawson's '99 Camaro.

"UGHHHHH. No!" I yelled, jamming my fingers onto the dash.

"What?" Dawson yelled back, acting appalled.

I smirked. "Dawson, we are not listening to this crap. I didn't listen to it back then, and I won't listen to it now."

What was blaring through the speakers of the Camaro was what I'd refer to as murdering music. All it was, was a bunch of guys screaming (literally, screaming) into their mics. They were screaming so loud, I couldn't even understand the lyrics.

"I get that you like this screaming crap, but I don't. Gimmie," I said, putting my hand out towards him and twinkling my fingers.

Dawson shook his head, a smile stretching along his face. "Nooooope."

I growled and then reached for his phone anyway. It was lying on his lap with an aux cord hanging out from the bottom. The second my hand landed on Dawson's jeans, his entire body went rigid.

I noticed the shift, still reaching for his phone, and then almost died.

My hand was resting right... on... his... dick.

Like, literally, I could feel his dick through his jeans.

My first thought, even before lifting my hand was, *Is it really that big?!*

Then, mortified, face blazing with heat, I snatched the phone and pulled it into my lap.

I expected Dawson to joke around and say something inappropriate because he'd been spewing those stupid, "That's what she said," jokes all day, even first thing this morning, but he said nothing.

Instead, he gripped his gear shift so hard that I was certain it would break off. His jaw muscles worked back and forth and then I felt pleasure ball up inside of my belly when I glanced up and saw his full, lower lip tugged in between his bright teeth.

He. Was. So. Hot.

I coughed, trying to hide the fact that I was so turned on that if he were to just stare at me, I'd probably have an orgasm.

I was almost wishing that Eric and I were on better terms so he could release some of this insane pressure I was suddenly feeling, but I knew now, after having my hand accidently rest on Dawson's lower region and then almost coming apart from the mere sight of his lip tugged in his mouth, Eric would no longer suffice in my sex game.

Would anyone?

My God, I was never going to be able to have sex with anyone ever again without imagining Dawson above me, ramming himself inside me and sucking in his bottom lip as I tightened around him.

To watch someone like him, come apart because of *me*...that would be equivalent to heaven. Dawson was irresistible.

He was irresistible when he was sixteen, but now? Now

he was so damn tempting that I would choose having him over my last breath.

Having Dawson would probably make going to Hell worth it.

Finally, evening my breath and calming my raging hormones down, I tried opening his phone to pick a different song.

I huffed, snapping my head over to his. "Password protected. Really? Why?"

Dawson swallowed, moving that strong and prominent Adam's apple up and down. *Whew.*

"One word: Breanna."

I thought for a moment. *Why was he with her again?*

"Well, what's the password?" I asked, ignoring my desire to prod him about Breanna. They were breaking up soon, I thought, so it didn't matter if I told him once again that she was *all* wrong for him.

Dawson looked out his side window for a second, then brought his eyes back to the road. His shoulders were pulled back and his eyes blinked rapidly.

Why was he nervous? It wasn't like I was going to dig through his texts and pictures. I rolled my eyes, ready to tell him just that, but he stopped me.

"Zero."

I peered at him out of the corner of my eye, but pressed the number zero on the keypad.

"Okay..." I said.

"Four." I pressed that button and then looked over at him. He took his fingers and drummed them along the peeling, leather steering wheel. "Two. Eight. Nine. Two."

I quickly pressed the remaining numbers onto the key pad and then sucked in a large breath.

I repeated the numbers in my head, like they were on a loop.

Zero. Four. Two. Eight. Nine. Two.

I slowly turned my head, driving my eyes right into the side of his head.

Then I repeated the numbers again: *zero, four, two, eight, nine, two*.

"How long has your password been that exact set of numbers?" I asked, voice barely above a whisper.

"It's my password for everything. But for that phone? Since I got it."

My heart strummed in my chest like a lone string being played on a guitar. His password was my birthday.

"I told you I never replaced you, Ivy. I never stopped thinking about you and I never stopped hoping you'd come home."

Dawson turned his head to me, stopped at a stop sign on an old dirt road right on the outskirts of our little, country town. We stared into each other's eyes for far too long. I had no idea what he was thinking, but the only thing I was thinking was how it felt like no time had passed between us at all.

Six years was a long time, but suddenly, just looking into Dawson's eyes, knowing he still cared about me just as much as he did when we were teenagers, made our time apart seem like *nothing*.

We were wrong that night, so long ago.

Nothing had changed between us.

I still loved him just as much, if not more, and I was pretty sure he felt the same.

He was still Dawson, just an older, *way* hotter version, still with a huge heart that may or may not still have my name written all over it.

TWENTY-FOUR

Dawson

"I cannot believe you talked me into this!" Ivy squealed, jumping out of my Camaro and slamming the door shut.

I laughed. "I can be very convincing." I shot her my best grin and she just couldn't help but smile, even if she was irritated with me.

"I don't doubt that for even a second."

Cicadas hummed in the background, no doubt lying helplessly in the hollows of all the tress that were surrounding us. The scent of crisp, autumn leaves and cow manure wafted around us with help from the gusty breeze. An occasional "moo" from a cow sounded in the distance, which was basically the soundtrack to our little town.

"I wonder if kids still come up here to make out?" Ivy asked, gazing out toward the open field of tall grass.

"Oh, I'm almost positive. I think I heard Max saying something about him having to come up here a week or two ago to scare them off."

Ivy's sweet laughter filled the air. "I'm gonna ask Bec.

I'm sure she'll know all about it. Those two seem to hate each other but I have a hunch that something else is going on."

My forehead furrowed as I thought back to the last time I saw them together. There was definitely something going on with them, and I was *almost* positive I knew what it was. I didn't say anything to Ivy, though, I was sure Becca would fill her in... eventually.

I leaned against the side of my Camaro, crossing my arms over my chest, and watched as Ivy climbed on top of the hood. Her tight jeaned legs dangled off the bottom as she kicked her feet back and forth. She brushed back a curtain of thick hair over her shoulder and gazed up at the stars. Her jaw was so delicate looking, and I couldn't help but let my eyes travel down the slope of her neck, all the way to the curves of her breasts.

The way she looked underneath the glow of the moon and stars made her appear like she was truly an angel. It honestly made it hard to breathe.

She was so flawlessly beautiful, it hurt.

Ivy kept her gaze upward as her voice broke through the quiet sounds of night. "I had fun today."

I genuinely smiled. "I did, too. It's nice going down memory lane, isn't it?"

She chuckled. "It's been a long time since I've been down memory lane." Then she paused and I walked a little closer to her. I could smell her shampoo as she shook out her hair, letting it dangle behind her back. "I tried to stay away from anything that reminded me of what *was*."

Me too.

"Well, what was, can now be," I quipped, breaking my gaze from her features.

"Dawson," she started, her voice no higher than a whisper in the wind.

I met her sparkling green eyes. "Yeah?"

A soft breath escaped her mouth. "Why have you settled?"

I crinkled my brow. "What do you mean?"

Ivy's voice was still quiet, like the pages flipping between a book. "I mean, why are you settling with Breanna? Or why *have* you settled with her? It's evident that she doesn't make you happy…"

I gulped, feeling nerves close in on me. I knew the truth was about to fall off my lips. I could taste the bitterness of it. "Because she was safe."

Nothing in her expression changed. Not even a flicker of her eyes.

I kept my sight locked onto her, feeling my heart spill the dark truth. "I knew that if things went south with us, it wouldn't hurt." My chest rose up and down quickly, like I was gasping for air. "I know you don't want to hear this, again, but when you left…" I clenched my eyes, wondering if I should continue on.

Then I heard her scooting closer to me, jeans rubbing along the hood of my Camaro. When I opened my eyes again, Ivy was only a few inches away, staring up at me with doe-like eyes. Like she was calling out to me, asking me to tell her what we both knew I wanted to say.

"When you left, you took something with you. I was empty. As if you took part of my soul…" I looked away, just for a second to gather myself. "I know how crazy that sounds. I mean, we were so young and we were the best of friends, so to say you were my soulmate…that sounds ludicrous, but the night of the fire and then every day after, I literally felt like part of my soul was missing." I shrugged. "I knew that Breanna could never take away something like that from me, so I just... I guess you said it best, I settled."

Ivy's eyes were quickly filling with tears and all I wanted to do was backtrack and take away everything I'd just said. I didn't tell her the truth to make her upset. What happened with us was inevitable. Some things that happen in life are simply out of our control. They happen for a reason. No one could have guessed that Ivy's parents would have died in a house fire, all caused by a stupid faulty wire, and no one would have guessed what would happen after.

Ivy and Mia moving away.

Me ending up with Breanna.

Ivy coming back.

Her and I both still feeling the same strong pull we had over one another, the way our bodies called out to each other...the most intense attraction that I'd ever felt in my entire life.

My heart skipping a beat when I saw her standing in my father's office after six years.

The way my heart thrummed in my chest when she was near.

"Ivy," I whispered, inching my body in between her legs. She widened them to let me stand between. I peered down into her eyes, searching for any indication that this was right. That she was feeling what I was feeling. "What do you want?"

She didn't dare move her eyes from mine.

"I want a lot of things, Dawson, but the thing is, you don't always get what you want."

Then her eyes moved down to my mouth and I knew right then that she was feeling what I felt.

Everything.

I answered quickly, "I do."

Then I pressed my lips onto hers.

The entire world ceased to exist.

The only thing I saw was *her*. The only thing I felt was *her*. The only thing I breathed was *her*.

Ivy's soft lips parted immediately, letting me take a hold on her. My hands snaked around her face, cupping her cheeks in my hands at the same time she pressed her middle up against my jeans. Her legs wrapped around my lower half, and I swear, I felt like I'd died and gone to heaven.

Kissing Ivy was everything I'd ever imagined and more. I never wanted to let go. I never wanted to know what it would be like to kiss another woman for the rest of my life.

This was what we were meant to do. We were made for each other. I could feel it all the way to my bones.

My tongue slipped in Ivy's warm mouth, enticing a soft moan from her, which only intensified my need to pick her up and carry her over to the open field to claim her. Ivy rounded her hips along my dick and my hands gripped her ass so hard, I was likely to leave marks.

I didn't care. I needed her to know how much I needed this.

How much I needed her.

Ivy's legs wound tighter around my hips as I carried her a few feet over to the back of my Camaro. Ours tongues continued to swirl together and Ivy's hands found their way to my hair, rustling the strands between her fingers.

"Ivy," I breathed, almost unable to form words. "I've waited my entire life for this."

Then she gasped and quickly bucked her body off of mine. Her legs flailed around my hips to the point that I had to release her.

When I looked down, all I saw on her face was mortification.

Her eyes were widened and her cheeks were flushed, then her hand came up and covered her mouth. Tears welled in her eyes and I had no idea what had just happened. It was like getting kicked in the balls.

"Oh my God," she muttered, slowly backing away from me.

I inched toward her, feeling my heart come to a screeching halt in my chest.

"Dawson, you have a girlfriend!"

Then reality came crashing along my shoulders. I brought my hands up to my head, driving my fingers into my skull.

What the fuck just happened?

I was so caught up in my need for Ivy that I forgot about the one thing keeping me from her the last few weeks.

Breanna.

I was still dating her, whether or not I'd made my mind up about breaking up with her. I was a cheater.

And that meant Ivy was a cheatee.

"Ivy," I started, bringing my hands down. She was staring at me with a blank expression on her face, void of all the emotions I saw earlier. "I'm so sorry."

She looked like I'd just run over her dog. Her mouth formed a small frown, and she instantly pulled into herself.

"Can you take me home?" she asked, voice near breaking.

"Ivy," I said again, her tear-filled eyes snapping up to mine.

"I can't even blame Breanna for hating me."

My heart dropped. Fucking great. Not only did I just cheat on Breanna, hurting her, but now Ivy was fucking hurt, too.

I had to fix this.

"This was my fault. Just..." I wanted to punch something. Or break something. I wanted to do anything but look into the face of the one girl who had my heart, knowing that she was now looking down on herself because of something I had done. "Just don't say anything, okay?"

Ivy's face was ambivalent. "Don't worry, I won't tell her..."

"No!" I shouted, clenching my fist, feeling my stomach form a pit. "That's not what I meant. I'm just trying to protect you. If Breanna found out, she'd... I don't know what she'd do but she's never been a nice person. You know this."

Ivy's eyebrow rose. "It seems like you're trying to protect yourself, Dawson. Don't worry..." she repeated, walking to the passenger side of my car. "I won't make a peep."

Anger flashed within. I let out a groan as I rounded the back of my Camaro. I stood only a couple inches away from her. "You know very well that's not what I meant. Just stop for a second."

"I want you to take me home." Another kick to the balls.

"Ivy," I protested. "I'm sorry, I shouldn't have kissed you until I was single."

Ivy's lip trembled as she lowered her eyes down to the ground. She dropped her head so low I could barely hear her. "Can you just take me home, please?"

"I'm sorry," I said, again. I wanted to crush her body onto mine, to make her feel better and to express how sorry I was that after six years of being apart, I choose to kiss her while I was still technically with someone else.

I was a fucking shit boyfriend and an even shittier friend.

"Just take me to my car, please. I... I just want to be alone."

I clenched my jaw together to keep myself from doing anything else that would get me in trouble or make her feel worse. I knew she was feeling awful. The one thing I knew for certain about Ivy, was that she *hated* hurting other people and she *hated* doing wrong.

She was an epic rule-follower as a teen and looking at her almost distraught face now, I knew she still was.

"Okay," I said, letting out a loud breath.

We didn't say a word the entire drive back into town. When I pulled up to my house, Ivy opened the passenger door and walked right through the door and into the kitchen. I was following closely behind her, but I stopped near the front door when I heard her upstairs gathering her stuff out of my bathroom and fumbling with her black bag full of clothes.

When she descended down the stairs, I stopped her from leaving. "You can just stay here; I'll stay with Emmett. Your house is still a mess."

She shook out her long locks. "I'll stay with Becca."

I protested. "Ivy, stop."

She finally brought her head up to mine. "Dawson, I'm not staying here only to wake up to Breanna in the morning. She'll see the truth all over my face."

My shoulders pulled back. "Breanna isn't coming here in the morning, Ivy."

She shot back, irritable voice and all. "Well I assume she'll stop by at some point to see her *boyfriend* that she hasn't seen all weekend and I'm not going to be here for the freaking reunion."

I blew out a heavy sigh. "You know that I'm breaking up

with her, right? Like, I didn't just kiss you for the fun of it tonight. I meant that kiss in every way possible."

Her face twitched, as if a wall just fell down right in front of our faces. "Just..." she closed her eyes, evening her breath. "Just... when you're done figuring shit out with her, then come talk to me, but for now...I'm going to Becca's."

Then she stormed past me and out the front door.

Once she got to her car, she stopped and looked at me standing in the doorway, and then to the structure of the house, a look of uncertainty on her face.

Then she slammed her car door shut and peeled down the road, tires spinning in her wake.

I knew one thing for certain – Breanna and I, we were over, and Ivy and I, we were just getting started.

I hope.

TWENTY-FIVE

Ivy

"Okay, start over."

I glared at Becca, who was lying on her stomach, sporting a freaking adult onesie with flying pigs on it.

"Which part?" I asked, annoyed.

Becca's hazel eyes lowered. "The kiss..."

I groaned, slapping my hand over my eyes. "This is serious, Becca! Dawson basically got me pregnant with a kiss and, uh, can we talk about the fact that HE ISN'T SINGLE!!"

"Okay," she sat up, crossing her pink, fuzzy, flying-pig legs underneath her. "He's basically single. So, stop. I'm almost positive that Breanna has cheated on him in the past, so whatever."

My heart hammered in my ears. *How dare she cheat on him!*

I felt sick. Dawson cheated on his girlfriend with me. He told me it wasn't my fault, that he shouldn't have kissed me (talk about a big blow to my ego), but it *was* my fault because I didn't stop him right away.

I couldn't. His mouth on mine was like silencing every sound on earth. His breath along mine, it sent goosebumps over every single inch of my body. All I wanted was more.

I would never get my fill of Dawson. Never.

But still, I knew it was wrong. I also knew that every single thought I'd had of him was wrong, as was crossing all those friends-to-lovers lines. I knew that being alone with him at the cow pasture was wrong because if I were Breanna, I wouldn't be okay with how we were acting toward one another.

Longing stares, playful nudges, touching one each other when we shouldn't have been. It was wrong from the beginning.

I never should have stayed at his house and I never should have traveled down memory lane with him.

Even if it did feel so incredibly right.

The truth was, I never saw Dawson as my friend for life. I saw him as so much more.

Even when we were teens and still in that awkward friend-zone place, I saw him as so, so much more.

"Just relax, Ivy," Becca said, drawing me out of my incessant thoughts.

"I feel bad, though," I whispered, lowering my head.

She came over and wrapped her arm around my shoulders, pushing me further down on the loveseat. "But you shouldn't. You should never feel wrong for loving someone."

I drew back. *Wait, did I say I loved him out loud?*

"Who said I loved him?"

Her plucked eyebrow rose. She half laughed, "Your teenage diary."

A small smile started to lift my cheeks. "Very funny."

She quipped, "Well it's true."

"We're different people now, though, and I'm no longer a fifteen-year-old with a massive crush on my best friend."

Becca said nothing, which was unusual, so I peeked over at her. She was biting her lip but her eyes were doing that thing that Tyra Banks always shouted about on *America's Next Top Model*: "Smile with your eyes! Smize, dammit!"

Becca was full-on smiling with her eyes.

I see you, Tyra. I get it.

"The kind of feelings that you had for Dawson, even if you *were* fifteen, never go away, Ivy. Even back then, everyone could tell that you and Dawson were just... it."

Confused, I asked, "It?"

"Yes, *it*. You two only had eyes for each other. It was *so* obvious to everyone but you two. Like the world didn't spin around you guys, you spun around *it*. You and Dawson had this bubble formed around you from the very beginning, like you two couldn't be separated by anything..."

Becca stood up and walked over to her bookshelf, bending down (a pig on her butt staring directly at me) and then said, "Ah-ha!"

She pulled out something from the bottom shelf and pattered back over to me.

I recognized what she held in her hand immediately. A yearbook from high school. I got one my freshman year, but unfortunately, it had gotten burned up in the fire – along with every other part of my life.

Becca flipped through the pages quickly, as if she knew exactly what she was looking for. I scooted closer, taking peeks at the blurring pages.

"Look..." she said, sliding the book over into my lap. It

still smelled of glossy paper, like the yearbook hadn't been opened since the day she got it.

I followed Becca's finger as she dragged it along the smooth surface, skimming over random pictures of people I barely recognized.

"Look at that picture and tell me that you two weren't totally wrapped up in one another." I swallowed as my heart lifted up higher in my chest.

I almost wanted to cry, staring down at the two young teenagers, totally captivated by one another. From the looks of the picture, we were in the middle of some type of pep-rally, with blue and black streamers flying through the air behind our heads. Everyone was posing for the picture; Becca in her cheerleading outfit, with a perky pony-tail, sticking her finger up as if she were saying "We're number 1!", then you had Casey (who now lived in California with her Army husband and three kids), sticking her tongue out and scrunching her eyes closed. Max was standing on the other side of Dawson, sporting his blue football jersey, as were a few other guys, and then there was Dawson and me – smack dab in the middle of the chaos, but we weren't even looking in the direction of the camera like everyone else. Dawson was staring down at me, smiling like a boy on Christmas morning, and I was peeking up at him, with the same type of smile. It really did look as if we were in our own little world, not even realizing that there were other people screaming all around us.

We had on the same smiles that we wore today, and last night, once again, wrapped up in our own little world. Dawson made the world seem a little brighter.

"See?" Becca piped, causing me to tear my eyes away from the photo. "If I believed in love, you and Dawson would be it, even after the last six years apart."

"I thought you hated Dawson," I said, wondering why all of a sudden she was rooting for him.

"I hated him when I thought he hurt you." I nodded in agreement because that was understandable, but there was one more thing I was confused about.

"Why didn't you tell me about the house?"

Her eyes squinted. "What?"

I pushed back, leaning my body against her soft couch. "Why didn't you tell me about he and his father building my house."

Becca's mouth dropped. "What?!"

"You really didn't know?"

"Know what? What house?"

I swallowed and filled her in on the fact that Dawson and his father had rebuilt my house and how Dawson now resided in it.

"HOLY SHIT. This could be a freaking movie, Ivy!"

I laughed, "It is. Haven't you seen the Nicholas Sparks movie?"

"Oh my God. Did he write you letters?! If so, I'm dead."

I laughed harder. "No, shut up. He didn't write me letters."

Becca gave me a side glance, pulling her blonde hair to one side. "Are you sure?"

I chuckled. "I'm pretty sure...but you really didn't know?"

She shook her head, looking around the room in complete and utter awe. "No. I didn't know or I probably would have told you. You know Dawson and I didn't really speak for years, and even though I don't agree with some of the stuff he did while you were gone, I know for a fact that he cares so much about you."

I urged her to continue.

She rolled her eyes and laughed. "You should have seen how pissed he was when you were sitting with his brother the other night at Ships."

"He looked mad but I wasn't really sure why."

"I thought he was going to kill his brother and then the other guy, Kip. My God, I thought he was going to blow." She laughed again.

"This is so confusing," I said, feeling like I was just in a car crash with epic whiplash.

Becca looked over at me, a grin covering her face. "There is nothing confusing about this, Ivy. You two belong together, and not as friends. Let him deal with his shit, and then you two will work it out... easy peasy."

It did sound easy. Like for once in my life, something would work out the way it was supposed to.

But...I couldn't help the weird, dreadful feeling that lurked over my shoulder.

Something would go wrong.

Nothing was ever this easy for me. At least, not for the last six years it wasn't.

"GREAT, thank you for getting it dry so quickly!" I hung up my phone after saying goodbye to Dawson's father, pretending I wasn't at all disappointed that it was Mr. Lanning calling me instead of him.

It was Monday morning and I was on my way to work. I had to leave Becca's forty minutes earlier than usual because her house was on the outskirts of town, and that meant I had to get on the highway, which also meant I'd get stuck in traffic.

Dawson was right. It was taking me forever to get into town.

It would have been so much better if I could have stayed at Dawson's again, but as of right now, I had no idea what was going on.

Did he break up with Breanna?

Did she kill him because she somehow found out that he'd cheated?

Was she going to be waiting for me at my house, to do the same to me?

I wasn't sure. At this point, I wasn't sure I *wanted* to know.

After spending yesterday with Becca yammering on about how Dawson and I were going to have much needed, pent-up-for-six-years sex soon, and then my sister texting me every five seconds, asking me how staying with my "long lost best friend/major crush" was, and if we'd done the deed yet, I wasn't sure I would be able to soothe the burn if we *didn't* have sex.

Like, what if he decided last second that he wanted Breanna instead of me?

I'd likely just die.

Which only made me feel weak.

My phone vibrated again in my cup holder, reverberating off the plastic sides. My heart leapt as my fingers jumbled with it. Hope blossomed in my chest, ready to break out in luminous colors, and then it was quickly zapped away.

Eric was calling.

Again.

Apparently, Dawson making those ludicrous sex noises in the background last time we'd talked was eating away at him. He'd texted me fifteen (yes, fifteen) times in the last two days and now had resorted to calling me.

I had a really bad feeling that he wouldn't stop

hounding me if I didn't meet up with him sooner or later, even if it was to truly end this little "I want you back" thing.

Something had to give, eventually.

He wasn't this clingy, even when we were together. My God.

My phone had stopped vibrating, only to start up again. I wanted to scream in annoyance.

"Jesus, F, CHRST!" I shouted, pushing my finger down on the side button and turning it off completely.

If anyone wanted to get a hold of me, they could just call work.

I was done with the stupid phone calls that weren't from Dawson.

And thankfully, the day passed by without a single phone call from anyone – other than a couple work calls.

I felt completely defeated and void of any other emotion as I pulled my car up in front of my house. I knew that Dawson wouldn't be here working today. Did I wish he was? Yes. But did I know better? Also, yes.

The question as to why he hadn't called or texted me or sent a fucking carrier pigeon ate away at me with every passing minute.

We'd kind of fought, and I'd never truly been in a fight with him before, not even when we were younger.

I didn't like it.

At all.

Rounding the front of my car and hopping up onto the sidewalk, heels clicking against the concrete, I told myself to suck it the fuck up.

I'd been let down before and I said it best the other night: you don't always get what you want, especially in this world. I was a true believer that shitty things happened to good people, and shitty things happened to bad people.

It just *was*. And the shitty thing was that maybe Dawson and I would never be a thing. Maybe we had simply just shared another amazing kiss, and that was just the end of it.

What a shame.

He was such a good kisser. A sexy kisser. Talented.

"Hey."

I squealed, dropping my phone and purse in one single movement, stepping backwards with a wide-eyed expression etched on my face.

"Jesus, you scared me!" I yelled, staring into those familiar blue eyes.

He was here. Dawson was sitting on my porch stairs.

How did I not see him before? OH, that's right. I was too busy telling myself to get over the fact that he hadn't called. But here he was, and just like that, my thoughts of getting over it went *poof*.

I would never be able to get over it. No way.

"You're very unaware of your surroundings," he mused, slowly standing up.

I fought a smile. "Why do you think I'm always tripping?"

He let out a throaty chuckle and felt it go directly down to my southern regions. After kissing Dawson the other night, I was even more linked to him. Like his mouth was just a small taste of temptation and now I was just left with wanting more. Needing more.

I wasn't quite sure what to do or say, so I kept my mouth shut after he laughed. A pregnant pause passed between us, me staring at him, him staring at me. I avoided looking into his eyes for too long, afraid I might get swept away like dust in a wind storm.

Dawson looked hot; that was something I couldn't take

my eyes off. He was wearing business-like clothes, just the same as the first time I saw him, back in his father's office.

His dark grey slacks hugged his thighs and his white dress shirt was unbuttoned at the top, like he was literally about to be photographed for Sexiest Man of The Year. I wouldn't be surprised if I walked into the grocery store later and he was on the front cover of *Glamour* magazine.

He wore rugged, working-man well, but seeing him all sleek and fancy wearing dress clothes – that was like pouring gasoline on a fire.

I was burning up.

"I broke up with Breanna," he said, as I passed by him to get to my front door.

I paused, my back to him, heart coming to a complete halt in my chest.

Fiddling with my keys, I unlocked my door and stepped inside, thankful that my house was, in fact, dry and all cleaned up.

I could feel Dawson behind me. His warmth and masculine scent wrapping around my body like a vine creeping along a tree trunk. I slowly spun around, swallowing my desire, and asked, "Did you already install my 5-star security system or should I go ahead and buy about fifteen deadlocks so she can't murder me in my sleep tonight..."

Dawson's face twitched, a small grin playing along those luscious lips. He stepped closer to me, causing me to walk further into my house and shut the door behind him.

The sun was setting in the background through my living room window, but the rest of my house was dim. Shadows danced along the far wall, sinking further and further away as the sun threatened to disappear for the day.

"I didn't tell her I kissed you." He swallowed, taking

another step towards me. "She told me she didn't want to know."

My heart climbed in my chest and my legs clenched together. Dawson's tone didn't hold his usual playfulness. In its place was something that came from my wildest and sexiest dreams. His voice was guttural sounding. Throaty.

"So what exactly did you tell her, then?" I asked, whispering.

Dawson took another step towards me, causing my heart to go into triple speed. My back pressed along the wall as I stared into his darkened eyes.

"I tried to tell her what had happened but she basically beat me to the punch, saying she knew that she and I could never be what she wanted and that she knew there was something lingering in my feelings for you."

I nodded slowly. That was good. She already knew, and that made me feel a little better about what had happened Saturday. But at this point, looking up at Dawson's hooded expression, I didn't care what she thought. I wanted Dawson in the worst way possible. I hated that I didn't care, but no one's perfect and if being with Dawson was wrong, I never wanted to be right again.

And I didn't just want him to satisfy the burning desire I felt within, I also just wanted to feel... *free.* I wanted to go back to feeling happy and carefree, like I was free-falling.

I tried to make a joke, "And then she tried to kill you?"

"She simply told me to go for it."

My brows crinkled. *Wait, what? Breanna told him to go for it... with me?*

That didn't sound right, but right now, I didn't want to start dissecting it.

"I'm sorry I kissed you, Ivy," he said, taking the final step over to me.

Nervous flutters filled my belly just as my heart took off in my chest.

"I'm not," I said, surprising myself and him. The tilt of his head and the way his eyes grew dark were a visual that I would never get out of my head. His mouth twitched upward for just a second, and then he brought his strong arms and anchored them beside my head, resting them along the wall.

"Are you ready for this? Are we ready to put a stop to this friendship bullshit and take a hold of what we both want but for some reason can't admit?"

GOD, YES.

I looked up into the endless blue of his eyes, dreamily hoping and praying that this was really it.

That I wasn't dreaming. That I wouldn't wake up tomorrow and come to a realization that the feeling inside of me wasn't real and that I was somehow stuck back in my mundane life, pretending that I was happy and high on life.

Because I wasn't.

I thought I was. I thought I had it all figured out, but I was so, so wrong.

"Yes," I breathed, and then every single thought was taken away from my brain and thrown onto the floor.

TWENTY-SIX

Dawson

This was it.

Every last hope and dream that I had buried deep within, underneath several layers of denial, was emerging so fast I would never be able to push them away again.

The second Ivy gave the okay, I claimed her like I'd always wanted.

My mouth descended on hers as my knee went in between her thighs. She opened them further, allowing me to press myself against her tiny body, and her hands wove around my head, crushing my face even harder to hers.

I moved my mouth over hers in a hungry way, like I would never be full. Her lips were soft and sweet, the inside of her mouth warm and inviting. My dick throbbed from just the mere look at her when she walked up her sidewalk with her black heels strapped along her ankles. My eyes traveled down the tight, grey pencil skirt and then paused on the stockings she was wearing.

I briefly wondered if they stopped at her thigh, and then

imagined how she would look with *only* those on, paired with her heels.

My dick instantly felt heavy and it was a desire that I couldn't quite hold back. The thought of me finally being free of Breanna and Ivy's flushed faced as she ran her eyes down my body – I was a goner.

Had I imagined Ivy and I having mind-blowing sex before?

Yes.

I couldn't count how many times as a werido teenager that I'd imagined her and I together like that, but now it was something feral. Like my life wouldn't go on if I didn't bury myself inside her.

Aside from my dick standing to attention any time I'd look her way, my heart did, too. It twisted and ratcheted in my chest, beating hard against my ribcage, begging me to attach itself to hers. The feeling was something I only thought hopeless romantics longed for, like those chicks who'd lose themselves in books like *Twilight,* hoping that someday they'd fall in love with someone so deeply that they couldn't live without them... but that's how I felt.

Like I could never live without Ivy.

She had left six years ago as my best friend, but now that she was back... she was going to be *so* much more.

She won't just be my best friend.

She'll be my everything.

Clawing my fingers through Ivy's brown locks, I moved my hands deftly to the back of her skirt. Her lips were still on mine, sucking and biting, moaning every few seconds, urging my fingers to move faster.

I pulled her slender hips away from the wall, just momentarily so I could unzip her tight-ass, sexy skirt, and then slide it down and over her hips, letting it fall gracefully to the floor.

Not having time to look down at what type of panties she was wearing, I moved my hand towards her blouse, undoing all the tiny buttons lining the front all the way down to the hem. I pulled my mouth away from hers, shoving her shirt down past her shoulders and over her arms.

My eyes took in the magnificent scene in front of me and I almost self-combusted from need. My heart stuttered and a surge of craving started at the top of my head and went all the way down to my ankles.

I have never wanted someone so bad, in my entire life.

Ivy was standing in front of me in the darkened living room, wearing nothing but a simple, silk, black bra, blank panties, thigh-high tights (*I knew it*), and heels. Soft, shiny brown hair fell over her shoulders and her chest rose and fell rapidly, pushing her breasts up and down with each breath.

My mouth literally salivated.

Ivy's normally bright, emerald eyes were dimmed and heavy-lidded as she moved her hands to my pants.

Her fingers fumbled with the button and zipper, taking longer than I'd like for them to fall down to my shoes.

I kicked my shoes off quickly and stepped out of my pants, kicking them away. I then undid the buttons of my shirt, pushing them through their rightful holes, and shrugged it off with the help of Ivy's hands pushing the fabric off my broad shoulders.

I crushed our barely clothed bodies back together, pressing my eager mouth onto hers. She tasted so sweet, yet so dangerous at the same time.

The second a small, breathy moan escaped her mouth

and landed on mine, I snaked one of my arms around her waist, and put my other hand to her breast. I dipped my palm down, underneath the padding of her bra and instantly felt her nipple tighten against my callouses.

"Fuck," I swore, inching her legs further apart with my bare thigh. I inched my head over her ear lobe, sucking and nipping it with my teeth.

"Dawson," she breathed, my name sounding like a fucking life-line on her lips.

"I know," I said back, still teasing her neck with my mouth.

I knew what she wanted and I was more than ready to give it to her.

The arm that was snaked around her waist moved back. I guided it down her thigh, stopping just at the top of her tights and then slowly used my fingertip and trailed a line all the way up to her middle.

The heat emitting from her pussy was something from another world. I growled, moving my lips back to her mouth while my hand eagerly went to the lacy bottom of her panties.

She was soaked.

The moisture coated my finger the second I moved the fabric aside and something grew hungrier inside of me.

I swallowed, pulling back slightly and plunged my finger inside to meet her warmness. I think I saw stars and I literally almost got off, just by feeling her tighten against me.

I barely even moved my finger inside her before I could feel her orgasm start to push through. It wasn't rare for me to get a girl off quickly, but this was a newfound discovery.

My little Ivy was a sex kitten.

My hand reached around to the back of her bra and I

unclasped it quickly, letting the straps fall over her shoulders. Neither one of us moved to take her bra all the way off; instead, it just rested along her flat stomach, the straps falling to her forearms. Her hands wove through my hair again, bringing my face to her breast where I used my tongue to swirl around the bud, over and over again all while driving her crazy with my finger, dipping inside.

My dick strained along my boxers but I shoved away my need, for just a little while longer.

I wanted to make her fall apart in my arms, and then drive so hard into her that she'd forget that the last six years were spent wasted without one another, because that's exactly how I saw it.

They were wasted without her by my side.

"Daw..." she started, left speechless as I crooked my finger a certain way, rubbing right along her sweet spot.

"Faa..." she stuttered.

My mouth still stayed on her chest, switching from one breast to the other, but my eyes traveled upward to watch in awe as she was overtaken by pleasure. Ivy's eyes were clenched tightly and her mouth was parted, a flush starting to creep along her neck and cheeks.

"Faaa.. fuck!" she yelled, clenching so tightly around my finger, I could feel it all the way to the tip of my dick

Her pussy clasped, ripple after ripple of ecstasy flowing throughout her body.

Ivy's knees buckled as she let out several uneven breaths.

I gave her a few seconds to collect herself, before slowly pulling my finger out of her. Her eyes finally opened and they flashed up to mine.

"Wow," she muttered, chest still rising.

Wow was right.

Honestly, I was so turned on that I couldn't see straight. Ivy was sexy as fuck with her glowing flush, spread along every inch of her body, and brightly-lit eyes, wearing nothing but some panties, tights, and a bra that was half on, her breasts just sitting out in the open, begging me to lick and suck, again and again until the end of time.

And then she smirked, biting down on her swollen lip. My dick was three seconds from busting a nut in my boxers and with her looking like *that,* I didn't even know if I could last half a second, after putting it inside her.

"Bedroom..." she exhaled, the small smile long gone. In its place was a hunger on her face that looked as if it'd never be satisfied. Her eyes were wild and begging me for more, for me to take her like we both needed.

I didn't say a word.

Instead, I picked her up, wrapping her legs around my torso, and led us straight to her bed.

TWENTY-SEVEN

Ivy

The second Dawson and I were in my bedroom, he placed me on the bed and pushed me backwards. I let him take charge for just a second, snatching my bra off my body and throwing it behind him, landing quietly onto the spotless floor.

But then I sat up and flashed my eyes to his wicked ones. It was dark in my room, the sun now long gone, welcoming the night sky, but I could still see the way his pupils dilated and the way his strong and dense chest rose and fell rapidly.

I slipped out from under him and stood on my floor, still in my heels.

Keeping my eyes trained on him, his brow furrowed and boxers tented, I bent down and slowly started to unclasp my heels. His eyes traveled down my body, mesmerized by the way my hands worked at the tiny, gold clasp near my ankle. I stepped out of the first heel, and then I did the same to the other.

I licked my lips, bringing my fingers to the edge of my panties, soaked to the point that I was relieved to slip them off.

They slid down, over my hips, all the way to my feet before I tossed them with my foot, where they landed near my abandoned shoes. Then, I took my hands and started to pull my at my thigh-high stockings, but Dawson's gruff voice stopped me.

"Leave them."

I felt the heat in his voice all the way to my core. Dawson was usually playful and care-free, but right now, his voice *dripped* with hungry sex appeal. Like he was a wild animal, about to pounce and strip me of my every thought.

I was ready.

I slowly pattered over to him and took my hands, placing them along his bare chest and shoved him backwards. His eyes widened and then dipped down to my breasts, full and heavy, ready for him touch and tease.

Crawling on top of him, I brought both of my stocking-clad thighs and straddled him, dipping my hands underneath the waistband of his boxers.

Desire clenched through my core, and I was literally throbbing for the need of having him inside me. I'd never felt a need this badly before. I needed him so badly it almost hurt.

My palms slid over his bare thighs, and then back up again, finally pulling down his boxers and freeing his dick.

I felt my eyes widen almost instantly, because he was, for lack of better words, as hard as a fucking rock. His dick strained, a bead of milky substance forming at the top the second my hand touched his shaft.

I wanted to devour him.

I peeked up at him, my hand gliding slowly over his rigidness, and I'd never seen a more perfect sight in my life.

Dawson's head was thrown back, his angular jaw clenched and his eyes shut tightly, closing out the world.

A thrill went down my spine. Watching Dawson come apart from my hand was out of this world.

It sent a completely new, mind-blowing jolt of lust through my body. I wanted him to come apart because of *me*. I'd never wanted to pleasure someone this intensely. I was actually excited to put my mouth over his rod and suck him until there was nothing left to suck.

I licked my lips again, moving my mouth down to his cock. He hissed between his teeth and I felt his upper body angle towards me and my mouth.

Taking my tongue, I ran it down the base of his length, and a line of curse words spewed from up above, but I kept going. My hands gripped his thighs as my mouth fully took him in. I sucked and bobbed my head up and down, moving one of my hands to cup his balls and fondle them as if they were made of crystal.

"Ivy, fucking stop," he groaned, causing me to smile along his dick. His hand found my hair, running his fingers through it roughly, at the same time he thrusted his hips up to my mouth. I took him in even further, still cupping his balls and then he pulled back, quickly.

He let out a growl as I peered up at him, his eyes were blazing with desire.

"I don't want to come without being inside of you," he said, driving his eyes into mine. "I've waited too long for this, for it all to end by your wicked, talented mouth."

I grinned but it quickly fell off my mouth as he grabbed my biceps and swiftly flipped me onto my back.

My hair spanned out around me as a surprised breath

fell out of my mouth. Dawson stared into my eyes as he slowly inched my thighs apart. His palm splayed on my inner thigh, moving his finger slowly over to my middle.

He only inched his finger in for a split second before removing it, a coy smile spreading along his features and then he moved upward, his dick only a breath away from entering me.

I held his stare, feeling myself get completely lost in his touch, his eyes, his breathing. I was completely smothered by his very presence and I wouldn't want it any other way.

Dawson bent his head down to mine, his warm breath fanning out over my face, and then captured my lips with his, moving them languidly over mine. His tongue swept inside but I couldn't focus on it because his dick had started to inch inside me as well.

It was a once in a lifetime moment with him.

It was like losing my virginity for the second time. It felt sacred. Dawson inside of me felt like I was beginning something new, but yet something that would never, ever get old.

Dawson sensed my mood change and pulled himself up, fully inside of me now.

"Are you okay? Is this okay?" His blue hues searched my face and I smiled, feeling tears brim my eyes.

I nodded, and brought my hands around his back, pulling him down further on top of me.

I needed to feel his skin on mine. I needed to feel him moving above me, claiming me with everything he had.

Being in this moment with Dawson felt like I was finally returning home after a really, really long time away.

He felt *right*, and I hadn't felt like I'd been right for almost seven years now.

Seven years too long.

He moved his body over mine, his cock pulling back and

then slowly entering me again. An emotional yearning flew through my body, my nipples tightening and my core burning with intense heat.

It was like a ball of fire bouncing around all over my body.

It was so much pleasure that I couldn't focus on anything other than the way my toes were curling and the way I was angling my body up towards his, basking in the way his dick felt as it rubbed inside of me.

"Holy fuck, Ivy," he muttered, pausing for a second and allowing me to ride his rod, curving my body up towards his, rubbing back and forth.

I felt my eyes shutting, but I still saw Dawson. I still felt Dawson. I felt like the rest of my heart, the part that I had taken with me when I was forced to leave six years ago, was literally climbing out of my chest and climbing right into his, nestling up to its other half.

"You're so damn beautiful, Ivy," he whispered, finally coming back down and meeting my thrusts again.

I was well over the edge by the time his words hit my ears. I spiraled out of control, yelling out his name in my release, feeling completely stricken with emotion.

Dawson thrusted a few more times before pausing. I felt his dick pulse inside of me, stuttering and then completely breaking loose.

My mouth parted in amazement as I studied the pleasure on his face. His eyes clutched together, forming small wrinkles around their edges, before he dropped his head down low, sweat beads forming on his temples.

He lowered on top of me, his heart rapidly beating against my own sky-rocketing pulse.

We lay like that for what felt like hours, but at the same

time, it didn't quite feel long enough by the time he rolled off me.

His cum slowly dribbled out of me, as I still lay flat on my back. And then that's when I realized, we didn't use a condom.

I was on the pill.

Had been since I started dating Eric, but Dawson...

Dawson *just* broke up with Breanna, and from what Becca had told me over the years, she was not a saint and I had a feeling Dawson hadn't been, either.

"Dawson," I whispered, feeling fearful at the thought of us being so caught up in each other that we didn't pause to think about anything else.

"Yeah," he whispered back, turning his head towards mine. I could barely see him in the pitch black of my room, but it only took my eyes a few seconds to adjust.

"We..." I bit my lip, curling up on my side. "We didn't use protection."

Dawson's entire body tensed. "Fuck, I'm sorry, Ivy. I just assumed you were on the pill or something..."

"I am—" I hurriedly said. "But... the pill doesn't protect against, you know."

Dawson slowly brought his hand under his head, hauling his torso up to stare down at me. His head tilted to the side as a small smile broke out along his lips.

"I've never, ever gone without a condom before."

My brow hitched. "What? You're totally lying."

He was quick to protest. "I would never lie to you. You know that."

A strange amount of happiness filled my body. I was the *only* one he'd been with without a condom? I wanted to jump around my room and scream like a freak.

"You never... with Breanna?"

He let out a snort. "Absolutely not."

I couldn't help the giddy smile breaking out across my face. "Good."

A beat passed before I heard Dawson open his mouth. "Ivy, that was..."

"Amazing," I finished for him. It was. The entire thing was just amazing, and that was honestly a poor word choice for what had just happened.

Slowly, I felt the bed dip and then Dawson was climbing over my naked body, once again. He rested his weight on his forearms, caging me underneath him, making me feel small and vulnerable.

"Do you feel it, too?" he asked, peering down at me, looking the same exact way I felt:

Exposed. So incredibly wide-open and unguarded.

Slowly, I reached my hands up, placing them along his muscular biceps.

"I always have," I answered.

And it was true. There had *always* been this automatic pull between us. Like I couldn't live my life the right way unless he was right there beside me. My life was darker without him in it.

I survived six years without him, but looking back, they were the dullest six years of my life. As if I needed him by my side to be truly *me*.

A small, hopeful smile passed by his lips.

"This was worth the wait," he murmured, lowering his lips to mine. His tongue coaxed my mouth open, and just like that, heat was emitting from down below. It was such a strong, powerful feeling that it completely took my breath away.

Dawson released my mouth, edging his knee between

my legs, opening them up once again. "Don't ever make me chase you again, Ivy."

His voice was almost pained, and I knew why.

This right here, was our breaking point.

There would be no going back from this.

Reaching my hands up behind his neck, I slowly pulled him down onto me, his face going into the crook of my neck.

Tears filled my eyes. "I won't."

Goosebumps broke out along my skin when I lowered my mouth to his ear, "I promise you, Dawson, because I don't think I could climb out of the endless void if I ever have to leave you again."

He said nothing; instead, he took his length and rushed to enter me again, allowing his body to make up for lost time.

Because that's what it was.

Those six years we'd spent apart, hurting and aching, pretending we didn't feel wrong... they were our *lost* years.

TWENTY-EIGHT

Dawson

"So let me get this right," my brother said, shuffling the deck of cards in his hand. "You broke up with Breanna, thank the fucking Lord, and then you went over to Ivy's and fucked her ... how many times?"

I punched his shoulder. "Shut the fuck up, I'm not giving you details on that shit."

Emmett's shit-eating-grin stretched across his face. Then he laughed. "Okay, but, so...Breanna was just... cool with you dumping her for Ivy? Because from what I remember from a few weeks ago, she was going fucking nuts that you and Ivy were 'just friends.'"

I leaned back in my chair, hand peeling away the label on my beer bottle. I thought back to last weekend, when I'd gone over to Breanna's that Sunday morning right after she'd returned from her trip, prepared to lay it all out in the open.

I honestly expected her to hit me or cry and blubber that she loved me (even though we both knew she didn't) and reiterate how she'd saved me from my own heartbreak years ago, but that's not what had happened...

Breanna had sat back on her couch, crossing her legs underneath her body, and smiled. A rush of uncertainty went through me and I was about to put my shields up, but then she surprised me.

"You and Ivy belong together, Dawson. It's okay."

I was stunned. I just stared at her, wondering where the catch was.

My brow furrowed. "What? You were going crazy a few weeks ago... but now, you're okay with me breaking up with you?"

She shrugged, looking around the room before bringing her baby-blues back to mine. "I care about you, you know that, but we both know that what we had... was nothing more than sex and companionship. There isn't that die-for-you type of love with us. Not like it is with you and Ivy. I know you're going to leave here and go to her,"

I opened my mouth explain, to tell her about the kiss, but she stopped me. "It's okay Dawson. I thought long and hard this week, after our last conversation..." Breanna's head dipped low and then she brought it back up, eyes squinting. "I can't even remember why I hated her all those years ago.

"My parents always talked so badly about her family, and she was like this mortal enemy to me because of how often my mom would diss on hers. Even in grade school, my mom forced me to participate in this stupid spelling-bee, all because she wanted me to beat Ivy."

Breanna chuckled, mouth opening wider. "Now that I think about it, it was crazy how psycho my mom always acted toward them and how she always forced me to go out of my way to treat her like shit."

I was a little taken back, not sure what to say. I mean, I

knew that Breanna's family and Ivy's never, ever got along. I knew it had something to do with their rival in dealerships, which seems so fucking stupid, but I didn't realize that it went *that* far. It made me angry for Ivy and it made me feel a little bad for Breanna.

"Do you want to know what my mom said when Ivy's parents died?"

I walked a little closer to Breanna, letting my guards slide down. "What?"

She nibbled on her lip, clasping her hands in her lap, working her fingers back and forth. "She said... 'good riddance.'"

My eyes widened as anger flew through my body. Not anger with Breanna, of course not, but what kind of person says that after someone burns up in a fucking fire? What the fuck?

"Wow," I said, and Breanna nodded.

"Yeah. It hasn't always been rainbows and shit with her, like everyone assumes. She puts on this perfect little façade of having a wonderful husband and daughter, getting lip injections and climbing her way up the ladder at St. Joseph's, becoming the Dean's right hand, but she's so fake and mean. She's always been so spiteful and it's taken me a little while, but I've realized that I don't want to turn out like her. At all."

My stomach formed a knot. "Why didn't you tell me any of this before? Like, when I was your boyfriend?"

Isn't that what boyfriends are for? To be there for their girlfriends? I sure as hell wanted to be there for Ivy, and she wasn't even considered my girlfriend yet.

Breanna shrugged again. "We didn't really have that type of relationship, Dawson." She laughed. "We talked about sex, and then had sex, and then...that was about it."

"I was a shitty boyfriend to you." Even more so since I had just kissed Ivy behind her back. Yep, Hell party of one for me.

She crinkled her nose. "I wasn't the best girlfriend, either. You and I just... aren't meant to be."

I nodded, agreeing with her because it was true.

We both knew who I was meant to be with.

I think everyone knew.

...I breathed out a long sigh and glanced back up at my brother, closing out my thoughts of Breanna. He was still messing around with the deck of cards and getting the poker chips ready. We hadn't had a poker night in a long, long time. Mainly because he'd been so wrapped up in Carrie, but now that Ivy proved the whole her-stealing-his-money shit, he'd dumped her and had started to be... Emmett, again. Well, the good Emmett.

Not the one that I had to bail out of a jail every few months.

He'd gotten his shit together, finally.

"Well, there were some things I didn't really know about her, and she'd worked through her shit, so we ended it on okay terms."

Emmett's eyes flicked to mine, head still tilted down towards the table. "Really? So what, you and Ivy are like... together for good now?"

I fought a smile. "Yeah."

Ivy and I had spent the last week and a half together, every single day. It was like a breath of fresh air, leaving work and going straight to her house. She'd spent the night at my place last night because of the new floors being installed at her house, but basically our days consisted of us working and then her grabbing us food and warming it up in the microwave and then forgetting about it because we'd be too busy christening every single part of her house.

I'd never had so much sex in my life, and I'm a dude, so that's fucking saying something.

It was just so different with her. It was unbelievable. Mind-blowing. The way her body slid above mine, moving to her own rhythm, throwing her brown locks back and letting out a moan – I could get off just by the sight of her.

I would never get sick of her pussy. I would never get sick of her perky, small breasts. I could never get sick of hearing her moan my name or the way her mouth parted just slightly from pleasure.

In fact, just thinking of the way she rode me last night had my dick springing to attention, even sitting at a table with my brother and the few guys who had just sauntered in.

This game was going to need to go fast as fuck because spending the day without Ivy was miserable, and turning that into the night, too, was brutal.

I was addicted.

Emmett nudged my bicep. "What?" I asked, carrying my attention back to his.

He let out a loud laugh, crossing his arms over his chest. "I asked if you told Mom yet."

I rolled my eyes. "Not yet,"

He shook his head, smiling. "She's going to be so fucking happy that you dumped Breanna."

I laughed. My mom despised Breanna. I had no idea why because they'd only met once. I didn't see my mom much, as she lives in the city and rarely comes into her old hometown anymore since the divorce, but the last and only time I'd brought Breanna with me to see her, my mom had

had a hard time keeping her face even and not acting appalled.

"Yeah, she is."

My phone dinged and I reached to grab it, but Emmett grabbed it first.

His face turned red and he laughed out loud as his eyes scanned whatever was on the front. I snatched it out of his hand quickly, seeing what he'd read.

Ivy- Becca is up on the stage, singing song country song with one of her co-workers and I'm sitting in the booth, alone, thinking about you and your dick. Why am I so horny all the time? Did you feed me some type of freaking horny love potion? I'm even finding things that aren't even remotely sexual... arousing.

I bit my lip, and took my right arm and drove it into my brother's stomach. He lurched forward, resting against the edge of the table. I looked down at him, smiling. "Don't fucking read my texts."

He chuckled through a groan. I went back to my message, ignoring him and the laughs from the other guys. One of them asked what was on my phone, but Emmett chose not to answer. Lucky for him.

I texted Ivy back.

Like what...?

Her message popped up quickly.

For example, I'm eating my fries... dipping them in ketchup.... Very, very slowly and the only thing I can think of is YOU ENTERING ME VERY, VERY SLOWLY. What is happening to me?!

I laugh out loud and quickly texted back.

My dick is magic. Don't worry, I'll leave here ASAP and pick you up and then we can play out this French fry and ketchup fantasy that you're having...

My dick literally grew hard.

I needed to get the fuck done with this game and pick my girl up.

It's what I'd wanted to do in the first place but I thought I should still act like I had some balls and hang out with the guys... even if it was the very last thing I wanted to do.

All I really wanted was Ivy.

THE SMELL of smoke wafted through the air as I walked up to the doors of Ships. Max was walking beside me, talking about one of his students and how he'd found him ramming a girl in the locker room before school the other day.

I couldn't believe it. Our laughter continued even as we walked through the bar doors, but mine slowly dwindled as I searched for Ivy. I looked towards the booths and felt utter disappointment when I didn't see her.

But I did hear her.

I moved my attention to the stage in the far corner of the bar and then I saw her. The sight of her took my breath away.

Max was still talking about the school incident, but I couldn't even form a coherent thought. I was too focused on Ivy up on the stage, shaking out her golden-brown hair, arms thrown up above her head, laughing and singing with Becca.

She was happy and beautiful.

And I couldn't believe that she was finally mine.

I couldn't believe that I no longer had to chase a ghost.

"My God, she's fucking beautiful," I muttered under my breath.

Max stopped talking, but I didn't look over at him. I couldn't. I was too enthralled in watching Ivy bask in her carefree, spirited ways. It was like I'd been taken back to when she was a teenager, when she didn't have a care in the world...she was always smiling and she always carried this lightness around with her.

"Yeah, she is..." Max said under his breath. I snapped my head over to his, surprised, but then I followed this stare.

He wasn't looking at Ivy... he was looking at Becca.

I smirked, watching him watch her.

I wonder if he knew that he was totally fucking into her? Because I was almost positive he didn't realize he'd said that aloud and that he was currently looking at Becca as if she walked on water.

I turned my head back, glancing up at my girl singing the chorus, and then her eyes met mine.

An even bigger smile formed on her face, white teeth shining against the pink of her lips. She kept singing and I walked steadily over to her, ignoring everyone in my way.

The second I got below the stage, with her and Becca still sharing a microphone, I quipped any eyebrow up and pulled myself up, too.

Becca's head tilted, wondering what the fuck I was doing, but Ivy...she just smiled and continued to sing as loud as she could.

She and Becca were on their second round, the chorus creeping up, and that's when I moved in front of Ivy, stealing the microphone out of her hands.

She laughed, eyes wide, and then I stole the show.

I took my free hand and grabbed hers, swinging her around and bringing her back to my body.

I belted out, *"Mamma Mia, here I go again, My my, how can I resist you? Mamma Mia, does it show again, My my, just how much I've missed you?"*

Ivy cackled with laugher in my arms. It was like the soundtrack to my life; hearing her laugh was like switching radio stations in my truck, trying my hardest to find that one song I wanted and when I would find it, it was like a gift. I would never turn it off and I'd always be searching for it.

"I love you, Ivy. I hope you know that," I admitted, right into the microphone, for everyone to hear. Her laughter faded, but her smile didn't.

Her green eyes glistened under the bright lights as she reached her face up to mine. I threw the microphone behind me, landing with a loud thump on the wooden stage, and then leaned her back, planting a kiss on her mouth.

Ivy wove her hands around my neck and applause went through the bar, drunk people hooting and hollering, a whistle here and there.

I continued to kiss Ivy, both of us forming smiles along our lips through the applauding. I pulled her up the second Becca's voice sounded through the bar, blaring into the microphone.

"And here you have it ladies and gents, a real-life love story!!"

I glanced over at Ivy, my heart growing fifteen sizes in my chest, and took her hand in mine.

The chase was over. Ivy was mine.

"THAT WAS QUITE the show you put on for all the ladies," Ivy said, walking through the door of her house.

I grinned. "The show was for you."

She turned back a fraction, eyes tipping over her shoulder. "I enjoyed it." Then she smiled wider before bringing her attention back to the front of her. Which was good, because Ivy was clumsy enough with her eyes facing forward, let alone looking back.

Once we were through the door and walking back to her bedroom, no doubt for her to change out of her work clothes and for me to watch, her expression changed from playful to serious.

"So," she said, stepping out of her heels. "I think you were right about Breanna."

I quipped an eyebrow, leaning my shoulder against the door jam. "How so? Did you see her?"

Ivy smooshed her lips together and nodded her head up and down. "And, dare I say, she didn't even throw a knife at my head. I was prepared to duck under the booth, but when she glanced over from the bar, she almost... skipped over me. Like her eyes saw me but her brain didn't..."

I chuckled and shook out my hair.

Ivy started again, "But in all seriousness..." She started to strip off her dress, standing only in a silk, see-through slip. I swallowed, not truly registering anything else she was saying. "...She didn't even so much as glare at me like usual. Maybe she morphed into a different person. Maybe a demon was inside her body all this time and it finally left, leaving her *real* soul to emerge." She shrugged, a small smile playing on her lips. "I guess I won't have to call Dean and Sam Winchester, although I was looking forward to it."

She was trying to get a rise out of me with her last comment. We'd played a game a few nights ago, asking each other a series of questions, all of which were completely ridiculous and not at all serious. She'd admitted that her TV sitcom crush was Dean from *Supernatural*, and I'd admitted that mine was Jennifer Aniston, in *any* TV show or movie. I then followed it up by listing all the similarities between her and Jennifer.

"Come here," I prodded, raking my eyes down her body and back up again.

"You come here," she said back, a coy smile on her lips.

I rose an eyebrow and licked my lips, giving her my best sultry stare. Ivy and I were testing each other more and more lately...specifically in the bedroom.

In the bedroom, our deep friendship with its comfortableness and laughter was long gone; in its place was this sexy, raw, and unforgiving pull between our bodies. My dick had never been so fucking happy.

"Nah, I think I'll stay right here and enjoy the view," I said, my voice throaty and husky, just the way she liked it.

Ivy's face twitched and then she narrowed her gaze onto my hand. I unhurriedly moved my fingers over to my jeans, pushing the button through the opening with one single shove, then I very, very slowly took my zipper and pulled it down, letting the sound fill the silent room.

Wild green eyes flicked back up to mine and a small grin started to creep along my face. I let my jeans fall to the floor in a single whoosh, where they landed around my ankles.

Ivy wiggled on her feet, still staring at me. I winked at her and then fiddled with the hem of my t-shirt, pulling it up and over my body and throwing it to the bed. I watched Ivy's neck break out with a rosy blush at the same time that her chest started to heave up and down a little harder than before.

Speaking of hard, that's exactly what I was. Hard, hard, hard, hard. Just staring at her, watching her become turned on...it was all it took for me. Just one single glance at the gleam in her eyes and I was done for.

She was so dangerously sexy in the bedroom.

She was the best of both words: so sweet and beautiful, but a God damn siren under the sheets.

I almost groaned out loud watching her eyes travel over my body. I flexed my pecks at her, a mischievous look on her face, which quickly disappeared when I dipped my hand into my boxer briefs, allowing my dick to feel a moment of satisfaction.

I pulled my waistband down while observing Ivy's widening of eyes and parting of mouth. I slowly took my steady hand and ran it along the base of my shaft, feeling tingles shoot down my legs.

I moved my hand a few more times, feeling my own breath labor. Ivy swallowed loudly and then she started to play along, too. She tiptoed over to me, still standing near the door, and kept her attention on my hand, rubbing my dick up and down. She pulled up her cream-colored slip, bunching it around her waist, and dipped her fingers into her lace panties. I started to pump faster and faster, feeling my balls deepening with a heavy pleasure. My heart beat wildly in my chest, anticipating her next move.

My voice was gruff. "Touch yourself."

A shot of pleasure went down my spine when Ivy's eyes grew hooded and clouded with ecstasy.

I glued my attention to her hand, slowly gliding her panties down to her ankles. She stepped out of them and kicked them over to the side, then used her other hand to bunch up her slip even more, giving me a full shot of her pussy.

Her delicate hand traveled up her thigh, a breathy noise coming from her mouth. I had to pause my hand on my dick, because I wasn't quite ready to come apart yet. As much as I loved coming, I wanted to do it while inside of her. I just didn't want to rush it.

I wanted to come fast but I wanted it to last, too. Quite the conundrum.

Ivy's breathing grew louder as she inched her fingers toward her warm center. I almost moaned out loud the second I saw her finger disappear. It was like watching a porno in real life. She was unbelievably hot. Her high cheekbones flushed, her mouth open, eyes on the brink of closing.

She only inched her finger in and out a few times before allowing a small moan to escape her mouth.

I'd had enough. I released my dick and reached out, pulling her body up to mine.

"That's enough, my turn," I gruffly said, pulling her slip right up and over her head. I crushed my greedy lips onto hers, tasting the beer she'd had, which probably was what had led her to do karaoke with Becca.

I picked Ivy up in my strong arms, wrapping her bare middle around my torso. I quickly laid her down on her back, not giving two shits that the bed was mere feet away from us. I wanted her on the floor, and I wanted to fuck her fast. I didn't want to waste time walking the three feet over there.

No time to waste.

Shoving my boxers down further, allowing my balls and dick to spring forward, I parted her legs, skimming over the way she said my name like her life depended on it, and rammed my steely, hard length into her tight, warm pussy.

I almost died.

The build-up was out of this world. Just watching her touch herself had me near exploding, and now that I was plunging in and out of her, I could barely handle it.

We have had so much sex over the last week that I've literally lost count, yet, here I was, still unable to last more than a few minutes with her clenching around my dick.

She moaned, throwing her head back on the floor. I took one of my hands, releasing it from behind her waist, and cupped the back of her head to protect it from the floor. Her legs spread wider, her back arching, her breasts pushed up and spilling out of her bra. I bent down and kissed the side of her ear.

"I love you," I said, again.

She brought her head up to mine, flushed face and deepening green eyes.

I'd told her I loved her tonight, after belting out some girly lyrics, but I'd never told her during sex before.

It wasn't that I didn't love her before, because I'd been in love with her since we were awkward pre-teens, but I had been waiting for the right time.

I was waiting to say it in the exact moment that made me feel like I'd die if I didn't spill the truth.

I loved her so fucking much. I loved her back then and I loved her even more now.

"I love you more," she whispered.

I pumped into her, faster and harder, grunting and moaning, trying to keep it together so she could find her release, too.

"Daws," she moaned, grinding her hips back and forth to meet my thrusting. She took her hand and traveled down to her clit and I literally had to shut my eyes because watching her do that was enough to kill me.

Within seconds of her circling herself, she clenched

around me and broke free like a fucking dam breaking. Her orgasm washed over me so deeply that I was coming at the exact same time that she was, and I can honestly say, that in all of my 25 years of life, and out of all the sex I'd had, this was the most powerful, mind-blowing orgasm I'd ever endured.

It was short-lived, though, because as soon as I felt the last few spurts of that pearly-white substance exploding from my dick, Ivy and I snapped our heads to the door.

Someone had come through her front door, shutting it loudly in their wake.

Then a girly voice, nearly identical to Ivy's sounded. "Ivy! Are you awake? It's only ten."

Ivy squealed, pushing me up and off her body. I paused on the situation for a second, imagining what Mia would do if she were to walk down the short hallway and into her sister's room, seeing me, ass totally exposed, boxers bunched down to my ankles, ramming the fuck out of her older sister.

Jesus, fuck.

I hurriedly stood up and pulled my boxers up, covering my near-gone boner, and ran over to my jeans. I slipped them up at the same time that Ivy threw on a t-shirt and sleep shorts.

I laughed out loud.

Even if we were fully clothed, Mia would know right off the bat that we had just had amazing, world-shattering sex. My chest and face were red and splotchy, my breathing still out of control. Ivy's face was covered with a reddish-tint and her hair was...honestly, it was to the point that she looked as if she was just thoroughly fucked, and that only made me want to go another round.

She hissed, "Stop looking at me like that!"

I laughed again and then heard Mia. "Ivy? Where are you?"

Footsteps echoed down the hall and soon enough, Mia, wearing an overly tight, fuchsia dress popped up in the darkened hallway, eyes bouncing back and forth between Ivy (sex hair and all) and then me, grinning unknowingly.

"EW! It smells like... SEX back here!!"

I fucking lost it. I howled with laughter and then Ivy started to giggle, too. Mia's mouth dropped open as she backed away. Once she was out of sight she yelled, "Come out when you two aren't spreading your stupid 'just had sex' endorphins around!"

I looked over at Ivy and she was holding back laughter. Her shoulders were shaking through her too-big t-shirt and her eyes were shut tightly.

"It does smells like sex back here..." I repeated, through another laugh.

"STOP LAUGHING!" Mia yelled through the house.

"I love us," Ivy said, looking up at me with those beautiful, forest green eyes.

I smiled. "Me too."

TWENTY-NINE

Ivy

Mia was lying on my couch, bare feet propped up on the arm rest with her arm draped over her eyes.

Dawson walked out behind me, tapping my bottom when we got to the living room. I yelped and turned back to playfully slap his chest. I loved that he still couldn't keep his hands off me, even after banging the fuck out of me.

I *loved* it.

"I really want to be grossed out right now, because it really does smell like musty, hard-core sex in here, but I just can't seem to truly be disgusted."

I folded my arms over my chest. "How do you know what musty, hard-core sex smells like?" (Cue me acting like an overbearing mother verses the older sister that I really am.)

Sometimes it's hard to act like a cool, big-sister/bestie when I have been almost like a mother to Mia since the night our parents died. We were both forced to grow up that night, but I'd always still acted somewhat like a mother to her, at least for the first few years.

Mia finally pulled her arm away from her eyes and glared at me. "I'm in my twenties, Ivy. You can stop with pretending like I'm a virgin because we both know I'm not."

I rolled my eyes.

I knew she wasn't a virgin and I'd given her enough talks about the Trojan man for her never to preform without protection, but still. I felt like it was my duty to continue on with that little tradition.

Mia sat up, closing her legs since she was wearing a dress and it was no longer just *me* in the house. "You two are like a Lifetime movie. One of those sickening, lovey-dovey, swoony ones. The kind where," she paused, bringing her hands up to form quotation marks, "boy meets girl and they become the best of friends, only to be ripped apart by an awful tragedy, and then they find each other again and fall madly in love." She smiled. "Boom. Lifetime movie."

I let out a small giggle and Dawson walked a little further in the room, draping his arm over my shoulder.

"You're right, we're the epitome of a Lifetime movie," he said, peering down at me.

Butterflies erupted throughout my belly as my heart fluttered. This was it. It was finally happening...Dawson and me, in sickening, swoon-worthy love.

Mia clucked her tongue. "So this is why you haven't been texting me like normal all week."

I scrunched my brows. "What do you mean?"

She opened her eyes wide. "You normally text me, like, 500 times a day, asking me if I've eaten, where I am, how my grades are, et cetera."

Walking over to her on the couch, I sat beside her, the

cushions enveloping me. I looked over at her profile. "Is that why you're here? To check on little ol' me?"

She laughed. "No, I was at a party and my roommate decided to be a bitch and lock me out."

Brow furrowed, mama-bear coming out to play. "First off, where is your key? And second off, why did she lock you out? Do I need to make a call?"

Mia laughed, looking at me like I was an idiot. "First off, you're not scary so stop, and second off, she's mad because I came home at, like, three the other night and accidently woke her up."

Confusion started to set in. "Where were you until three? And why the heck are you dressed like that? I demand you change right now!" Mia's dress was completely inappropriate; I didn't think I'd ever worn something that short.

Mia laughed again, as did Dawson, who had taken a seat across the room in my other brand new couch. Now that my house was nearly done, I had finally been able to get some furniture in here last week. I went with a lovely loveseat and couch combo – per Dawson's recommendation for how small my living room was.

Mia rolled her eyes when she answered. "Can you chill, please? I was at a party, and yes, before you get all mad, I'm a college student. It's what we do and we also dress like this for said parties."

Dawson cleared his throat. "It's true, although I'm not sure I'm a fan of you wearing something like that, either. It seems... wrong."

Mia pouted. "Okay, please don't tell me that you two are going to gang up on me now that you're together. Ivy and Uncle Tim are already overbearing enough; I don't need an older brother, too, Dawson. And, I'm not the loser kid that you used to know. I've grown up."

I snorted. "Barely."

Mia gave me a death glare, which only made me laugh.

Dawson chuckled, looking totally adorable. "Fine, fine. But if you need me to beat someone up, I will." He flashed his award-winning smile, all while flexing his arm muscle, and I swooned, right there on the couch.

"We all know I can take of myself." Mia popped up. "In fact, I smacked some jock tonight before coming here. Which is why I'm here so early."

I watched Dawson's expression grow dark, then I turned and angled my body towards Mia, eyes going directly to her boobs. *I'm totally burning that dress. Can you hear that? It's our father rolling over in his grave.*

"What? What happened?" I asked.

She shrugged. "I got all dressed up for his stupid party, that *he* invited me to, and when I got there, he was sucking face with some chick. The second he saw me, he grinned at me, thinking I would be totally okay with it, and it made me mad so I smacked him, and then left."

My mouth opened into a gaping hole. My sister was such a little bad-ass. She always had been. I needed her balls.

Dawson's laughter boomed throughout the room, causing Mia to stand up and bow, declaring, "Thank you, thank you very much!"

I sat back, huffing with annoyance, but really, I was enjoying seeing Dawson and Mia together and getting along. They hadn't had much of a relationship back when we were younger due to the awkward age gap, so it was kind of nice watching them interact.

"And, piggy-backing off the subject of my now-enemy

who goes by the name of Dierks," she said, coming back to sit down. "Guess who else I saw on campus the other day?"

Perplexed, I asked who.

"Mrs. Connors. Do you remember her? She basically hated our family."

I almost yelled. "Why the heck was she there? And did she do anything?"

Mrs. Connors = Breanna's mom, aka the woman who hated me and Mia, and who was probably still holding a grudge against my parents, even though they weren't even here to defend themselves anymore.

"She works there," Dawson answered.

A pit grew in my stomach so large that I think it swallowed my heart.

"Did she say anything?" I asked, looking back to my sister.

Her eyebrows folded. "No, I'm not even sure she saw me. I did a double take because I wasn't sure if it was her or not. I barely remember her from when we were younger, but she had that stupid, bleach-blonde hair tied up into a tight bun like she always used to, so I knew it was her. Plus, I saw her name in one of my pamphlets awhile back and then it just kinda clicked. I turned around at the last second because I ran into the person in front of me, causing a near-fall with the sidewalk." Mia laughed.

I didn't know she worked there. What did she even do? From what I remembered, she used to help run the dealership...or, something with the books or accounts.

"So you've got the clumsy gene, too?" Dawson asked, laughing.

Mia stuck her tongue out. "I'm not nearly as bad as this one," she answered, pointing at me.

She and Dawson fired back a few jokes about me falling

down and running into things constantly before I realized that Dawson was standing, looking over at me.

"Huh?" I asked.

Dawson's face twitched with humor. "I said I was going to head home tonight so that you and your sister can hang out."

"You don't have to go," I answered, almost sounding desperate.

Dawson chuckled. "It's fine, babe. You hang with your sister." Then he walked over to me, pulling me up to my feet. I felt the blush running across my cheeks.

I grinned. "I like you calling me babe."

A Crest commercial worthy smile appeared. "I like calling you babe."

We both turned our head at the sound of Mia making puke noises. Then she stopped and smiled. "I'm just kidding. I love you two together. Even my twelve-year-old self thought you two were the coolest couple ever."

I laughed. "We weren't even a couple back then."

She rolled her eyes. "Tell that to twelve-year-old Mia who watched her cool, older sister stare across the dinner table with Cupid eyes at her 'best friend.'"

I laughed again and walked Dawson over to the door. He bent down, slipping his shoes on and leaned in, his scent wrapping around me like a blanket.

"I'll come by tomorrow, after work?" he questioned, bending down to brush his lips over mine.

I reached up on my tiptoes, planting an eager kiss on his lips, slipping my tongue in for good measure.

He whispered, "Careful, now."

I smirked. "Yeah, come by after work. I'll cook."

I heard Mia say, "You cook?"

Rolling my eyes, I shot her a dirty look.

"Love you," Dawson said, pulling back and smiling at me once more.

I smiled back. "Love you more."

Then he walked out the door and I turned around to a squealing Mia.

"What are you screaming about?!" I shouted.

"YOU GUYS ARE SO CUTE!"

Yes, yes, we are.

I WAS LITERALLY DRAGGING at work. Like, eyelids blinking so slowly that I might have caught a 5-second nap in between the blinks. Mia and I stayed up way too late going over everything that was going on with Dawson and me and her filling me in on the stupid, ass-hat jock who thought he could play my sister.

I was still pissed about it now, hours later, sitting at my desk.

My phone rang, causing me to shake off my anger and put my customer-service voice on (we all have one, don't pretend you have no idea what I'm talking about).

"Hello?" I said cheerfully.

"Hey, it's me," Abigail said, incognito.

I laughed. "Why are you whispering... and why are you calling me from the next office over?"

Abigail was probably the only other person in the office other my boss, Mr. Daniels, who had actually tried to be friendly with me. The tellers—they weren't so thrilled with me getting this job over them. Seniority and all.

I get it.

But I was also really good at my job, so whatever.

"So, The Hawk is coming in for a meeting with you."

I crinkled my brow, looking around my small, 5 x 8 room. "Who is The Hawk? I don't know codenames yet."

She groaned through the phone. "Her name is Debbie Connors. I don't really know much about her since I only moved here a year ago with Chase, but her husband owns the real big dealership in town, and she's such a pain to work with. Like, seriously, even Mr. Daniels avoids her."

The only words I heard Abigail say were "Debbie Connors" and "dealership."

"She's coming, like, now, so get your freaking game face on."

"Hah," I mumbled. "Thanks for the heads up."

If anything, I didn't need my game face – I needed a freaking shield and sword.

This couldn't be a coincidence. The pit deep within my stomach from the little intel I'd gotten from Mia and Dawson last night, referring to Breanna's mom working at St. Joseph's, was growing even larger.

I swallowed, evening my breathing and cracking my neck a few times. This was going to take every ounce of energy out of my very, very tired body to play nice with her.

Every little jab she'd said to my parents when I was younger was flipping through my mind like the pages of a text book. Every glare and roll of her eyes when my parents would walk into a sporting event for me flared over my skin.

I thought I hated Breanna, but it turns out, I really just hated her mother.

My door opened with a cheerful-looking Abigail, red hair pulled into a low pony. "Ivy, Mrs. Connors is here to speak with you regarding some of her and her husband's accounts."

Slowly, I stood up from my chair, taking my hands and

smoothing my dress down the front of my legs. "Ah, yes, thank you."

And then... she walks in.

I had a momentary lapse of time where I traveled back to the past and pretended that I was sick this morning, calling off work, so I could avoid my current situation. I would have stayed in bed all day and convinced Dawson to do the same. He would have made me a big breakfast in bed, and then we would have had each other for a lunch. It would have been perfect.

But, here I am, in this tiny office, smelling of more flowers from my ex-boyfriend, whom I still had not talked to, a fake smile plastered on my face staring at Breanna's mother.

I wonder if she knows.

Probably.

"It's so good to see you, Mrs. Connors," I said with as much excitement as I could muster up. Which wasn't much, let me tell you.

"Hello, Ivy dear."

"Please sit." I ushered her to the chair furthest away from the door; that way if I had to escape, she couldn't trip me on my run out the door.

"Thanks, Abigail," I said, glancing at my coworker. She made sure Mrs. Connor's back was turned before rolling her eyes and mouthing, "Good luck."

I held back a snort.

"So, if you just give me a quick second," I intoned, moving back behind my desk and sitting down on my comfy chair, "I'll pull up your accounts. Is this regarding the dealership or your personal accounts?"

Her voice was like ice being flicked at my forehead. "There's no need for that." Her sentence was blunt and to the point. I slowly peeled my eyes away from the computer, heart thumping with anger.

"And why's that?"

Mrs. Connors and her stupid, bleach-blonde hair pulled into a stupid, tight bun on the top of her head, with her stupid, matte lipstick and matching shirt, sat back in her chair, her shoulders pulled back and a conniving grin on her face.

"You're just like your mother, you know that?"

Now, usually, I would have taken that as a compliment because my mom was absolutely amazing. She was the type of woman who went above and beyond for her family, baking homemade cookies for Christmas with Mia and I by her side, making sure my dad had a packed lunch every day to take to work.

She was a stellar human being, which is why it was so unfair that she was taken from this earth so soon. She made it a better place. Or maybe she just made *my* world a better place. Either way, she was incredible.

"Thank you," I droned, acting as if I was bored with the conversation.

"You think you can come back to Oak Hill and take things that aren't yours? You're just like her." Her face twisted with disgust. "Despicable."

Chills broke out along my arms. I moved my hands to my lap so she wouldn't see how badly I was clenching my fists. I didn't care if she wanted to talk about me. I didn't. I'd grown a pretty thick skin over the years, but bring up my mom, and I would rip her fucking head off.

I kept my voice even, although my mind was going a thousand miles a second. "I'm not quite sure what you're referring to. Did I accidently take your parking spot? Or the wrong bag of potatoes at the store? Did you already claim them?"

She rolled her eyes so hard that I half-expected them to come out. "You're just like your father in that sense, trying to make people laugh when nothing is funny."

"Okay, now that's enough," I uttered, feeling blood rush through my veins.

"Did you know that your mother..." I held my breath, watching Mrs. Connor's face look as if she had a bajillion Lemonheads in her mouth. "Did you know she took your father away... from *me?*"

I raised an eyebrow. The way she said "me" sounded as if she thought she was the Queen of fucking England.

"I have no idea what you're talking about," I retorted, still clenching my fists.

She crossed her legs, anger pulsating off her body. "Your father and I, we were best friends in college. We were best friends in high school, actually, but more so in college, and the second your mother walked up to him in her stupid cheerleading outfit... he was gone."

My heart stuttered in my chest, just for a second, but it did. I knew my parents met in college. I'd heard the story over and over again when Mia and I would ask my dad to tell us about it before bed, but conveniently, this part of the story had been left out.

I wasn't quite sure what to say to Mrs. Connors, so I didn't say anything. I was supposed to be acting professional. This was a new job and it was one I couldn't afford to leave. Literally. I had bills to pay and Mia's school. The scholarship only paid for half of her tuition; the other part was on my shoulders.

Sure, I could get a new job somewhere else but this was

the only bank in Oak Hill. I wasn't leaving again, no matter what.

I wouldn't leave him again. I wouldn't.

"So imagine my reaction when I'd heard that you took Breanna's boyfriend away from her. How *dare* you?"

Mrs. Connor's voice rose a little at the end and I quickly averted my attention to my glass door, hoping someone, anyone, would hear the commotion going on. *Why didn't I record this?* I should have known she would come in here being her usual psycho self.

"I didn't take Dawson away from Breanna. They broke up on mutual terms, Mrs. Connors, and I would like to explain to you that this is a personal issue and right now, I am at work, so if you could like to discuss your accounts with me, that is fine, but otherwise I'd like you to leave my office."

She cackled, her entire body shaking with an evil laughter that made my teeth ache. "Listen here, this is what's going to happen. You will end it with Dawson and you will give him back to Breanna. Down here, in Oak Hill, we don't give up what's ours. Not anymore, we don't. I was played once by your family, I won't fall for it again."

My mouth fell open and I had to hold back a laugh. "Are you threatening me because Breanna and Dawson broke up, and now he's with me? Because from what I learned, Breanna is just fine."

She scoffed. "She doesn't know what she wants; give her a few weeks and she'll realize what a mistake she's made by agreeing to this ridiculous breakup. Breanna needs someone to take care of her, and Dawson did... that is, until you came back into the picture." Mrs. Connors let out a sigh. "The second you throw him away, he'll come back for Breanna. You just watch."

I was stunned. The whole forming sentences skill was long gone. You'd think that she was the who had been broken up with, not Breanna.

"That's not going to happen, Mrs. Connors. Please leave my office or I'll call security."

She laughed again, leaning forward slightly so I had a clear view to her glare.

"Here's the thing, darling. You either end it with him and give him back to Breanna, or you can say goodbye to your sister's scholarship."

That had me pausing and she realized it by the smile that broke out on her face.

"Oh yes, that's right. Didn't you know? I'm head of the scholarship committee at St. Joseph's, and guess whose pocket I'm in?"

My stomach churned and I could feel the dread hanging over my head like a cumulonimbus cloud. I pinched my leg, distracting myself from what was actually happening.

Breanna's mom was threatening me. She was black-mailing me to break up with Dawson... because of my mom taking my dad away from her? I could barely wrap my mind around it. She needed to be fucking committed.

My voice was near cracking. "You're blackmailing me to break up with Dawson... for what?"

I was simply confused. So, so confused. Everything inside was jumbled like dumping the pieces from a very wacky puzzle all over the floor.

"Because even if your parents are *dead*..." Her words sliced through my skin, tears instantly springing to my eyes. "I'll never let them win. Ever."

Gathering myself for a second, teetering back and forth over my decision to either throw my stapler at her head or to cry, I asked, "You hate my mom that much, from years ago, that you'd try to ruin my and my sister's lives? What is wrong with you?"

She shrugged. "Life isn't always sunshine and rainbows, Ivy dear. You should know that better than anyone."

My heart felt like it had been punched. My lunch threatened the back of my throat. I felt stuck. Completely stuck.

I had to tell Dawson. I had to tell someone. Better yet, I would call Breanna and tell her to get her fucking nutjob of a mom out of my office.

What in the actual fuck is happening?

Mrs. Connors stood up from her chair, to hover over my desk, flowery perfume hitting my nostrils.

"You end it, or I swear to God, I will end your sister."

Blood rushed to my ears as I stood up, too. "And how you expect to do that? What evidence do you have to take her scholarship away?" *Please be nothing. If I ever needed my sister to be a goody-two-shoes, it would be now.*

She smiled. "All it'll take is one word to the Dean and he'll rip that scholarship right out from under her and get her kicked out of school." She tapped her red fingernail on her chin. "Good luck getting into another four-year college after being thrown out of St. Joseph's."

I ground my teeth. Even if I didn't abide by her wishes and Mia got kicked out of college, she wouldn't be able to get another scholarship even if she *did* apply to another school and get in. I couldn't afford to pay for full tuition, and there was no way I could get a loan for her. I wouldn't even be able to co-sign a loan for her, given that I'd just taken out a chunky amount for my mortgage. I almost wanted to laugh out loud thinking about Uncle Tim trying to co-sign. *Yeah, right.* He was sweet but he had absolutely no credit.

"Do it, Ivy. You don't get to win this time."

I wanted to say no. The very words were on the tip of my tongue. *Just say no, Ivy. You'll figure it out. You'll find another way... But would I?*

I'd given up everything to get where I am right now.

I quickly tried to come up with another plan. I would tell Dawson. He could fix this. He could...

"No one can help you, Ivy. You're stuck and you know it and you also know that you'll do anything for Mia, which is how I know I'll walk out of here a winner."

I flicked my eyes up to her, feeling my hands tremble by my sides.

I always thought that Breanna was the devil, but I was wrong...

Breanna was just the poor, little spawn of the devil.

And that devil just took my fucking heart.

THIRTY

Dawson

I'd been sitting at Ivy's house for an hour now. My legs bouncing up and down, my knuckles being cracked every few minutes. *Where the fuck is she?*

This morning I had a weird feeling come over me. I couldn't shake it all day, not once. My stomach ached. I couldn't focus worth shit.

I thought it was because, for once, I'd actually woken up without Ivy's warm body pressed to mine. I thought it would pass once I got to work, but it didn't. If anything, the feeling grew larger. So large that I finally broke down and called Ivy's work phone.

One of the bank tellers told me she went home early. I found that strange. Why wouldn't she call me and tell me she went home early? Was she sick?

I instantly told my father that I had to dip out early because Ivy was sick. He didn't put up a fight. He could see the distress on my face and told me to go, and to tell her he hoped she felt better.

I wanted to smile at him with astonishment because my father wasn't usually the nice and sappy kind of guy, but that was just the thing about Ivy—you just had to love her. There was no other way.

When I pulled up to her house, nearing three, her car wasn't there. The feeling I had this morning overtook my body and I started to truly worry. I ran up to her house, skipping over her newly concreted steps, and knocked a few times before grabbing the key under the mat and going inside.

I was met with new floors and the smell of fresh paint that had been applied last week, but that was it. Ivy wasn't home.

Pacing the living room, I called her phone four times before going outside and sitting on the porch.

I told myself I'd just wait. She was probably at the store, gathering canned soup and some crackers for whatever illness she came down with. I thought back to what she'd eaten last night at the bar, which wasn't anything unusual. She drank a little, but nothing to the point that would make her sick.

As each minute passed, the nervousness in my stomach got worse.

I looked down the road a few times, and then dialed Max's number.

"Hey, man," he answered.

"Is Becca with you?" I asked, out of breath from pacing the porch. The wind picked up in the distance, howling and swirling leaves around.

Max stuttered, "Uh, no... uh. Why would she be?"

I groaned. "Where is she?"

He started to stutter again.

"Max, I know you fucking know...tell me."

He could try to hide his attraction and awareness of Becca's every move all he wanted, except for right now.

"She's at practice. She coaches cheerleading. What's wrong, dude?"

I exhaled. "Something. I can't find Ivy and apparently, she went home sick today, but she's not home. Go get Becca and have her call me as soon as possible."

Max's voice was calm, relaxed. Unlike me at the moment. "I'm sure she's fine. What could be wrong?"

My heart clenched, my voice on the verge of breaking. "I just know something's wrong, Max."

He must have heard the distress in my voice. "I'll go find Becca. We'll call you in a sec." Then he hung up.

I wasn't waiting for Becca to call me.

THE DRIVE to Becca's house should have taken me at least forty minutes, but I made it there in twenty, heart near stopping when I pulled up behind Ivy's Camry.

I put my truck in park and flew out of the driver's seat, running up to the front door. I pounded my fist on it like my life depended on it.

I stood there, breathing in and out of my nose, trying to prepare for the worst. When the door finally opened after what felt like a lifetime, my heart dropped.

Immediately, I knew something wasn't right. Ivy looked normal but the way she pulled back into her body, wrapping her hands around her torso, shoulders slumped... I knew.

"Ivy?" I asked, grabbing her chin and directing it up towards my face.

She swallowed loudly, looking anywhere but in my

eyes. I studied her, observing the way her eyes were puffy and her usual mascara long-gone.

"Ivy, what's wrong? Is it Mia?"

Her pale lip trembled and fear shot through me, but then she shook her head no.

"What's going on?" I said, softly, trying to coax it out of her.

Her words broke me in half. My world stopping moving. "I don't think you and I are going to work."

One minute passed without a single peep from either of us.

The next minute passed and I lowered my hand.

The third minute went by and...nothing.

I was giving her time to explain. I was giving her time to break out in laughter because there was no fucking way she was being serious.

But she was.

I saw it in her eyes.

I watched the sparkle and glimmer she had when staring at me disappear. It damn-near killed me.

"Why?" I finally asked, still not fully believing what was happening.

My heart twisted in my chest with every breath she took. It felt like it was being wrung out every few seconds, as if someone had a hold of it and was squeezing it until I just gave in and stopped fighting the feeling of pure despair trying to suffocate me.

Her voice wobbled as she stepped back through the threshold of Becca's tiny house. "I just don't think we can be anything more than friends."

She could barely get the words out, and I studied her so fucking hard I could probably carve a sculpture of her with my eyes shut.

She was lying.

Flat-out lying to me.

I knew when she was lying and she was.

Even as kids, she was a shit liar. Her nose would twitch, her small nostrils flaring just slightly. Her eyes would dart to the side and her mouth would form a straight line.

She was lying... but why?

I stepped back with one foot, then the other. Never taking my eyes of her.

She finally brought her head up and I saw it plain as day; she was utterly broken.

This wasn't right.

Ivy was forced away from me six years ago, it was inevitable. We were too young to truly do anything about it.

But now?

I'd be fucking damned if she was taken away from me this time.

There was no going back now.

I told her I would never stop chasing her, and I *always* keep my word.

THIRTY-ONE

Ivy

"What in the actual hell, Ivy!" Becca shouted, throwing her hands over her mouth.

I knew I could trust Becca. I had trusted her six years ago when I left. I had begged her not to tell Dawson anything, and I knew that if I asked her to keep another secret, she'd do it, and I had to tell someone.

I wasn't sure if Dawson would look for me at her house or not, but when I heard the pounding on her door a couple hours ago, I instantly knew it was him.

It was almost as if I could sense him, and I would be lying if I said I was upset to see him. It made the last little sliver of my heart that was keeping me alive, happy. I wanted him to fight for me. I wanted him to fix it, but he couldn't fix what he didn't even know was broken.

"We cannot let her get away with this! Hell, I'll pay for Mia's college. Just tell her to give up her scholarship and transfer. Plus, does bitch-face even really have an 'in' with the Dean? Like, come on!"

I shrugged, eyeing the open wine bottle on Becca's table. I hadn't drank anything. I wanted to. I wanted to guzzle the bottle, maybe even take it to bed with me so that way, when I woke up and realized that this wasn't an awful dream, I could just drink more. But I felt absolutely sick to my stomach. Like there was a bowling ball lying inside, making me feel heavy and just...sick.

I just felt sick.

Trying to smile at Becca, I said, "You're a teacher. You're poorer than I am."

Her eyes moved to mine and then she chuckled. "You're right, but Ivy, this isn't right. We cannot let this happen. There has to be another way. You and Dawson are not breaking up because Breanna's mom has a hard-on for him."

"It has nothing to do with Dawson." I shook my head. "I mean, she said that Breanna would realize that she belonged with him or whatever, but it wasn't really about her or him. It was about *me*. It was about my mom, which is ridiculous because my mom is dead! Both of my parents are dead! Why isn't that enough for her?!"

My lip began to tremble as the waterworks started to whirl.

It wasn't often that I cried or felt sorry for myself. I knew what real pain was and I knew that crying wouldn't solve anything but right now, I was feeling pretty fucking sorry for myself.

I was feeling even sorrier for Dawson because the look on his face earlier was the most sickening thing of this entire situation and honestly, I felt a little bad for Mrs. Connors, too, because she was obviously sick in the head.

Okay, I wasn't really feeling bad for her, but she must lead a pretty terrible life to be this evil.

She was pure *evil*.

At least now I know where Breanna got it all those years ago. Her mom was probably whispering in her ear at night while she was sleeping ways to make my life a living hell.

Just add Breanna to my list of people to feel sorry for, too.

"We will figure it out, Ivy. Just calm down."

I shook my head, tears slowly falling down my face. My heart felt like it was gone. I wasn't even sure how I was still alive.

I felt like the Tin Man.

I watched Dawson pull back and stare at me, jaw clenched tight, working back and forth. His chest lifting and falling fast, hands clenched down by his sides. The more he studied my face, the angrier he became. My heart thrashed in my chest, banging off every single bone in my body. My heart was begging me to tell him the truth, to work something out.

Just wait for me until Mia is done with school. Pretend to love Breanna when you really love me.

Let's hit Mrs. Connors with your truck.

Do some work on their roof and accidentally let the entire thing collapse on her.

To be honest, I couldn't even think straight.

I felt exhausted and overwhelmed.

"Can I just stay here tonight?" I asked Becca, furiously wiping at the tears on my face.

"Of course, Ivy." She quickly walked over to me, sitting down on the couch, wrapping her warm around me.

For a brief second, I thought the one thought that I hadn't had in a long, long time.

I wish my mom was here.

HOW DID I ever survive living without Dawson for six years? It'd been two days and I literally felt like I was missing a freaking limb. We officially had the shortest spurt of love in the entire world.

How long was it for Romeo and Juliet? Longer than a week, right?

I mean, yes, I'd loved Dawson forever. I'm pretty sure I loved him in 7th grade when I spotted him across our middle school gym for the first time, but I'm referring to the actual love-making, gaga eyes, I-love-you kisses when we'd part for the day. Only a week? Why did it feel so much longer than that?

Why did it feel like I'd been with him for my entire life? Like my soul had always been tethered to his. I wasn't sure I believed in reincarnation but now I was second-guessing myself.

Maybe Dawson and I had always been together, in other lives, somehow finding each other again in the next life.

I hoped past me didn't have a heartbreak that hurt this bad.

Because it sucked.

I'd been ignoring all texts and phone calls because I didn't even want to speak.

Since I'd decided to leave Becca's, through her protests, she'd been over to check on me a couple times. I called off work, which I shouldn't have, but I did. I told myself I'd give myself the weekend to get my shit together and then pull on my big girl panties (the ones with the tacos on them, because... #tacos) and deal with the issue head-on.

How was I going to do that? I had no idea, but I was coming to the conclusion that I wasn't going to let a grown-ass woman, who wore her hair too tight and who held grudges on dead people, dictate my life.

I just had to figure out what to do first.

I was strong.

I was intelligent.

I was no longer a pushover. She may have gotten Breanna to bully me when I was younger, but I'd been through way too much in my life to be pushed around again. I was not that same nerdy, awkward fifteen-year-old.

Fuck Mrs. Connors.

Even her name pissed me off.

Which was good. Anger was like putting gasoline on the fire. It would fire me up to the point that I would un-ball all the paper wads that I'd thrown on the floor, trying to write out a plan for "Operation Take Back Dawson & Get. Mrs. Connors Fired".

I lay back on my bed with a whoosh and focused on my laptop sprawled open on the other pillow.

"WWOBD?" I said aloud.

What would Oliva Benson do? I'd been watching episodes of *Law and Order SVU* all day, trying to figure out a way to turn into a detective to get myself out of this ridiculous mess. I just needed some time. That's what I told Dawson, and I hoped when this was all over, he'd understand why I'd said that.

It wasn't because I didn't love him.

"Okay, Detective Benson, what the hell would you do if you were me?" I said, again, to no one. I drummed my fingers on my chin and ran my other hand through my ratty hair. I looked a hot mess but I didn't have time for a shower! Who had time for a shower when they were trying to come up with a plan to fix their life?

Not me.

My eyes flashed to the screen: Oliva and Ice-T were crouching over a screen, replaying some footage from a kidnapping. Then I gasped.

"CAMERAS!!!!" I hopped off my bed in a rush, getting tangled in my messy covers, landing with a thump on top of the several torn notebook papers.

The bank had cameras. Like, lots of them. Duh! And I would almost bet my left arm that they had audio. If a robber came in to pull a bank job, the police would likely want footage with audio. Bank security systems were top notch – or at least, I hoped. They should be if they aren't.

I pulled on my jacket, adjusting my leggings so they were actually straight to my body and not twisted like I'd slept in them all night (which I had) and darted out the door, snagging nothing but my keys and my phone.

The sun was bright over my head, causing me to squint as I reached my car. Its glare on the hood damn near had me wrecking as my tires spun out from underneath my Camry.

It took less than ten minutes to get to the bank. I stole a glance at myself in the mirror, which was scary. But that was good. I'd called in sick this morning and I definitely looked the part, so kudos to me for planning ahead.

I threw my car in park, not even bothering to grab my usual parking spot and hopped out of the car, hoping with all my might that my plan would work.

I was almost positive that Mr. Daniels would believe my story, about Mrs. Connors. They all feared her and they all dreaded her. Abigail made it very clear that people scattered when Mrs. Connors would walk in the door, so if I could get him to let me have the footage to take to the Dean at St. Joseph's, then there would no mistaking her blackmail scheme.

It would be right on tape, so even if she were to tell the Dean something about Mia, he would know she was lying.

I hoped.

I only made it three feet to the door when I ran right into someone. I wasn't paying attention; I was too wrapped up in praying to God that my plan would work.

"Oh, shit. Sorry!" I mumbled, moving around the innocent bystander.

"Ivy?"

I paused, feet stilled in front of the bank doors.

"Wow, they just told me weren't here today and here you are... I think it's fate."

Eric's black suit looked stiff and prim, just as he'd always looked before, except now, I wasn't at all fazed by it.

"What are you doing here?" I asked, annoyed. I had shit to do.

My to-do list went like this:

1. Plead with my new-ish boss to give me footage (with audio).
2. Drive to St. Joseph's.
3. Meet with the dean.
4. Give him the footage and explain the issue.
5. Confirm that he wouldn't take Mia's scholarship away and doom her for any other college in the state.
6. Dramatically exit the building and drive straight to Dawson's and spill my heart out.
7. Have amazing make-up sex.
8. PUNCH MRS. CONNORS in the face.

Nowhere on that list was the name Eric.

Nowhere.

Eric stepped back, face forming into a frown. "Are you sick? Let's head back to your place. We can talk there." He walked over to me and gently grabbed my arm to usher me back to my car.

I snatched my hand out of his grasp. "Eric, I'm sorry, but I can't talk with you right now."

Why the hell is he even here?

"Ivy, please. I drove all this way to talk to you because you can't seem to answer your phone."

My heart started to beat faster in my chest, feeling as if time was slipping through my fingers. I was on a deadline to get my life back together and to fix this ordeal with Dawson, but Eric was like one of those stupid Whack-A-Mole things. He just kept fucking popping up.

I'd turn my body one way and he'd move there, too. I'd go the other way and there was his face, inches from mine.

"Eric, move. I have something to do!" My voice was frantic and it had him pulling back for a second.

"Ivy, please. I just drove four hours..."

No one asked you to come, bucko. I was about to kick him to get him to move, but then my phone started to shriek in my pocket. I let out a loud breath, feeling more anxious.

Pulling my phone out, I gave Eric an incredulous glare.

I saw Mia's name on my screen and my heart fell. I looked at the small numbers at the top of my phone, noting that it was just after three.

She had class at this time.

I swiped my finger over, evening out my voice. "Hello?"

She screeched. "Where the hell are you!?"

My voice wavered with panic. "At the bank. Why?"

"Uh... have you talked to Dawson? I'm really, really confused right now."

Just the sound of his name had my heart blasting up to space. "Why?"

Mia breathed loudly into the phone. I took my other hand and rubbed it anxiously over my face, glancing once at Eric, who was looking at me with apprehension. Eric and I may have broken up and ended on bad terms, but I knew he still cared about me. *Obviously.*

"So, I was just called into the dean's office."

My throat began to close as my hands started to shake.

I had to get the tape, and I had to get it now. *What if it's too late?!*

Mia's voice trembled, "Why didn't you tell me you were paying for half of my college, Ivy?" I was about to answer, but she kept going. "The dean told me everything. About you paying for the rest of my college and how Mrs. Connors threatened you and tried to con you into breaking up with Dawson... which I don't even understand that part but I was informed of how she was going to get my scholarship taken away, leaving you to foot the rest of the bill. What were you thinking?! Why didn't you say something?!"

My mind was currently spiraling all over the place.

"Wait, what? How did the dean know all that?"

"DAWSON!" she yelled. "He came in and told the dean everything, and then we all had a meeting and he asked if I knew anything about the situation. Which I didn't, so thanks for keeping me in the dark. I'm so mad at you right now... but I can't really be since you're so damn selfless. GAH."

My eyes were wide and my heart was frantically trying to escape my chest to win a race I didn't sign up for. "Where's Dawson?" I asked, out of breath.

I ignored Eric who said, "Dawson? The old best friend,

Dawson? Is that why you've been ignoring me? Are you with him now?"

"He's probably headed to you. He left before me because the dean wanted to talk with me a little longer about the situation. Did you not tell Dawson, either? I'm so damn confused."

Breath escaped my body. Dawson. I had to go get Dawson.

"I'll explain later!" I said, hanging up the phone.

I took one more look at Eric and said, "I'm sorry. I'm in love with my old best friend!"

And then I took off running to my car like I was back on the track team, trying to win our school finals.

Dawson, I'm coming for you.

THIRTY-TWO

Dawson

Becca used to be the one person I hated. I mean, after she yelled at me and slapped me when Ivy left six years ago and then wouldn't tell me where she was, I loathed her.

I held a grudge so deep that I didn't think I'd ever fully be on "okay" terms with her, but now, I was going to get a statue made of her and put it in my front lawn. She'd called me late Wednesday night, only a few hours after I'd left Ivy standing on the porch of her house, and told me everything.

Shortly after I'd left Ivy, I'd headed straight to Breanna's because honestly, she was the only person I knew who had that much beef with Ivy – well, other than her mother.

Breanna was stunned and completely confused when I'd stormed through her house, yelling at her. Her mouth formed an "O," and her shoulders shot up to her ears. She put her hands out like she was caught stealing something.

Yeah, stealing Ivy!

She said she had no idea what I was talking about. She pleaded with me over and over again that even if she wasn't

Ivy's biggest fan, she wouldn't do something like that to hurt me.

I wanted to believe her. I felt like she was telling the truth but it was the only solution I had for Ivy's behavior. Ivy had told me she needed time.

She didn't need time, and neither did I.

We both knew what we felt.

Something wasn't right.

I left Breanna's feeling worse than I had after leaving Ivy. I hoped to find an answer, I hoped to find a reason as to what the hell was going on, but Breanna was just as shocked as I was. Before I made it to my truck, she came running down her driveway barefooted.

"I'll do some recon, okay? Maybe my mom does have something to do with this. I wouldn't put it past her."

I clenched my jaw and nodded while turning around and climbing into the driver's seat. I pinched the bridge of my nose so hard my eyes started to water – at least that's what I was going with. I wasn't going to admit that I was about to cry, because I was a man and men don't cry.

Unless they lose someone like Ivy.

I drove straight home, avoiding going to Ivy's. I knew she wasn't there. She would more than likely be staying at Becca's. Max was sitting on my porch when I rounded my truck and started to walk up the sidewalk.

"You okay?"

I didn't answer him because I wasn't okay.

"Becca's with her now," he said after my non-response.

That got my attention. "What did she say?"

He stood up, turning to go into my house. I followed him, heart skipping a few beats. "She texted and said she was waiting until Ivy went to sleep and then she was going to call you. I told her I was here, so give her a few and she'll fill us in."

Finally. Some fucking hope.

We sat in silence in my kitchen. My leg bouncing up and down, my hands rubbing the back of my neck every few minutes, and then his phone rang.

He answered it quickly and put it on speaker.

Becca's voice started off in a whisper, "Dawson..."

"What's going on, Becca..."

Max stood up, holding the phone in his hand, and walked closer to me.

"She asked me to keep her secret, but I did that the first time and *nothing* good came out of it, so I swear to God, if she stops being my friend after this, you better spend the rest of your life making it up to me."

"Tell me, Becca," I pleaded, sounding less desperate than I felt.

My heart fell to the ground, the really hard ground, as she explained the situation. I wanted to *kill*. I'd never even wanted to hit a woman before, and here I was, pacing my kitchen, trying to hold back my anger before I lost it.

Once Max hung up with Becca, we got to work.

Like I would let Breanna's mom fucking rule my life and Ivy's. Was she fucking nuts?

The answer was a big fat yes with a capital Y.

It took a day to get the footage from Mr. Daniels, and it was the longest day of my life. I was lucky that Max had Mr. Daniels' in class and that Max was his favorite teacher because Mr. Daniels had been extremely leery on the phone when I'd explained the situation.

He told me he would review it and then let me know what he found. He told me that Ivy had called in sick, so it definitely matched up with the situation, and that he knew

Mrs. Connors on a personal level, and then... he left it at that. I wasn't sure if that meant he knew her enough to know she wouldn't do something this insane or the opposite.

When he'd called me, after six o'clock the following evening, he'd told me to come pick up the tape because it was all there. Every last word.

I was so elated that I told myself I'd go to the security company after all this was over and thank them for such fucking amazing technology.

Fucking yes.

The dean was absolutely appalled and Mia's face told me that she knew nothing of the situation, not even that Ivy was paying for the other half of her tuition.

I left the office, giving them time to speak, before rushing to my truck to tell Ivy that it was all over. That it would be okay, and that also, she needed to fucking learn to lean on me when things got hairy, because she wasn't alone anymore.

She didn't have to fight her battles by herself any longer.

She had me.

And I wasn't going anywhere.

Once I got to her house, I realized her car wasn't there. I sighed. I felt like I had been chasing her all over town the last few days. Not that I was literally chasing *her*, but more like chasing her demons away. One in particular: Mrs. Connors.

I threw my truck into park and got out, walking up her porch steps, and took a seat. Much like I had done a couple days ago when she'd never returned home.

I finally let out the long breath I'd been holding, feeling a little at ease; almost everything was settled. But there was still that little bit of ambivalence lingering in the back of my mind, because I still didn't have Ivy back. Not yet, so the tension in my neck continued to strengthen.

Squealing tires rang in the distance, which almost had my head snapping off my shoulders. It sounded like a car crash had been mere seconds from occurring. I stood quickly, inching my head towards the street, and then I saw Ivy's car quickly approaching.

As soon as she was in front of her house, the car came to a screeching stop, her small body jolting in the driver's seat, brown hair flying past her face.

I would have chastised her for driving like a maniac, but I was too damn relieved to see her and her rushing body, falling out the driver's side door.

"Dawson!" she yelled, taking off into a full sprint, except she only made it a few feet because her jacket was caught in the door she'd not so subtly slammed. Her body flew backwards as confusion fell over her face.

I chuckled, unable to keep a straight face. I would never get sick of her clumsiness. Never.

Finally, I started to walk towards her as she freed herself from the car door/jacket debacle.

"Dawson!" she shouted again, full on running and jumping into my arms.

I wrapped my arms around her waist, squeezing her just as hard as she was squeezing me. My head went into the crook of her neck, inhaling the smell of her shampoo.

"I'm so so so so so so so so sorry!" she mumbled, burying her face into my shirt.

I held on a little tighter, basking in her touch, and then slowly released her. Ivy pulled her body away from mine and peeped up at my face. Her forest green eyes were wide and full of fear. "I'm sorry, I just didn't know what to do."

A sad smile covered my face. "The only thing you have

to be sorry about is the fact that you thought you had to handle this on your own."

She looked down, taking those vivid green eyes away. "I just...don't really know how to *not* handle things on my own. I felt...stuck. Like I was drowning."

"Ivy," I said, bringing my hand upward and placing it under her chin. I tipped her face towards mine so I could look down into her eyes. "You're gonna have to learn to let me help you, because I'm not going anywhere."

Tears quickly appeared before she crushed her body back on mine. "Good, because I don't want you to."

We held onto one another for a little while longer, the chilly fall air causing her hair to whip around us like we were in some type of tornado, together, holding on for dear life.

"So, what happened? What's going to happen with Breanna's mom? What did the dean say? Mia told me you were there in a meeting with him. How did you do it? How did you even know? How did you get him to believe you?"

I laughed, rubbing my hands up and down her arms to warm her up. "Let's just talk about it later. I just want to hold you right now."

Her shoulders relaxed into mine, once again smooshing her face onto my chest. I was about to pull us up onto the porch and inside the comfort of her home when a sleek, black car pulled up behind hers.

My eyes watched the man inside. He stared at us with a grim expression on his face, wiping his hand roughly over his chin.

"Ivy?" I asked, still staring at the man. "Who is that?"

Ivy backed her body away from mine and turned around to look in the direction that I was pointing.

She groaned. "That's Eric."

Blood boiled so quickly in my veins that I thought I was going to explode.

"What the fuck is *he* doing here?"

Ivy turned around at the harshness of my voice and then she chuckled. My brow furrowed as I clenched my jaw together.

"Okay, simmer down there, Hulk. Jealousy isn't a turn on for me..." She looked away before adding, "Okay maybe it is, but only a little bit."

I didn't laugh. I was still fixated on the douche in the car who thought Ivy was worth giving up. Fucking idiot! But then again, his loss was my gain, so maybe I should be tipping my imaginary hat to him.

"What is he doing here?" I ground out.

Ivy's eyes glimmered with humor. "Dawson... your ex-girlfriend's mom just tried to blackmail me into breaking up with you so her daughter could have you." She blinked, more humor spreading along her delicate features. "Now, I know that it wasn't really about you and me and it was more about this idiotic grudge she was holding over my... dead parents, but still. You cannot act this jealous because my ex-boyfriend shows up after I ignored him for, like, two months."

She was right, but I still didn't like it.

Ivy perked up on her tiptoes, kissing me softly on the mouth. She wrapped her hands around my neck, calming me down with just a single kiss. My eyes closed involuntarily as I let myself fall into her little trick.

Once she pulled away, my eyes opened quickly. She was smiling up at me with that beautiful, soul-sucking smile, and I caved.

"Fine. But can you tell him to leave before that kiss

wears off and I throw him through the windshield of his car?"

She bellowed with laughter. "Of course. I'll be right back." And then she winked.

I stood back, crossing my arms over my chest, staring intently as Ivy leaned down and talked to her ex through his car window. I watched as Ivy's eyes slid to mine with a small smile on her lips and then back to him. She pulled herself upward and gave him one last wave as he pulled out, never once looking in my direction.

The second she walked back over to me, I pulled her into my arms, lifting her up so her legs were wrapped around my torso.

"Okay," I said, pulling her flush against my middle. "Your ex is gone, mine is probably committing her mother to a psych ward," I laughed. "Now..." Ivy brought her head down to me, forehead resting on mine, her eyes searching every inch of my face. "Now there's nothing in our way...right?"

Her tongue swiped her bottom lip, causing a burning feeling to ignite in my lower stomach. Then she smiled that coy smile and answered, "Right."

"Good, now let's go make up," I hummed, sneaking in a few kisses below her ear.

We didn't even make it to the bedroom.

EPILOGUE

Ivy

The morning headline of the paper read as: Forty year old woman, wife of number one dealership owner of the last three years, escapes Oak Hill's looney bin, only to be captured and taken back into custody within an hour after escape.

Okay, I'm kidding. But Breanna's mom did get put on administrative paid leave after the whole blackmailing ordeal, and was given the option to step down from St. Joseph's main campus to work at the branch in a neighboring city, after completing a series of counseling sessions regarding her emotional issues.

She obviously took them up on their offer, as her family urged her to do so. I have yet to see Mrs. Connors or her husband, both of whom probably still hated my family, but Breanna and I had been around each other on more than one occasion, usually at Ships, and I'd never felt the need to guard myself with a table, so that's good, I suppose.

Breanna had texted Dawson shortly after the incident

and asked him to give me her dearest apologies. I rolled my eyes but accepted the apology anyway, which seemed to make things a little less awkward.

I found out that Becca had been the one to fill Dawson in on everything, allowing him and Max to pull on their detective hats and come up with the same plan I had, although they had been a little quicker on their feet, and beat me to the punch.

Mia got a part-time job, despite me telling her not to and to just focus on school, but she was absolutely livid that I had been paying the rest of her tuition behind her back. Uncle Timothy was on my side and said that she should just be thankful and continue to excel at her deepest studies, but Dawson sided with her.

He wasn't a fan of me always putting people before myself, which is what most of our bickering was over, but I usually won by slipping my shirt over my head, causing him to forget what we were fighting over in the first place.

Dawson and I were still in the beginning stages of our relationship, but it didn't feel that way. It felt like we'd been together forever; we knew each other's darkest secrets, our worst fears, where all of our soft spots were, and most of all – what we wanted for our future.

It was an easy answer, for the both of us.

All we wanted was each other... (and for Mia's unexpected visits stop interrupting us when we were... indisposed).

"Are you ready to go in yet?" Dawson asked, looking over at me applying my lipstick in passenger seat of his truck.

"Almost," I answered.

Tonight we were spending our evening at Ships to hang out with Emmett and some of his friends for his birthday.

Max was meeting us there, as was Becca and a few of their co-workers.

I had still been working with Emmett on his books as a little side job until I picked up a few more clients (in which case I planned to leave the bank). Dawson's father had been hinting around for me to take over the books for Lanning Construction, since their normal accountant was thinking about retiring, as she had been their accountant since the very beginning.

It felt like everything was finally falling into place for me, which was a little unnerving. I wasn't used to things being so... *easy.*

"Babe, you look perfect. Let's go."

I playfully rolled my eyes at Dawson before throwing my lipstick back in my purse and zipping it up.

"Fine, let's go. I can't wait until your brother opens his gift."

Dawson turned to look at me again. "His gift? What did you get him?"

I giggled, causing Dawson to flash his pearly whites toward me. "I signed him up for Tinder."

Laughter filled the truck as Dawson threw his head back before saying, "He's going to kill you."

I giggled again. "I love messing with him. He's like the older brother I never had. But in all seriousness, he needs a lady friend. He's been so lonely since Carrie. Every time I go into the shop he talks my ear off. He needs a girlfriend."

Dawson shook his head, a sigh escaping his mouth. "Come on, troublemaker. Let's hurry before he gets here. I'll buy you a drink that'll go nicely with your evilness."

I shot my eyebrows up. "Like a Rum and Coke? That's what all the bad girls drink."

Dawson laughed again, hopping out of the truck while shaking his head.

As soon as we made it inside, he went over to the bartender and ordered our drinks. I saw Kip and another tattoo artist sitting in the back booth, each with sleezy girls by their side. I brought my hand up and waved briefly before sauntering back up to Dawson to snag my drink.

"Here ya go. A Rum and Coke for my little rogue."

I grinned. "I love you."

Dawson's brow furrowed for a second before a smile appeared. "I love you too, but where did that come from?"

A warm sensation wrapped around my heart. "I was just remembering when you came here shortly after we made it official and sang that *Mama Mia* song and told me you loved me in front of the entire bar."

Dawson's mouth tipped up at the side. "I'll do it again if we can finish the night off the same way..."

A pull at my stomach had my entire body tingling thinking back to what had happened *afterwards*. "How long do we have to stay tonight, because I'm ready when you are."

Hooded eyes met my expression and I bit my lip. Dawson reached up with his empty hand and slipped it out from beneath my teeth.

"Careful now, or you won't be able to give Emmett his gift."

As soon as the words left his mouth, the bar door opened up and in walked Emmett. My eyebrows shot up all the way to my forehead when I spotted a cute, petite girl wearing designer jeans and a dressy blouse trailing after him. At first, I thought it was just a random girl walking into the bar but then, she turned her shy face up to him and smile weakly, like she was nervous. I could tell she felt out of place almost instantly, and she *looked* out of place.

Dawson peeked down at me, his expression matching mine. "I guess he won't be needing that Tinder account after all..."

Then he grabbed my hand and pulled me towards our friends, shooting me a heated look that meant we would *definitely* be leaving early.

The End

ABOUT THE AUTHOR

S.J. Sylvis is a lover of reading and writing and just recently graduated with her graduate degree focusing on English and Creative Writing (the only fun parts were the writing classes). Besides writing, S.J. Sylvis loves coffee (specifically caramel iced coffee, but really, any coffee will do), binge-watching Gilmore Girls, going to the beach and spending time with her family! She currently lives in North Carolina but is often moving as her husband is in the United States Marine Corps and they go where the military sends them!

www.sjsylvis.com

ACKNOWLEDGMENTS

Thank you to my husband, Joe, for always supporting me and for urging me to continue with writing. You are so supportive and I wouldn't want to do this life with anyone else!

Thank you to my friends and family for all of your love and support. It's comforting knowing that you all are there to pick me up when I feel defeated. Another thank you to my author besties for answering questions, allowing me to bounce ideas off of you, and for simply reminding me that I'm not alone in this journey.

A huge thank you to all my readers, especially my S Club Sylvis' readers! You make writing so much fun!

To Stephanie, my editor, thank you for polishing my work. I am so incredibly grateful for your grammar knowledge and for all of your support!

Lastly, thank you to all the bloggers and bookstagrammers who help spread the word about my books. Your unwavering support is amazing! You are my biggest cheerleaders! Thank you from the bottom of my heart.!

Xo,
S.J. Sylvis